JAMES OSWALD

NOWHERE TO RUN

WILDFIRE

First published in 2021 by
WILDFIRE
an imprint of HEADLINE PUBLISHING GROUP

1

Cataloguing in Publication Data is available from the British Library

Hardback ISBN 978 1 4722 9046 5
Trade Paperback ISBN 978 1 4722 9049 6

Typeset in Aldine 401BT by Avon DataSet Ltd,
Arden Court, Alcester, Warwickshire

Printed and bound in Great Britain by Clays Ltd, Elcograf S.p.A.

HEADLINE PUBLISHING GROUP
An Hachette UK Company
Carmelite House
50 Victoria Embankment
London EC4Y 0DZ

www.headline.co.uk
www.hachette.co.uk

NOWHERE TO RUN

For all those who find themselves
living at the end of the line.

1

It was probably a mistake coming to the pub on a Friday. But then again, my whole life's been a series of mistakes.

Take my current situation. I'd only intended to spend a few weeks away, an escape from the press, since their dogged determination to catch me unawares still verges on the psychotic.

Aunt Felicity put me in touch with an old friend of hers who had a cottage on the coast near Aberystwyth. That felt remote enough to evade even the most persistent of the Fourth Estate. So, I packed up the trusty Volvo, by some miracle remembered to empty the fridge, and escaped London for some well-deserved time off.

Then, just as I was beginning to sort my head out enough to contemplate going back to work, a helpful fellow in China developed a cough and the whole world tumbled down around me.

I guess I could have gone back to London and locked down there, but actually Wales isn't all that bad. I've even started trying to learn a bit of the language. Bore da, shwmae and all that. Not that I get much chance to practise. I don't know many folk around here, and everyone's been very good at social distancing. Of course, they might all do that with us English anyway. There's only so much isolation even I can take though, so I've been making a habit of visiting the local from time to time, if only to listen to other voices and see a face that might be different to the one staring back at me in the mirror every morning. It's not something I'd contemplate in London, going to the pub alone. Too much opportunity for a quiet drink to be spoiled by some unwanted attention. Llantwmp has proven to be much more civilised in that respect.

It's nothing special, the Black Lion. Mostly I sit in the beer garden, nursing a pint and wearing my thickest coat. The bar's like something from a cheap 80s sitcom. Walls covered in horse brasses and unidentifiable bits of old agricultural machinery. There's a juke box and a little platform in one corner that suggests bands play of an evening, but it's clear that nobody's picked up a guitar around here in months. There's a telly on a high shelf in the opposite corner, and this is the first time I've seen it on. Some rugby match. Two teams of swarthy men playing with their odd-shaped balls. I never could quite see the point.

'Pint of Brains and a couple of cheese and onion, is it?'

The landlady is straight out of central casting. Short, round, big hair, arms I'd not want to wrestle with. But Cerys's smile is always friendly and genuine, even if I can hear the slight judgement in her voice. Fair enough, it's not the healthiest of diets. If they did proper meals in here maybe I'd eat better, but from the look of the place not much.

'Cheers, Cerys.' I wait for my spoils, the chance for a bit of a chat somewhat ruined by the Perspex screens cutting the bar off from the rest of the room. At least I've got my phone.

'You're in later'n usual,' she says as she slides my pint across the bar through the little opening that makes it feel like I've just made a bank withdrawal.

'Evenings getting lighter, right?' I tap the payment, shrug my shoulders. 'Not so cold for sitting outside, either.'

'Well, you'll probably not be alone. Fridays are a bit more

busy now the games are back on.' Cerys nods in the direction of the telly at the same time as the door opens and two men stumble in. I've seen them before, kept out of their way. I think they work on one of the small fishing boats that sails out of Aberaeron. They certainly look like they've spent time at sea. One of them has a beard that would see off a grizzly bear, but no hair at all on top of his shaved and polished head. The other looks like a rat that fell into a bucket of used engine oil. Their gaze latches onto me uncomfortably, until Cerys finds the remote and turns up the volume on the telly to distract their attention. I give her a quick nod of thanks and escape out the back with my drink.

The sun was shining when I walked down the hill from the cottage, but by the time I take up my usual spot in the beer garden it's gone. I can't tell if the grey overhead means rain soon; I'm too much a creature of the city for that kind of wisdom. It's a bit chill to be sitting outside though, even with my coat on. Eating the crisps warms me up a little, but the beer chills me right back down again. Perhaps I'd have been better off back at the cottage. There's a wood burning stove and a seemingly endless supply of logs.

As I check my phone for messages, the two fishermen come out into the beer garden. Too much to hope I'd have the place to myself then. I call it a beer garden, but it's more the loading yard out the back of the pub, with a few cheap wooden tables arranged suitably distant from each other. They don't need to sit anywhere near me, since the place is otherwise empty, but of course they do. I glance up briefly, not catching their eyes, then go back to my pint and my phone, hoping they take the hint. So much for Llantwmp being more civilised than London.

'Look like you could do with some company, hen.'

Like I'd entertain either of them for a second. I've seen more appealing prospects on the underside of my shoe.

'C'mon sweetheart. How's about—'

3

I hold up a hand to silence whichever one's speaking. Possibly Greasy Rat, although since I've not looked away from my phone screen I can't be sure. I'm busy composing a text to Karen Eve back in London, but mostly I just can't be doing with their shit.

'Snotty bitch,' the other one says, and I almost turn to give him a piece of my mind. A survival instinct honed by far too many similarly unwelcome and uninvited experiences holds me back, although I do have to correct what I was trying to type on the screen. Text sent, I down the remains of my beer. It might have been a nice evening, a couple of pints and a chance to clear my head, but now all I want is to get out of here. Away from these two before they do something even more stupid than Slaphead's hairstyle. They're sat between me and the pub door, so I leave my empty glass as I turn towards the other way out, the one where the delivery vans come in with the beer.

'Don't be like that, hen. We're only after a bit of fun, see?'

There's something about the tone that shatters my patience. Facing the two of them, I put on a fake smile, like an air hostess with a machine gun hidden behind her back. 'Sorry, boys. Not interested. I'm afraid you'll just have to suck each other off tonight.'

Then, before either of them has time to register what I've said, I turn and walk out of the pub garden.

Yes, I know, petty. Trading insults with a couple of losers isn't exactly mature, but they had it coming. And I'm getting tired of being stuck in the middle of nowhere. Or at the far end of nowhere, given how close this village is to the sea.

I had hoped maybe to have had time for another pint, enough to take the edge off before climbing the hill up to the cottage and an early bed. But my encounter with the two of them has left me jittery. Time was, I'd not have been fazed by the likes of them, but it's barely a year since I was almost killed by a would-be

4

rapist not more than a few hundred yards from my flat in London. It didn't end well for him. Sometimes, late at night, I still hear the cut-off scream, the crunch and crack of bone as the car ran over him. I hear it now, even in the fading light of the evening, and it makes me shiver.

I need to walk.

The beach stretches in a shallow arc from the hill where my cottage is, all the way south towards Aberaeron. Describing it as a beach is generous, since it largely consists of shingle and rocks. A couple of caravan parks grace the inland side. I'd make a snarky comment about it being a pretty awful place to come for a holiday, but in truth it's not that bad. And it's not as if every-one can afford to fly off to Ibiza for a week of sun, even if they were allowed to right now.

I don't walk far. Behind the clouds, the sun's half in the sea already and a cold wind is picking up the waves, throwing salt spray at me. I'd wager that there's rain on the way, but since this is Wales that wouldn't be a difficult bet to win. A half hour is enough to clear my head of the sudden anxiety that had swamped me, so that by the time I walk past the pub on my way home I'm back to being calm, relaxed and ready for bed.

It's the scent that alerts me first, a mixture of sweat and grease and body odour, but mostly too much deodorant. Or not enough. It brings back that sick feeling I thought I'd got rid of. I don't need to turn to know that at least one of my unwelcome friends from the pub has decided to follow me. Dogs usually hunt in packs, so my guess is the other one's not far away.

When it comes, the attack is swift and brutal.

Had I been less aware of my surroundings, maybe headphones on and zoning out to some music, I wouldn't have stood a chance. As it is, the smell isn't my only clue. Greasy Rat comes at me from behind, silent except for the soft patter of his feet on the pavement. Slaphead steps out from the corner of the nearest building, presumably intending to surprise me, cut off my escape and let his friend do all the hard work. What he doesn't realise is that I've been watching them both reflected in the window of a parked car on the other side of the road since I first noticed the stench of them. The rest is all about timing.

Slaphead smiles broadly, as if greeting a long-lost friend. Perhaps he's hoping to confuse me enough for Rat to grab me from behind. I don't give either of them the satisfaction. At the last moment, I duck and spin, stamp my boot down hard in front of his leading foot. Rat's momentum does most of the work, but I help him along with a hard shove in the back. His yelp of surprise turns into a shriek of pain as he hits the pavement badly. If he's lucky, that wrist's only sprained.

'You fuckin' bitch.' Slaphead's closer than I expected, coming for me with a snarl of rage. He's a brawler. I take one step towards him, see the flicker of uncertainty across his features. It's all the opening I need, that and his slightly wide-legged seaman's stance. My boot connecting with his bollocks drives all the air out of him in a satisfying 'whoof' noise and he crumples, first to his knees and then onto his side, hands cupping his bruised pride.

The punch catches me out of nowhere, snapping my jaw shut with a crack that would make my dentist wince. I'm lucky not to bite my own tongue off, and for a moment everything goes a little dark around the edges. I can't say whether it's an error on my part or just my sense of balance momentarily fucked, but I feel the second punch whistle past me rather than see it. Greasy Rat is back on his feet, and even though he's holding his injured wrist close to his body, he's handy enough with the other fist. Shame he seems to have spent time on the punchbag rather than the bench press like his bearded friend.

'Oh, for fuck's sake.' The words come out under my breath rather than as a direct insult. Not that Greasy Rat cares. He jabs in with another punch, far too well telegraphed for me to let it land. I grab his wrist as it goes past, and spin him round. He smells bad, so I'd really rather not get close, but needs must when the devil calls and all that. He screams as I get his other wrist behind him and force him to the ground, wishing I had some cuffs on me, or even a zip tie. A quick glance across at Slaphead, still lying on his side with his hands wedged between his thighs, reassures me he's not going anywhere soon.

'Fuckin' kill you!' Greasy Rat shouts, although his situation suggests otherwise. He's a wriggler though, and I've got no backup. Stupid, Con. You should have thought that through. I get him in a choke hold, even though I know I shouldn't. He keeps on struggling, but I can feel him getting weaker. Hopefully soon I can let him go, confident it'll take him longer to get his strength back than it will for me to disappear. After I've got photos of both of them to pass on to the authorities, of course. They might not get charged with anything, but they'll leave me alone if they've any sense.

Greasy Rat's almost out of it, Slaphead is still curled up in a foetal position, clutching his privates and letting out the occasional whimper.

I figure we're done here.

I'm just about to let go when I hear an all-too familiar sound behind me. The whoop-whoop of a squad car siren shatters the quiet.

Wonderful. The cavalry has arrived.

2

I can't believe this is actually happening. At least the two goons who attacked me are being transported in a different vehicle, but there's no reason I should be in the back of a squad car right now. Even less reason why I should be in handcuffs. Part of me wants to argue with the arresting officer, but that small voice of reason keeps me quiet. I can go with it for now, let this run its course. Then I'll demand a public apology.

Aberystwyth Police Station is a surprisingly modern red brick building on the outskirts of the town. Or at least, what would have been the outskirts before someone thought it a good idea to dump a modern housing estate right on the banks of a river. I've been past a few times, so I know that the river in question is actually the Rheidol, not the Ystwyth. Nobody's yet given me a decent explanation as to why the town decided to name itself after a river that doesn't run through it rather than the one that does, and I doubt I'll get one from the duty sergeant.

I lower my gaze, flutter my eyelids and do my best meek victim impression as I'm led into the building, pleased to see that my attackers have been processed ahead of me. I'll be happy not to see them again outside of a courtroom, although the realist in me already knows it's unlikely this will get that far.

'Name?' The duty sergeant is an older man, buzzcut grey hair and leathery skin. He looks bored, but I've met enough of his type down the years not to be fooled.

'Fairchild. Constance Fairchild.' I study his face nervously for any flicker of recognition, while debating whether to add 'Detective Constable Constance Fairchild, for what it's worth'. That would open up a can of particularly awkward worms though, not least of which is why I haven't let the local Constabulary know I'm currently living on their patch. Since he doesn't appear to read any of the tabloids, I decide discretion is the way forward here.

'Constable Jones tells me you were brawling in the pub garden of the Black Lion, down in Llantwmp. That right, Miss Fairchild?'

Brawling? For fuck's sake. That would imply equal fault on both sides, when those two bastards near enough jumped me. Calm thoughts, Con. No point escalating an already difficult situation.

'If by brawling, you mean fending off a couple of potential rapists, then yes.'

That gets me a raised eyebrow, but nothing else.

'Look, just put my details into the computer and I'm sure we can get this all sorted out quickly, eh?'

The sergeant squares his shoulders, rolls his head as if readying himself for action, then picks up an elderly clipboard. I've said the wrong thing. I don't need a brush with the local law. Not now. He fishes a pen out of his top pocket, clicks it a couple of unnecessary times, then stares straight at me.

'Name, address, date of birth. Then I want you to empty your pockets onto the counter here. We'll see about getting your details onto the system in due course.'

I count to ten. Silently, of course. I'm not stupid. Well, not that stupid. Then I do as I'm asked, and repeat my name, address, all the other stuff this annoying old jobsworth demands. I haven't got much on me, since all I'd planned on doing this evening was go to the pub for a quick pint, take a stroll along the beach and then head back to the cottage. Jobsworth insists on taking my bootlaces though, and then I'm marched along a corridor and into a holding cell. Promises of a cup of tea if I'm good. At least nobody says 'Don't go anywhere now!' in that annoying Welsh accent of theirs. That would be a step too far.

It's only as the clang of the cell door closing fades, the jingle of the duty sergeant's keyring counterpointed by his out of tune singing, that I let my shoulders slump and admit defeat. Turning, I go to survey the cell that will be my home for at least the next couple of hours.

Which is when I realise. I'm not alone.

It's highly unusual for a cell to hold more than one person at a time. But then again, it's quite unusual for a victim of assault to be arrested and thrown in a cell in the first place. OK, so when the two constables arrived, I did happen to have one of my assailants in a choke hold and the other was on the ground cupping his bruised testicles. But even so, aren't we meant to be in the grips of a pandemic? It's not really possible to keep two metres apart in here, and neither of us is wearing a mask. The fact I've been given no instructions makes me suspect this is a mistake, although I'll not rule out some stupid prank. Coppers can be cruel that way. I should know, I am one.

My cellmate is a young woman, maybe twenty or possibly younger. Her long hair is probably blonde, but so dirty I can't really be sure. A mess of tangles and curls, it hides half her face and hangs loose over her shoulders. I'm guessing they took away her scrunchie along with her shoelaces. She's dressed in loose-fitting casual wear, a stained pink sweat top and baggy grey jogging bottoms. Her white socks gleam beneath the overhead light. She looks at me with a level of suspicion I've not seen since I last walked the beat, if you don't count every single time I've tried to have a polite conversation with my teenage half-sister Izzy. I'm almost transfixed by the pale blue of her eyes.

'You police?'

Two words are enough to identify that she's not from around here. Eastern European at a guess, which opens up all sorts of reasons why she might be in a holding cell in Aberystwyth Police Station.

'No. Not police.' I shake my head slightly, then point at my laceless boots as if that makes everything clear. She glances at them briefly, but the suspicion remains in her eyes.

'I'm Constance, but people call me Con.' I've not moved from the space immediately in front of the cell door yet. My cellmate is sitting at the far end of the narrow bench that juts out from one wall, her knees drawn up to her chest. I point at the opposite end. 'OK if I sit?'

She shrugs, but says nothing. I approach with caution, but she doesn't move when I sit down and lean my back against the wall. I hope it doesn't take the custody sergeant long to input my details. A night in the cells wasn't exactly on my agenda.

'Why you here?' the woman asks. As she looks up, her hair falls away from her cheeks to reveal the yellow of old bruising under one eye, and there's a scab over a cut on her lower lip.

'Got in a fight, didn't I? Two blokes jumped me as I was leaving the pub. Thought they'd have a little fun. Don't think one of them's going to father any children any time soon.'

That raises a thin smile, short-lived but enough to brighten her face for a moment.

'You not from here.' She lifts one hand towards the high window and the orange streetlamp visible beyond it. 'Not speak like them.'

I smile back. What is it about this woman that raises my

sympathy? We're both strangers in this town, both down on our luck. That's probably enough, but there's something more about her I can't quite put my finger on. 'No. I'm not Welsh. Grew up in England. Not far from London. I worked there for a while, too.'

'So why you here? Is end of line.'

It's a very good question, and one I'm not sure I have a ready answer to. I draw my feet up onto the ledge, arms hugging my knees. 'I needed to get away. From London, the job, everything. Friend of a friend had a cottage going spare. It's away down the coast a bit from here. Thought it'd be for a couple of weeks, maybe a month. Then, well, you know what happened.'

She stares at me, the hostility easing with each word, but still lingering. I'm trying to work out if I've seen her somewhere before, her face hauntingly familiar. I've certainly seen women like her around the town, sheltering in doorways and bus stops. Aberystwyth doesn't have much of a drug problem, but it's there when you know what to look for.

'What about you?'

She shrugs. 'I run away from boyfriend. Nowhere to go. Is still cold on the streets at night, no?'

And a cell is much warmer, even if it's hardly comfortable. I don't like the way she says 'boyfriend' either. It sounds far too much like 'pimp'. Or am I reading more into this than is there? Damn, I shouldn't be reading anything into this at all. Another hour, tops, and I should be out of here.

'Is Lila,' my cellmate says, her voice weary. 'My name. Lila.'

'Pleased to meet you, Lila.' I hold out a hand to shake before remembering we probably shouldn't touch. Not with the lack of hand-washing facilities. She doesn't move, but the suspicion has faded from her eyes, even if I get the feeling that's more down to exhaustion than trust earned. I let my hand drop and start to form another question, but before I can ask it the clack of a key in the lock has us both turning to the door. It swings open to reveal the custody sergeant, an angry scowl on his face.

'You.' He points at me. 'Out. Shouldn't be in here, anyway. Stupid bloody constables can't even get the right cell.'

I stand up slowly, turn back to Lila, give her a smile and a nod. Then I follow the sergeant out into the corridor. He makes sure to lock up, peering through the little sight hole before addressing me.

'Why didn't you just say you were a police officer when we picked you up?'

'Because I'm not. You made me empty my pockets, right? Did you see a warrant card?' I enjoy the fleeting confusion on his face before realising I'm being petty. 'I'm guessing you had a call? Was it DS Latham or DCI Bain?'

Now the confusion deepens into a frown, and the sergeant waves a hand to hurry me along the corridor back towards the processing area.

'Don't know what you're talking about,' he says as we step out into the waiting room. There's a man sitting on one of the uncomfortable plastic chairs, looking for all the world like this is the most natural thing to be doing. His thin, aristocratic face, tidy white hair and smart but casual tweed suit are totally out of place in a police station, but he seems quite unconcerned. I know him, of course. He's my landlord, and one of Aunt Flick's oldest friends. As he sees me enter the room, he beams at me with a smile so bright it would fade paint.

'Constance, dear. Heard you got into a spot of bother at the pub.'

Gareth, or Lord Caernant to those who aren't family friends, hauls his old body out of the chair and strides across the room to give me a hug. Then he remembers social distancing is a thing and pauses, shifting awkwardly.

'You didn't need to come and get me,' I say, even though this is marginally less embarrassing than the alternative.

'Nonsense. Amy would never forgive me if she found out I'd left you in the lurch.' His lordship looks past me. 'We good to go, Ben?'

I catch the remnants of a scowl as I turn to see the custody sergeant. I knew Lord Caernant was a pillar of the local community, but I'd not expected this. Neither had the sergeant, apparently.

'I'll fetch her things, sir.' He gives us both the slightest of nods, then walks over to the counter. None of us say anything while he unlocks the door, heads into the office beyond and quickly returns with a clear plastic bag containing my belongings. I take it from him with a quick thank you, and retrieve my bootlaces.

'The girl in the cell back there, Lila. She been in trouble before?'

'Friend of yours, is she?' The custody sergeant, Ben, has a sneer in his voice. But then he's had a sneer in his voice since I first heard him speak, so maybe he's one of life's natural sneerers.

'Just curious. She looks like she needs help, not locking up.'

'I'll be sure and tell the arresting officer that, Detective Constable. And you'd best not be leaving the area without letting us know where you're going. Just in case we need to speak to you again, see?'

I give him my best patronising smile. 'You've got my address, I'm not going anywhere.'

'Felicity warned us you had a knack for getting into trouble. Thought she was making it up, if I'm being honest.'

I've met a surprising number of lords, earls and other nobility down the years. Hell, I should correctly be addressed as Lady Constance, though the less said about that the better. Lord

Caernant probably thinks he doesn't fit the stereotype, but he has the eccentric manner down to a tee.

Take his car, for instance. Most people would consider driving a Rolls Royce that's probably more than twice as old as I am to be something of an affectation. Gareth drives his because it was his father's car and it hasn't broken down yet. Replacing it would, to his mind, be wasteful and unnecessary.

'You really didn't need to come and bail me out, you know? Not that I'm complaining. Thank you. I wasn't looking forward to the fallout of that getting back to London.' I settle into the soft leather and watch the road ahead, poorly lit by elderly headlights.

'Far be it for me to pry, but what exactly happened? All I know is that Cerys called and said you'd been carried off in a Black Maria. Not that they're black these days.' He sounds like he's disappointed it's no longer the Fifties, even though he's barely old enough to remember those years.

'It was all a bit of a misunderstanding.' I tell him about my visit to the pub, my encounter with Slaphead and Greasy Rat. A shame I never had a chance to snap photos of them with my phone. Now I'll have to find out their names the old-fashioned way. 'If the police hadn't shown up when they did, I'd be tucked up in my bed now.'

A few more miles rumble along in silence before Lord Caernant speaks again. 'There is one thing that confuses me though, Constance. When I approached Ben Griffiths in the station back there, he was surprised to find out that you're a detective. Why didn't you just tell him? He's a bit brusque, I'll grant you, but he's a good enough chap if you know him.'

I can see the lights of Llantwmp up ahead, which means the turning onto the steep drive up to my cottage is almost upon us. 'It's complicated. I know what Aunt Flick's told you, but I really don't know whether I am a detective or not any more. Not sure if I'm still a police officer of any kind. That's why I'm here, you see? Leave of absence to sort my head out. Give the press a chance to forget me.'

'I saw some of the things they wrote. Ridiculous. Why do people even read that nonsense? None of anyone's business, anyway.'

I feel the tension ease from my shoulders. I don't like talking about what's happened to me, even with friends. I've only known Gareth for a few short months, and while he might be an old friend of my aunt, he's also my landlord.

'You can stop here. I'll walk up the hill, thanks,' I say as he indicates to pull onto the track. 'No need to risk your under-carriage on the potholes.'

'Nonsense. This old dear's more than capable of getting up there.' He pats the steering wheel affectionately, but slows to a halt at the side of the road nonetheless. 'It's turning her around at the top that's the problem.'

'Thank you, again. It was very good of you to rescue me,' I say as I clamber out. 'Please give my love to Amy. Or perhaps I should say Lady Caernant.'

Gareth looks at me with wide eyes. 'Only if she can't hear you. Which reminds me. Since you're now officially part of our social bubble, she wanted me to invite you over for supper sometime. I serve a mean cocktail, and if you bring a change of clothes you can kip in the spare room.'

I'm tempted to ask which one, given that Plas Caernant is almost as big as my childhood home, Harston Magna Hall. It's late though, and I really want to crawl into my bed now. 'Sounds wonderful. I'd love to. Thank you.'

He smiles. 'I'll let her know and we can set a date then.'

I watch the car move silently away, then start the trek up the hill to the cottage. The clouds have thinned now, the occasional glimpse of a star visible in the inky black sky. I'm out of breath by the time I reach the point where the narrow track widens into a small yard. My trusty old Volvo estate is parked close to the back door, its dented white paintwork glowing slightly in the night, lit only by a thin moon flitting between clouds. The wind's whistling over the cliffs a few hundred metres further on, bringing with it the scent of the sea and a chill for my bones.

I search through the clear plastic bag for my door key before I freeze to death. Inside, the cottage is exactly how I left it rather more hours ago than I'd intended. I pause a moment in the narrow hall and let the tension seep out of me. There's something about this place, its old stone walls giving it a timeless solidity, that lets me relax in a way I never could in London, certainly never could in Harston Magna. The only other place I've felt this at ease is Newmore, up in the Highlands. Or possibly Madame Rose's house on Leith Walk. This cottage has that same sense of security about it.

Through the kitchen doorway, I spot a bottle of single malt whisky, but I'm too tired even for that. I drop the plastic bag on the side table where the phone lives, then clamber up the steps to bed.

3

Weirdness magnet, that's what my brother always called me. I think he's probably being a bit unfair, but there might be a little truth in it. I've certainly had more than my share of trouble in my thirty-odd years on this planet. Almost as if it seeks me out.

Not that I was expecting anything much to happen when I came into town this morning, not after yesterday's run-in with the local constabulary. Aberystwyth isn't exactly a hotbed of violence and intrigue. It's a sleepy little university town that's as far west as you can go without falling into the sea, and as far from London as I can get without leaving the country. Unless you count Wales as another country, which I know a lot of folk around here do. I'd expected to be here a few weeks, but I'm not entirely upset that it's turned into months.

I've grown to like it here. The people are friendly enough, and the pace of life's blissful after the past few years. I'd not realised how close to a breakdown I was until I stepped away from the madness.

But I've got to eat, and that means making the occasional trip from the cottage up to the town, even if I was here just yesterday, courtesy of my new-found friends in the local police. There's a supermarket, but I prefer the little independent stores in the town centre. The vegetables in the grocers on Chalybeate Street still have dirt on them so they must be healthy, right?

Grubby carrots achieved, it's as I take the turn up Queen's Road, heading back to the car, that I spot them. Two men and a woman, walking towards me on the other side of the narrow street. On the face of it, there's nothing unusual about any of them, but the way they're moving sets all my internal alarm bells ringing. She's boxed in between the two men, her body language unhappy. She looks well enough dressed, perhaps a bit too much bling, more make-up than is strictly necessary for this time of the day. The two men are older, maybe thirty to her twenty, and they'd be a great choice for an identity parade. One's got a hand on the woman's shoulder, almost as if he's steering her. And that's when it hits me. I recognise this young woman because she was in the cell with me yesterday evening.

Lila, wasn't it? At least, I think it's her.

My foot hovers at the edge of the pavement, but then I freeze. Get a grip, Con. You can't fight everyone's corner, and you've no idea what the story is here. These shopping bags are heavy too, not to mention the bruises from yesterday's misadventure slowing me down.

There's a moment though, where it could swing either way. Lila notices me, eyes going wide. Is that the faintest shake of her head warning me? Before I can make up my mind, the man with his hand on her shoulder notices the subtle interaction. He stares at me, and there's no doubting his animosity. I can feel the tension boiling off him, even though he's on the other side of the road.

A car turns at the bottom of the street, swiftly enough for its tyres to squeak against the tarmac. A big 4x4 with blacked-out windows and a personalised number plate, it slows when it reaches the group across the road, then comes to a halt. I can't see past it, and there's nothing I can do anyway. Before I know it, everyone's inside and the car pulls away from the kerb, up the hill towards Heol-y-Bont, Bridge Street to you and me. It turns at the top and disappears, the whole episode over in a matter of seconds.

As I reach my own car, haul open the stiff passenger door and place my shopping carefully so that it won't fall over on the way home, I can't help wondering what that poor young woman's story is. Could I have done more to help her? I guess I'll never know.

I try my best to put the incident out of my mind as I carry on with my shopping, but it's not easy. I know nothing about the young woman in the cell apart from her claim that she'd run away from her boyfriend. I'd assumed by the way she'd said 'boyfriend' she was in some kind of sex work, and most likely not willingly. That alone makes me want to help; it's why I joined the police in the first place. Her general air of ill health put me in mind of drug abuse, too. But in truth, we spent less than fifteen minutes together. Seeing her in clean clothes and make-up she looked healthier, although not necessarily healthy. It's amazing what a bit of concealer and a red lippy can do. I've worn that disguise myself, often enough. But am I overthinking this?

Drugs and prostitution are probably not the first things that come to anyone's mind when they think about Aberystwyth, if they think about the place at all. But I've been trained to notice things, and that's a hard skill to switch off.

Anywhere there's more than a handful of houses will have a drug problem. Harston Magna's a tiny little village and you can still score pretty much anything you want if you know who to ask in the Green Man. Aberystwyth's a university town, which means students, which means drugs. It's also a seaside town, far from the big metropolises of London, Manchester and

Birmingham. The kind of place where people who drift out to the edges end up with nowhere left to go. It hides its deprivation well, but it's there if you look.

I'm driving out past the Welsh Assembly Government building when I see the 4x4 again. There's so many on the roads these days that I couldn't normally be sure it's the same one, if it wasn't for the personalised number plate. That's something people never consider. Sure, it might look cool, might even spell out your name, but it's also memorable. This one doesn't have any obvious meaning to me, its numbers and letters spaced correctly. But it's much older than the car, older even than my Volvo.

On a whim, I decide to follow the vehicle. With its dark tinted windows I can't see if the woman's still inside, but I'm nothing if not curious. It goes up the steep hill to Penparcau, which is my route anyway. Before we get to the top and the coast road, it takes a sharp turn into a housing estate without bothering to indicate. I follow, more sedately, as it drives past the Welsh primary school and deeper into the estate. Mostly 1970s two-storey terrace houses, there are a few more modern three-storey apartment blocks built into the hillside, unwelcoming under the low clouds that threaten rain.

When the 4x4 pulls in, I drive past as if I'd never been following it in the first place. At least my Volvo looks more at home here than it does. I pause at the end of the street and get a half-decent view through my rear-view mirror, watch as one of the men climbs out, opens the rear passenger door and helps out a young woman.

Lila.

The hand around her arm grips too tight to be helpful, and any doubt I might have is extinguished by the way she drags her feet, obviously unhappy to be here. A toot of horn reminds me I'm blocking the road. There's nothing to do, except wave an apology at the driver of the car that's crept up behind me, and set off once more. I loop around the houses, but by the time I come back the 4x4 is gone and there's no sign of its passengers either. Stupid, Con. You're here to do your shopping, not play detective.

Out on the coast road, passing through Rhydefelin on my way south towards Llantwmp and home, I fancy I see the 4x4 once more, climbing the hill ahead of me. Too far away to read the registration plate, I can't really be sure. This stretch of road's not made for speed either, and by the time I'm at a point where I can go faster, I'm stuck behind a tractor. You have to love rural living.

I don't see the 4x4 again after that, so either it's found some clear road or it's turned off somewhere. By the time I've turned off myself, and negotiated the steep, tight farm track up to the cottage, I've almost convinced myself the whole thing was nothing but a waste of time. An unnecessary distraction.

Almost.

4

I think it's when I fill the Volvo with petrol only a couple of weeks after the last time that I finally realise I've slipped back into old habits, and not necessarily good ones.

Going to Aber once a week, sometimes less, has meant a tankful has lasted months. But I've been finding excuses to come into town, driving around the housing estates in Penparcau, looking for that 4x4 or Lila. The only thing I haven't done is ask Karen Eve in my old NCA team to run the registration number, some small part of me still accepting that I'm not currently a detective constable and this is not a case that needs investigating.

There have been other reasons for coming to town, of course. I can persuade myself pretty convincingly if I have to that multiple visits to the National Library of Wales are totally necessary for research into the book I'm not actually writing. Then there's the new clothes I had to buy after I threw away the ones I'd been wearing when I was attacked. The smell of Greasy Rat's rancid breath and Slaphead's pungent beard oil might have been only in my mind, but repeated washing of my jeans and top did nothing to get rid of them. I still don't know the real names of my two attackers, although I suspect Cerys in the pub would tell me if I asked. I've not been back there since the attack though, so that's another reason for coming into town more frequently. My meagre stocks of beer and wine have needed replenishing.

But mostly it's because of Lila. I don't believe much in fate or destiny or whatever. Mine isn't some desire for karmic justice, more a dawning realisation of what she represents. I know far more about County Lines than most members of the public; that's been a big part of my job for years. The young woman trying to leave her 'boyfriend' fits the profile of someone who's been sucked into a criminal underworld and is desperate to escape. Or simply survive. Even if I have no real idea of who Lila is, it makes me want to do whatever I can to help. She's not that much older than my half-sister, Izzy. I can't stand by while someone like her is being abused by grubby, older men. So, I've been doing a bit of discreet surveillance.

The more I look for it, the more of the town's seedy underbelly I find. There are distinct immigrant communities, waves of incomers washed up, all suspicious of each other. Eastern Europeans like Lila aren't even the most recent to arrive here. There's been an influx of Syrian refugees, one running a very nice little cafe and bakery that I could spend a lot of time in if I could afford it. The signs of deprivation are all around when you start looking too, from the Big Issue sellers outside the station and on Great Darkgate Street to the huddled forms of rough sleepers in grubby doorways and rather more beggars than a so-called developed nation should be happy about. There are signs of drug use too, although as yet I've not seen anyone catatonic after taking spice. Only a matter of time, is my guess.

And somewhere along the line, I've picked up a tail.

I should have expected it, I suppose. If there's drugs and sex work here, there'll be local CID keeping an eye on things. Someone's bound to have noticed the battered white Volvo that's parked up on the edge of the worst estate for hours at a time.

No doubt, they've run the plate and know who I am now, which is probably why they follow me rather than pull me over. It's a timely reminder that I really shouldn't be doing this, though. I've no warrant card, no backup, no authority whatsoever. And I've not managed to find Lila or even spot the 4x4 with its personalised number plate in over a week of looking. It's getting late, anyway. Maybe it's time to give the whole thing up.

My unofficial escort follows me for a couple of miles out of town before pulling into a layby. It's an unmarked Ford Mondeo, a couple of years old, essentially anonymous, which is the whole point I suppose. I keep a watching eye behind me all the way back to Llantwmp, but clearly I've passed beyond their juris-diction, or any assumed capacity to cause trouble.

Something feels different as I park up in the narrow space in front of the cottage and climb out of the Volvo. An unexpected scent on the air, perhaps? A sixth sense feeling that I'm not alone. It puts me immediately on my guard. The door's locked, but does the handle feel warmer than it should? As if someone else has touched it? No, you're being paranoid, Con. This cottage is so remote, tucked away in its own little gully. No one would know it was here.

Still, I'm tense as I unlock the door and push it open. There's that scent again, not any perfume I'd ever wear, but strangely familiar all the same. Cautious, I edge into the hall, check the open kitchen door to see if there's anyone there.

'Ah, Con. There you are. I was beginning to wonder if you were coming home today.'

Sitting with her back to the cooker, calm as you please, a mug of coffee in one hand and a large glass of my precious single malt whisky on the table in front of her, is my boss.

'I have to say, you do know how to hide, Detective Constable.'

I like my boss. Well, technically, she's my boss's boss. Diane

Shepherd was first introduced to me as Superintendent, but she's ex-military and should probably be referred to as General or something. I was never big on the ranks. Still, I always presumed that the army went in for discipline and sticking to the rules.

'Shouldn't you be wearing a mask?' My own, in dire need of a wash, is crumpled up in my pocket.

'Why? Are you sick?'

I open my mouth to say no, then remember my time in the cell with Lila. She didn't look terribly well, but it was more that she'd been beaten up than that she was feverish. And I'd got far too close to Slaphead and Greasy Rat for comfort. It's been a week, but they say symptoms can take two to show. Even after a negative test.

'Let's just say my social distancing plans got thrown a little recently.' I pull out a chair and sit down. Then I immediately get up again, fetch a glass from the drainer by the sink. Shepherd watches me the whole time, but says nothing until I've poured myself some whisky and topped it up with a little fine Welsh spring water from the tap. It's early for me, but if Shepherd is here, then I'll probably need it.

'So I heard. And you've been sticking your nose in places it's not meant to be, too. Spending rather too much time in the worse end of Aberystwyth for someone who's meant to be off work.'

I shrug at that. Seems I must have been tailed before today. There's no way Shepherd could have got out here from London in the couple of hours since I first noticed it. Either that or it's taken a whole week for the news of my short stay in the cells to filter through.

'I had hoped you'd be back in London by now.' Shepherd stares straight at me. 'Karen's not happy with having to do all the legwork.'

That's not what she told me in her text earlier today, but I let it go. Shepherd's here for a reason, and I don't believe for a minute it's because my name popped up on the PNC. Or even that she wants me back at work. Both could have been done with a call, or by an underling.

'You know, I never said I'd be coming back at all.'

'You did. I remember the conversation well. And if I'd believed you then, I'd never have suggested you turn your compassionate leave into a furlough.' Shepherd looks into her coffee mug, then puts it down on the table and picks up the whisky instead. Savours a mouthful before speaking again. 'You're a detective, Constance. Good at it, too. A bit chaotic, maybe. Certainly not the best at following orders or rules. But you get results. You don't give up until the end.'

'And what if this is the end?' I take a slightly larger sip of whisky than I'd intended, feel it burn in my throat and at the back of my nose. Don't sneeze, Con. 'I tried therapy, just like you suggested. And you know what happened?'

Shepherd stares at me with those annoyingly understanding eyes of hers, says nothing.

'Three weeks in and he quit. Not just me, the whole therapy gig. Jacked it all in and went off to be a delivery driver or something. Said he couldn't take it any more. My therapist.'

A twitch at the corner of her mouth lets me know Shepherd's trying not to laugh at that. She has a point, it's hilarious on the face of it. If it's not happening to you. Lately rather too much has been happening to me, though. My little bubble of calm has been burst. Violently.

'I don't know if you heard, but two men attacked me not a mile from where we're sitting. They were going to rape me, and yet I was the one who ended up in a cell.'

Shepherd frowns at that, even as she sips. 'Word did reach me, yes. Sounds like you took care of yourself, though. You always do. And you managed to spring yourself without calling in any favours, which is very resourceful. Helpful, too.'

I'm suddenly tired of this conversation and the way we're dancing around each other.

'Why are you here, Ma'am?' I put my glass down, slopping a little of the precious liquid over the edge.

'I had a call from the local CID about you this afternoon. I was in the area. Thought I'd check in on you. See what trouble you're getting yourself into.'

'Really? In the area? You do know this is the arse end of nowhere, right? The literal end of the line?'

Shepherd tilts her head, gives me a look I imagine mothers give their wayward infants. Not my mother, of course. She was always hands off. And now she's dead.

'Have you any idea how much cocaine comes into the UK through Wales? Heroin, too, although it's gone out of fashion lately. And there's a steady stream of trafficked women. The major ports are locked up pretty tight now, so the gangs have switched to bits of the coast we can't watch so closely.'

I think again of Lila, knees drawn up to her chest, hair unkempt, face bruised. Then of Lila all dolled up, a couple of older men escorting her somewhere. I shudder. 'If there's an operation underway in this area, shouldn't I know about it? If only to keep out of your way?'

The ghost of a smile flickers across Shepherd's face. She reaches down to the floor and retrieves a soft leather bag from beside her feet. No square-edged briefcase for her. From within its depths, she produces a thick A4 envelope and slides it across the table to me.

'Operation Cantre'r Gwaelod. Think I'm pronouncing that right.'

'The petrified forest? Legend of the sunken city?'

Shepherd shrugs. 'I've no idea. It's all Welsh to me. Had a meeting in Carmarthen this afternoon. Dyfed-Powys have been pursuing some interesting leads, but every time they think they're getting close, it all unravels.'

I put a hand on the envelope instinctively, then stop myself from opening it. I don't know if I want this at all, let alone right now. Shepherd's face remains inscrutable, but I can see the tiniest droop of her shoulders when I don't immediately fall for her ploy.

'Maybe they need to find out who's taking bribes then. Or who's got a gambling problem.'

'I think the local police are more than capable of sorting that out for themselves.'

Outside the kitchen window, I hear the crunch of wheels on gravel. It's getting dark, and the sensor trips the outside light as a car pulls up to the door. Shepherd pushes back her chair and stands, slinging the bag over her shoulder. She pauses only long enough to throw back the last of her whisky, points at the envelope as she places the glass down on the table. 'That's all classified, so no letting anyone else see it, right? And you're only seeing it so you know why I'm asking you to leave well alone. I know you mean well, Constance, but sometimes good intentions lead to ill.'

I scramble to my own feet, feeling aches I'd not noticed before, the leftovers of my fight with Greasy Rat and Slaphead. 'Leaving already?'

'It's a long drive back to London, and your couch doesn't look all that inviting. It'd be unfair to make DS Latham sleep in the car, too. Bad enough he's going to have to back it down the lane.'

I follow Shepherd out, and sure enough as soon as she appears, DS Latham climbs out of a shiny black Mercedes. Where he's been while I've been talking with the boss is anyone's guess. He barely registers my existence as he hurries to open the passenger door for the boss. She turns back to me briefly before climbing into the rear seat.

'You're looking well, Constance. The sea air obviously does you good. But don't get too used to it, eh? We need you back at work soon.'

I say nothing, only watch as Latham gets in, starts the engine and begins the laborious process of backing down the lane in the gathering dark. I could go out and help, even open the gate into the field where he could turn around. But he's such an arsehole he'd probably get stuck and blame it on me. Instead, I take a few breaths of the cool evening air, give my uninvited visitors a little wave, and then go back inside.

5

Isn't it always the way that, no matter how exhausted you might be, a troubled mind will never let you sleep? I'd mooched around for the evening after Shepherd's visit, all the while studiously ignoring the top-secret briefing notes on the kitchen table. I'd made something to eat, and read a book until the letters began to swim before my eyes. Then I'd given up and gone to bed. For months now, I've been falling asleep the moment my head hits the pillow. But not tonight.

I thought I'd become used to the darkness and utter silence that surrounds this little cottage in the middle of nowhere. Now I find myself lying on my back, staring at the faintest shadows on the ceiling. It's so quiet I can hear the blood pumping in my veins, the crinkle of the duvet cover as I breathe in and out, the almost imperceptible tick-boing of my watch on the bedside table. In my London flat, these noises would be drowned out by the roar of the city, the room painted orange by the glow from the street lamps. Here their absence leaves me with too much space to think. I've managed a week without reliving the moments when I was attacked outside the pub. Deep inside, I knew that I'd have a reckoning sooner or later.

It's not quite a panic attack, but I can feel my body almost shaking as I relive the incident, over and over. I can tell myself I was never in any danger, and that's probably true. Those two men were half-cut, and were certainly not expecting someone trained in self-defence. And yet my heart patters away like there's a frantic bird trapped in my ribcage. I can't help but wonder whether Slaphead and Greasy Rat might not merely slink away, lesson learned never to mess with an angry redhead. They might instead bear a grudge, seek me out. What if they know where I live? What if they've been nursing their injuries, waiting for the right time for revenge? This cottage is so remote, there'd be no passing squad car to save me. What if they brought friends?

Stop it, Con. You're fine. Just too tired to sleep.

Maybe I should get up and go back to the kitchen. Another glass of whisky will chase the demons away, at least for a while. But I left the envelope on the table, I will surely open it, just like Shepherd wants me to. I'm not stupid enough to think she was only stopping by to tell me off about Aber CID's complaint, certainly not daft enough to think she'd give me a confidential operation briefing just so I can keep out of its way. She doesn't want me back in London helping Karen with the paperwork. She wants me here, sticking my nose in where it's not wanted but careful not to tread on any more toes.

Dammit, how does she know me so well?

More hours of tossing and turning. I must sleep a little, but the churn of thoughts never quite goes away. Eventually the darkness starts to shift, the pre-dawn light seeping into the room like a slow tide. I give up, climb out of bed and drag myself to the shower.

The envelope is still on the kitchen table, daring me to open it as I go about the serious business of coffee and toast. Outside, the day is clear and bright, only a few clouds in the sky. Perfect weather for a walk along the clifftops. If that doesn't clear my head, then nothing will.

I just need to scan those briefing papers first.

★ ★ ★

It's a couple of hours and a full cafetiere emptied later when I finally step outside, lock the door, and set off for the cliffs. To the south, Llantwmp beach stretches away in an immense arc of grey shingle, but the cottage is nestled into a small hollow at the top of a steep hill that marks its northern end. Where the sea meets this hill, it's as if some ancient giant has carved half of it away with his magical sword, leaving sheer cliffs that plunge hundreds of feet into the water. On a clear day, it feels like you should be able to see the coast of Ireland. Not that you can, of course. It's too far away, and too low. There are boats though, larger ships lining the horizon while smaller ones chug along the coast. Lobstermen and crabbers, the sight of one below me, not far out at all, reminds me again of the two men at the pub. And of Operation Cantre'r Gwaelod.

From what I read, brushing toast crumbs off the pages as I skimmed the report, most of the drugs come in through the small ports and a few private moorings. The packages are on larger vessels, dropped in among the lobster creels in the dead of night and picked up with the dawn by local inshore boats. So far, no one's been able to work out the pattern, if there even is one, of where the drops will be and when. The police have had a few lucky breaks, but always small scale and never quite managing to trace the source or find out the destination. Reading between the lines of the briefing notes, I get the impression the few successful busts are more of a diversion than anything. Designed to throw us off the scent while darker deeds are going on elsewhere.

Us.

I catch myself thinking that way as I clamber over a stone stile from one grazing field to the next. The sheep in these parts are small and hardy; they have to be to survive the gales. Constantly washed and blow dried, no wonder they're so white and fluffy. Unconcerned by my arrival, too. One glances up at me, but the rest have their heads down and aren't going to let anyone come between them and the wiry grass.

Us.

Am I really ready to go back? Do I want to? Is Shepherd right about me, that I need to keep looking for answers? I've certainly not found any in the months I've been here. Maybe I've not been looking at all, just running away from any decision.

The path winds down into a narrow gully, waves lapping noisily at the sides and crashing onto a small stone beach at the bottom. A few rusted iron spikes in the cliff and some unidentifiable old machinery suggest that this was once a place where cargoes were landed, boats hauled up and away from storms. It's sheltered from the wind that's picked up as the morning has progressed. I sit, take out the flask I brought with me, and gaze out to sea with a warming mug of coffee and a couple of biscuits. Seagulls wheel and scream overhead, and that little boat I saw earlier is puttering from buoy to buoy, hauling up lobster creels. I don't see any suspicious packages in this catch.

My phone buzzes in my pocket, a text come in. For a moment, I assume it's Shepherd with some strange request. Maybe she wants me to destroy the notes, pretend I never saw them, and go back to being my carefree happy-go-lucky self. When I stare at the screen though, I see a message from Gareth, or should I call him Lord Caernant? Supper tonight, cocktails served at six. I ping off a quick reply of thanks and acceptance. I'm usually fine on my own, but I could do with some company for a change. Especially if that company is serving cocktails.

The clouds have rolled in again, and the sea is turning choppy as I slip the phone away and pack up my flask. I'm still no closer to knowing what I should do, but whatever it is I think it'll be better done indoors. When I reach the clifftop, the wind batters me like an assault. I hunch myself against it and hurry back to the cottage, but the rain comes on hard when I'm still half a field away. Hood up and running, I'm out of breath by the time I reach relative calm in the lee of the gable end wall. Which is probably why I'm almost at the door, key already in my hand, before I see the figure huddled on the threshold. She notices me first, looks up with haunted, dark-rimmed eyes, a mixture of fear and desperation twisting her face. I recognise her, though. How could I not?

'Lila?'

'How did you even know where I live?'

We're in the kitchen. I know, social distancing and everything, but what else could I do? The rain's come on strong now, battering against the windows as the wind shakes the stubby trees outside. I couldn't exactly have left her on the doorstep.

'When they come for me. Not long after you go.' She stares into the mug of coffee I made for her, cupping her hands around it as if the heat is as important as the caffeine. Maybe it is. She's not well dressed for the weather.

'That's not exactly an answer.'

'Is in waiting room. How you call it? Where they take details, write down on paper.'

'The processing room, yes?'

'We wait there while police man talk to Kieran.' She somehow manages to spit the name without actually spitting. I don't need to ask who she means. Boyfriend, pimp, dealer. Probably all three. Almost certainly the one responsible for the bruises that make her look like a panda. Was he the man I saw with his hand on her shoulder? Was that his 4x4 I've been looking for all week?

'They all hush hush. In corner so no one hear. Police man. He take something from Kieran. Give something back. Is money, papers, I not know. But I see other papers on counter? I take while nobody seeing. I have look. See?' Lila shoves her hand into her coat pocket and pulls out a folded sheet of A4. When she passes it across to me, I recognise the form the custody sergeant used to fill in my details before I was marched off to the cells. Name, mobile phone number, address, date of birth. Jesus Christ.

'So why come here? We met for all of, what? Half an hour? Not even that.'

Lila stares at me with those bruised eyes and a gaze that has seen far too much in too short a life. 'I run away. The police give me back to Kieran. He hurt me. Make me work two times hard. I not take it any more. Run away again. But I have nowhere to go.'

Whereas, I do. A quick glance at the clock on the microwave tells me it's early afternoon. I'm meant to be going over to Caernant Hall tonight. Cocktails at six, Gareth said. I was looking forward to that. Was looking forward to some lunch, too.

'You hungry?' I ask, the question emerging before I realise what I'm doing. Lila's face creases into something that might be a smile, might be her about to burst into tears. She nods, but says nothing.

'Well, I'm not sure there's much here, but I'll see what I can do.'

I find some bread that's a bit stale but not mouldy, cheese cracked and dry because I forgot to close the wrapper on it. Lila doesn't seem to mind, attacking her cheese on toast as if it's the finest thing she's ever tasted. We don't talk much while she's eating, which at least gives me time to think.

'Is there nowhere you can go? A hostel maybe?'

She had been starting to relax, but now a genuine fear etches itself across her face. 'I not go there. Is not safe.'

'Really? Why not?' I've a suspicion I know, but I ask anyway. Today is not shaping up how I'd thought it would.

'Kieran find me if go there.'

'Kieran. That's the boyfriend you ran away from, right?'

Now Lila looks at me as if I'm an idiot. 'You have boyfriend?'

I ignore the question. 'So he's more of a bloke who mostly looks after you, right? Gives you somewhere to stay, feeds you. And in return you do . . . stuff for him.'

Lila's eyes narrow at the word 'stuff', or maybe it was the pause. She doesn't come across as a typical drug addict, and I'm not getting a sex worker vibe from her either. It's hard to pin her down as anything, really. I'm not even sure how old she is. Certainly young, maybe much the same age as Izzy, which is probably why I'm even speaking to her.

'Is something like that. He promise he get me papers. He give me money, some nice clothes.' She pulls at the collar of her coat. Not the one she was wearing when I saw her in town, but neither is it the stained hoodie from the cell. It's faded, patched, looks like a hand-me-down. Her jeans are torn and dirty, trainers more hole than fabric. Any sign of make-up is long gone, the fading bruises around her pale grey eyes the only colour in her face. Did she walk here, all the way from Aberystwyth? What kind of desperation drives a person to do that?

'And what did he ask in return?'

She stares down at her hands, embarrassed, and I reappraise how young she must be. I've no idea who this Kieran is, but I know I don't like him already. Or the filthy men he sells her out to for their sick pleasures.

'Just that? Or does he get you to do things for him? Maybe . . .' I search for the words. '. . . take packages places for him?'

Lila's gaze comes back up to my face at that. 'I take trip sometimes. Go from here to big city. Manchester, London, Birmingham.' Her accent makes Birmingham sound far more exotic than my memories of the place. 'I go with luggage. Stay one night, maybe two. Sometimes there is man. Better when there is no man. When I come back, I leave luggage behind.'

She shrugs at the last few words, which means she knows

well enough what she's doing on these trips. I wonder why her, and not some local from a sink estate, but the answer's clear enough. She's here illegally, so this Kieran has her under control. She can't run; where would she go? Aberystwyth nick, apparently. But they just picked her up from there. So, she came here. Christ, she must be desperate.

'Where are you from?' I ask. 'Originally?'

Again that look of suspicion. 'Why you ask?'

'Because I'm trying to work out what to do with you, Lila. I'm not a social worker and this isn't a hostel for refugees.' I'm a plain-clothes police officer on extended leave of absence, trying to decide what I really want to do with my life, and this isn't helping.

'I grow up in Ukraine,' she says eventually. 'Was nice. I have two big brothers. Mother and father with good jobs. But then men came, start fighting. I was at school one day. Learning speak English, yes? Big explosion. Lots of noise, dust, people running and screaming. I run too. All the way home to my family. But house, it is gone. Just hole in ground.'

She falls silent, head drooping as if she's too tired to hold it up any more. I don't know much about what's been going on in Ukraine, but her story sounds plausible enough. How she managed to make it all the way from there to Aberystwyth is a tale in itself, I'm sure, and one I don't think I want to hear right now. But she came to me for help, she desperately needs help. Who am I to turn her away?

6

I grew up in a massive country house in Northamptonshire, before being shipped off at an early age to a boarding school in an even bigger stately home. To me, Gareth's house, Plas Caernant, is nothing particularly special, although its setting in the foothills of the Cambrian Mountains, surrounded by endless miles of ancient forest, is picturesque. The house is a little smaller than Harston Magna Hall, although it has a much bigger walled garden than my father's estate, and a spectacular stable block around the back. I've been here a few times since moving to the cottage, so all in all the view doesn't impress me.

The same can't be said for Lila.

'Your friends live here?' The awe in her voice is something to hear.

'My aunt's friends. They're quite a bit older than me.'

I called Gareth while Lila was making use of my shower and, judging by the smell once she was finished, all of my toiletries. I'd been going to ask him if I could postpone, but as soon as I explained why he'd simply laughed.

'Bring her along too. Sounds like someone I'd very much like to meet.'

And so here we are, since there was no way I was going to leave Lila alone in the cottage, and nothing else I could easily do with her in the short term. Long term? Well, I'm still working on that.

'Is big family to have such large house,' she says as we climb out of my old Volvo and stare up at the ivy-clad walls. If I knew more about architecture I'd probably be able to say when it was built, but I don't so I can't. It's old, though.

'Actually, it's just Lord and Lady Caernant. They never had children.'

'No children?' She looks at me with eyes so wide I find myself reassessing her age. I'd put her in her early twenties, but there's a teenager's innocence in her expression now, and once again I'm reminded of Izzy.

'Ah, Con. You've arrived. And right on time.' We're interrupted from further conversation by the appearance of Lord Caernant at the entrance. Even though she's standing on the other side of the car, I can sense Lila stiffen. For a moment, I wonder if she recognises our host from somewhere, and my mind does a rapid branch through a dozen possibilities before I realise she's simply scared. To his credit, Gareth appears to notice this too, approaching slowly and coming first to me.

'It's good to see you again.' He stands a few feet away, leans in for a pretend hug, social-distancing style. A bit daft given we're all about to go inside together. 'And this must be your unexpected guest.'

Lila still stands beside the car, close enough that she could open the door and jump back in again should she choose. It's an oddly tense moment, but then this whole afternoon has been odd. I make introductions as best I can, aware that I'm bringing a drug mule and possible sex-worker to the home of a sitting member of the House of Lords. Though put like that, it maybe doesn't seem so outrageous after all.

'Amy's in the kitchen. She'll be with us in a moment, I'm sure.' Gareth leads us through to a room that is relatively small by the standards of the rest of the house. A log fire blazes in a huge fireplace and in front of it, two deerhounds laze on a threadbare rug. One of them raises its head to see who has come in, thumps its tail a couple of times in greeting, then collapses back down again. The other could be dead for all the interest it pays us, although I know it isn't.

'Cocktails, I think.' Gareth points us at the sofa and chairs before turning his attention to a sideboard stacked with bottles. 'Please, sit down. We don't do ceremony here. You did bring a bag, like I told you?'

I shake my head, trying to indicate Lila without rudely pointing. 'I'm sorry, Gareth, but given the circumstances I thought it best if we didn't stay.'

'Nonsense, dear. I've already made up a couple of spare bedrooms.'

We're interrupted by Lady Caernant, who sweeps into the room like a fading Hollywood star. Her stare would make any person quake in fear, although I've had worse from the teachers at my old school, as well as a few hardened criminals, come to think of it. I shrug and smile, which used to work for the teachers, less so for the criminals.

'And you must be Lila.' She focuses her attention on my young companion, face switching instantly to welcoming. 'Gareth told me you'd been in trouble with the police.'

I feel sorry for Lila in that moment. I don't know Lord and Lady Caernant well, but they're friends of the family and I am used to the idiosyncrasies of the British aristocracy. Lila's English is a lot better than my Ukrainian, but she is so very out of her depth here. It would probably have been kinder to drive her back to Aberystwyth police station and persuade Sergeant Griffiths to take her in again.

'I . . .' She starts to say, but Lady Caernant waves the reply away.

'Never mind. You're our guest tonight, so we need say no more about it. I'm Amy, by the way. Can't be doing with this lord and lady business.'

'There you go, Con.' Gareth hands me a huge martini glass, almost brim full with clear liquid, a single olive nestling at the bottom. When I sniff the surface I get plenty of gin but not any noticeable vermouth.

'And what about you, Lila? A cocktail before dinner?'

Lila looks puzzled. 'Cock . . . ?'

I stifle a laugh that might be more to do with the alcohol vapours going up my nose than anything. 'I'm not sure Lila's old enough to drink.' Certainly given how skinny she is, one of Gareth's martinis wouldn't be a good idea.

'I not drink booze,' she says. 'Kieran, he always drink. Beer, whisky, vodka.' She pronounces it 'wodka', but the look of anguish on her face stops any of us laughing.

'Booze make him angry. I not like him when he angry.'

I do my best to convey my apologies to Gareth without it being obvious, but Amy has already sat down and taken one of Lila's hands in her own.

'I imagine you've seen a great many things in your short life, dear. You're safe here, though. Nobody's going to get angry or violent within these walls.' She pauses for a few moments, letting the room fall silent save for the crackle of logs in the fire. 'Now, since supper's ready, why don't we all go through to the kitchen and eat?'

There's something very special about eating at the kitchen table in an old house you know has a dining room large enough to seat two dozen. Or maybe that's just another hang-up from my childhood. I hated formal dinner at Harston Magna Hall, the utter silence of that cold, draughty, cavernous room. My father was never much of a conversationalist at the best of times, but he insisted the dinner table was no place for idle talk. My brother, Ben, would spend meals pulling faces, trying to make me laugh so that I'd get into trouble. My mother could see what he was doing, but never told him to stop or came to my rescue.

So, it was always a relief when both parents were away. Then we could have our meals in the kitchen, watched over by Joan the housekeeper. The massive old range cooker kept the room warm, and the food was always simpler. We usually had more of it as well.

Such is the way at Caernant Hall, too. The kitchen is the heart of the house, and clearly where Amy spends most of her time. We've barely sat down before the two dogs wander through, one raising a hopeful nose towards the still-empty table. They slump down in front of the Aga, then have to be shooed away so that our hostess can open the oven doors.

The meal is good. A simple but hearty stew followed by apple pie and proper custard. I could almost be back at St Berts, except there aren't twenty other girls sitting at the table on long benches, elbows pulled in awkwardly for lack of space. Conversation tumbles around inconsequential things, and Gareth is sticking to subjects that are unlikely to be awkward for Lila. For her part, my new friend says little, instead working her way methodically through all the food put in front of her. She eats slowly, savouring each mouthful in a way that makes me wonder once more about the life she's been leading since a badly aimed artillery round blew her world apart.

'Delicious as ever, Amy,' Gareth says, when everyone has had their fill.

'Is wonderful. Remind me of home.' Lila's smile is betrayed by the shiny wetness of her eyes. She looks down quickly to try and hide her tears, but I see them all the same. How different this must all seem, how alien. Just a week ago she was in a police cell after trying to escape an abusive man. She's a victim of modern day slavery, sexual abuse and God only knows what else, and I know now that I'll do everything I can to get her away from all that. I'm just not sure what. Not yet.

'How would you two like to see the Holy Grail?'

Gareth speaks in such a light-hearted and jovial manner, it takes me a moment to parse what he's just said.

'Holy . . . what now?'

'Gareth, are you sure?' Amy sounds cautious, and she's frowning deeply. Her gaze flicks towards Lila before she can stop herself.

'Of course, dear. We're all friends here, aren't we?' Gareth ignores her tone and pushes back his chair to stand, a little wobbly after that large martini and several glasses of very good claret. I'm not entirely sure what to do, or indeed what they are talking about, but Lila stands up too, so I do the same.

'Well, it's your responsibility, your decision.' Amy dabs at her lips with her napkin, then shakes her head like she's seen it all before. 'Go on then. I'll deal with the dishes while you're showing off to our guests.'

We both follow our host through the house, past the small sitting room with the open fire and along a dark corridor. The floor is made of slate flagstones, the walls lime plastered and whitewashed so that the place has the feel of some medieval church rather than someone's house. I've consumed rather more alcohol than is perhaps sensible, which doesn't help with the spooky atmosphere either.

At the end of the corridor, Gareth stops and guddles around in his jacket pocket before producing a large iron key. On his second attempt, he manages to insert it into the keyhole of a heavy wooden door. Beyond, stone steps lead down into the gloom.

'This all used to be hidden, back when the house was first built. Catholics were being persecuted all over the country. The old families had priest holes and hidden chapels so they could carry on praying in peace.' Gareth flicks a switch before setting off down the stairs. I follow, Lila close behind me, and we're soon at another, larger door. The space beyond it is dark, but from the chill in the air, I can sense that we're in a big room. Something in the distance glints dully, until Gareth flicks another switch and takes my breath away.

We're standing in a chapel, underground and hidden away, but no less grand for that. The ceiling vaults high overhead, the stone carved in an ornate and gothic style that puts me in mind of Rosslyn Chapel outside Edinburgh. Wasn't that where the Holy Grail was meant to be hidden, anyway? Or was that just Dan Brown's imagination running wild?

Beside me, Lila says something in what I presume is Ukrainian. I don't need to understand her words to know the awe behind them; I'm feeling the same emotion myself.

'This is incredible.' I take a few steps into the room, my head swivelling as I try to take everything in. The glittering I saw in the darkness turns out to be a golden cross on an altar at the far side of the chapel, flanked by a pair of spectacularly ugly gold candlesticks. Behind them, nailed to a wooden cross on the wall, an almost life-size Christ suffers for all our sins.

Lila steps forward, halfway to the altar along the narrow aisle, then kneels and crosses herself, head bowed. Gareth gives her a moment, then goes to her side. He places a gentle hand on her shoulder, helps her to her feet, and leads her to a small alcove in the corner. Their faith makes me uneasy. I can't deny their devotion, or the magnificence of this hidden, private chapel, but I have never been a believer. Religion is a tool for controlling people, as far as I'm concerned. Still, there's no denying my curiosity, so reluctantly, feeling as though I have no right being here, I follow.

By the time I reach them, Gareth has opened up a pair of carved oak doors to reveal a narrow cupboard that appears to be hewn out of the bedrock. Inside, nestling on a red velvet cushion, is what looks like a manky old piece of driftwood, found on the beach after the sea has polished smooth one half of it and eaten away the other.

'That, my dear, is all that remains of the cup from which Jesus Christ drank at the last supper. Gifted to Joseph of Arimathea and used by him to catch the lord's blood at his crucifixion.' Gareth reaches into the alcove and picks up the piece of wood with hands that tremble from something far more potent than alcohol. As the light falls on it, I see that it is, indeed, a cup of sorts, although badly broken and inexpertly mended over the years. I doubt very much it's more than a few hundred years old rather than a couple of millennia, but I'm not about to spoil the moment as he passes it to Lila. The look on her face makes her seem even younger still, a wide-eyed wonder I wish I could experience.

'It's seen better days, of course. But they say if you drink from it you will be cured of all your ailments.'

At that, Lila quickly offers the bowl back to him as if she's terrified she might drop it. Gareth merely waves towards the other side of the chapel and steps past her.

'Would you like to try it?' he asks, clearly not expecting an answer. Lila follows him, and I fall in behind the two of them as we're led to a small stone font. Gareth lifts off the wooden lid to reveal clear water within. He takes the cup from Lila, dips it in the water, then offers it to her.

'Drink,' he says. 'It's not poison.'

Lila is trembling now, and I wonder how this can be more terrifying than what she's already been through in her short life.

'If you're worried about the water, it comes from the same source as the rest of the house. There's a spring deep under the mountains. You won't find anything more pure, anywhere on earth.'

Something about Gareth's words, his soft Welsh accent, must reassure her. Lila nods once, then takes the cup and raises it to her lips. She drinks the water down quickly, as if it is some horrible medicine that must be endured. In a way, I suppose it is.

Nothing happens. No chorus of angels or sudden beam of holy light. It's all a bit of an anti-climax. Lila hands back the cup, her hands no longer shaking, and Gareth lifts it slightly in my direction.

'Would you like some, Con?'

For a moment, I'm caught in a bit of a dilemma. This isn't a piece of the Holy Grail. I don't believe in that nonsense any more than I believe in Christ, God and the rest of it. I really don't want any part of the charade, however impressive the set dressing might be. But to refuse would possibly upset my host, and almost certainly give Lila something unnecessary to worry about.

'Oh, why not?' I try to make it sound inconsequential. 'I've been feeling a bit bruised ever since those two goons jumped me. Maybe this will help.'

The water's cold and refreshing, even though I can smell a mustiness coming from the old wood of the cup. Broken, the bowl doesn't hold much more than a mouthful anyway, so the whole procedure is done in moments. I can't say that it has any effect on my general aches and pains that the martini and claret haven't already dealt with, but I say a polite 'thank you' as I hand back the Caernant family heirloom.

'Best lock this away safe again.' Gareth carries the grail to its hidey-hole, where he lovingly dries it with a clean white cloth before returning it to its velvet cushion. Lila crosses herself and bows her head to the altar before leaving the chapel, although I'm content to simply gawk like a tourist at the craftsmanship that has gone into its construction. Gareth puts the lights out and the doors are once again locked. In silence, we climb the stone steps back up to the ground floor of the mansion, but once the final door is closed, Lila speaks up.

'Thank you. This is very kind thing you have done for me. I know not how to repay. I never tell anybody your secret.'

'I'm sure you won't, my dear.' Gareth beams a toothy smile and raps a knuckle on the door. 'This won't open for just anyone, you know. It let you in, so it trusted you.'

Something in his words reminds me of another of Aunt Felicity's friends, the enigmatic fortune teller and occult curio dealer Madame Rose, who helped me out in Edinburgh last year. It's exactly the kind of mystic mumbo jumbo she would spout. Remembering her, and the first time I met her, gives me an idea about what to do with Lila. Come the morning I'll need to make a few phone calls.

Amy is waiting for us in the small sitting room, as are the two dogs who seem a little put out to find that the fire is burning low. I hadn't realised quite how late it was getting, but the clock on the mantelpiece suggests it's close to midnight. Something unspoken passes between Lord and Lady Caernant, and her smile notches up a gear.

'It's quite something, is it not?' She addresses the question to both me and Lila, but her focus is on the young woman. I'm picking up a bit of a 'welcome to the cult' vibe I wasn't expecting, and slightly regret having agreed to drink from the cup now. Mostly I'm tired, so when I say 'amazing,' and stifle a yawn at the same time it maybe comes across as a little rude.

'Sorry, Amy.' I cover my mouth. 'Didn't get much sleep last night, and that meal was excellent. I'd no idea we were down in the chapel so long.'

'Time has a habit of moving differently down there, in its own little world. And no need to apologise, you look all done in, Con dear. Come on, I'll show you both to your rooms.'

Before I can move to follow, one of the dogs ambles up and sniffs me. I'm not the most doggy of people, but these two are so laid back it's hard to be afraid, even if they are the size of small horses. I give the creature a scratch behind his ears, and receive a tail wag in return.

'You've made a friend there,' Gareth tells me. 'Old Gelert doesn't usually like people much, so you should be honoured.'

I look down at the hound, about to protest that he's not that old, surely. He's all skin and bone, his coat a mixture of grey and white, so it's hard to tell. But the eyes that look back up at me are clouded. I give him a final scratch, then follow my hostess out of the room.

Lila and I have been given bedrooms opposite each other on a narrow corridor towards the back of the house. If my tired mind is right, then they're above the kitchen, and their relatively small size suggests servants' quarters from an earlier era. My room is warm and the bed far more comfortable than it has any right to be. Even so, I wait up, listening, for a long time after I've closed the door. It's been a strange day, and I can't quite understand why Gareth and Amy both welcomed and trusted Lila so quickly and completely. They're old-fashioned, but they're not stupid. They knew she had been in police custody, and yet never asked why. Now she's free to wander around this mansion and help herself to anything of value she might find. Anything that would fit in a pocket, at least.

But then I remember her awe in the subterranean chapel, her obvious religious devotion. I remember, too, the defensiveness when I first met her in the cell in Aberystwyth, and the desperation when she appeared at my doorstep. I don't yet know how much of her story is true; that's something to begin chasing down in the morning along with working out what to do with her. For now, all I can do is be vigilant and hope I haven't inadvertently brought a cuckoo into the nest of my aunt's eccentric friends.

The muted sound of a toilet flushing a little further down the corridor is followed by the soft pad of footsteps and the click as the door across from mine is opened then closed. I wait for a while longer, listening to the creaks and groans all old houses make. After a while, I ease open my own door and stare into the darkness. Light spills out from under Lila's bedroom door for a moment, then disappears with the click of a switch. I'm being foolish, worrying what she might do, but I stay frozen to the spot for a while before accepting she's probably asleep by now. It's my exhaustion making me paranoid, nothing else. So I finally surrender, close the door and climb into bed.

7

I can't remember the last time I woke up feeling actually refreshed. More often than not, something's aching, and lately I've been troubled by nightmares of past horrors. My mother's dead body, a boy with his heart cut out, a man's scream cut short as he goes under the wheels of a speeding car. Snippets of trauma that leave me confused and unsettled. Sometimes it's just a pressing need to pee that wakes me.

But not last night. Last night I slept like the dead.

Given the amount of wine and the strength of Gareth's martinis, I should have woken with a raging thirst and pounding head, but I feel better than I have for ages. It's not until I'm up and dressed that the worries of the previous night return.

My phone tells me it's not yet seven, but when I step out of my bedroom I see Lila's door is already open. I rap my knuckles on the wood. When there's no answer, I dare to glance inside. Her bed is empty although obviously slept in. She has nothing but the clothes she was wearing, a mixture of her own and some things she borrowed from me yesterday. None of it is here, but as I gaze around the room, I can hear snippets of conversation filtering up from below. Not the actual words so much as the cadence and intonation of speech. She must be downstairs already.

51

Gelert the deerhound greets me at the bottom of the stairs, a warm wet nose shoved against my stomach as his whole body moves with the wagging of his tail. I scratch the top of his head and he walks beside me happily, claws tapping against the flag-stones, as I move along the corridor towards the kitchen. The other dog looks up from its place in front of the Aga, but my attention is more on Amy and Lila, sat deep in conversation.

'Oh, Con. You're up. Hope you slept well.' Lady Caernant stands as soon as she sees me. She bustles over, about to give me a hug, then pauses as though only just remembering the social distancing rules. I'm not sure they really apply any more, since we've been in the same house together overnight, but I mirror her apologetic shrug.

'Coffee?' She sidesteps me, heading to the Aga and a percolator blepping away on the edge of the warming plate.

'Please,' I say as I pull out a chair opposite Lila and sit down. She's tousle-haired from sleep, and I can't see much of the bruises that gave her panda eyes the day before. There's none of the trapped wild animal about her either; amazing what a little friendly hospitality can do.

Amy places a mug of fine-smelling coffee in front of me and gestures toward the jug of milk. Inhaling the aroma gives me a sudden feeling of homesickness, as I remember the times spent drinking coffee with old Mrs Feltham in the flat below mine in London. I really need to make a decision about my life. Get back there and back into the fray.

'Lila was telling me a bit about her home in Ukraine. Such a terrible tragedy.'

Her words bring me out of my musing and I glance across the table at the young woman. She shrugs, as if losing your entire family and ending up a drug mule in the arse end of nowhere isn't so bad. She still has a haunted look in her eyes.

'I was thinking,' I say, then pause as I try to find the right words. 'There's a place I know. Up in Scotland. You'd be safe there, away from everything. Away from Kieran.'

I can see as soon as the name is out that it's the wrong thing to say. Lila might have come to terms with the tragedy that brought her to Wales, might have relaxed a little in this warm, safe place, but she's still terrified of the monster. She huddles in on herself, hands clasped together in her lap, gaze down.

'Scotland?' Amy says. 'That's . . . a long way away.'

'I know, but that's kind of the point, isn't it? And it's a refuge for women escaping exactly the kind of abuse Lila's been put through. They've other sites. There's probably one not far from here. But this one's special?' I make it a question, since I'm really not all that sure myself.

'You're talking about the Downham Trust, I take it.' Amy sits down at the head of the table. 'Burntwoods?'

Why does it not surprise me she knows the place?

'That's it, yes. Izzy. My sister. Well, I guess technically she's my half-sister, right enough. She found out about it and managed to escape there. A pity she didn't stay put.'

Amy reaches over and pats me on the arm, which makes a mockery of the whole no-hugging thing, but I'm a bit past caring. 'I know. Felicity told me all about it. Your family, eh? And now you're helping out other strays.'

'I not stray,' Lila says, her voice as indignant as a slighted teenager. It's the first thing she's said since I came in, but it's clear she's both listened to and understood our conversation. 'Scot Land. Is Glas Gow no?' She somehow manages to pronounce both country and city as two words.

'Glasgow is on the west of Scotland, yes. Have you been there?' If she has, then it could be more of a problem getting her away from trouble than I thought.

'One time. I not understand what they say. Is like English, but not like English. You know?'

Amy laughs at that. 'I think that's a fairly accurate description of Glaswegian, although there's some accents in Wales would give it a run for its money.'

'Burntwoods is on the other side of the country. Near Dundee. And it takes in women from all over, not just Scotland. You'll be safe there. I can give them a call, if you'd like?'

Lila doesn't answer straight away, and I can almost see the thoughts tumbling through her head. She's had a little over twelve hours of kindness and welcome in this house, and she clearly doesn't want to ever leave now. What a life she must have endured.

'We need to get you away from Aberystwyth, Lila,' Amy says. 'Away from the people who've been using you. This place Con's talking about? I know it. I've been there. They'll look after you for as long as you want.'

'How will I get there?'

It's the question I've been dreading ever since I first thought of Burntwoods. On the plus side, the fact that she's even asked means that Lila is seriously considering the idea. But on the minus there's only two ways to get her there. I can take her to Carmarthen and put her on a train, at which point she'll likely disappear and probably end up as a drug mule and sex worker again. Or I can fill up the Volvo with petrol and drive the four hundred or so miles to the refuge. At least I could drop in on Madame Rose and Janie Harrison on the way back, I suppose. And who am I kidding? I was always going to do whatever I could to help this young woman; she reminds me too much of Izzy not to.

'How do you fancy a road trip?'

I know something's wrong even before we reach the top of the track leading to the cottage. I can't say what it is exactly, something my subconscious has noted or some mystic warning maybe.

54

I find myself slowing the car before the final bend, crawling into the narrow yard. The first thing I notice is what looks like rubbish strewn across the ground. The second is that the door is wide open.

I don't pull all the way into the yard, but instead back into the gateway to one of the fields that surround the cottage. The gods are looking down on me as, for once, the gate is open. The farmer must have gathered his sheep to the farmyard down the hill. Christ, I hope I don't meet them all coming back that way if I need to make a hasty exit.

'What is . . . ?' Lila's face has gone even paler than usual, her hands grasping the chest strap of her seatbelt in anxiety.

'I don't know. Stay in the car. Lock it after I get out.' I kill the engine, grab the keys and pull out my phone as I open the door. A bitter cold wind brings with it the scent of salt spray. I approach the cottage from an angle that minimises the chances of my being seen through either the kitchen or living room windows. Closer inspection of the mess lying in the yard reveals it to be the contents of the bin that was under the sink in the kitchen, along with some of my clothes. I keep close to the wall of the cottage, listening for any sound coming from inside, although it's almost impossible to hear anything above the constant moan of the wind. Crouching low, I risk a peek in through the kitchen window, then stand up when I see it's empty. I make a slow circuit all the way around the building, checking the other windows, until I end up where I started. Nothing moves and there is no sound from inside that I can hear. I step in, wrinkling my nose at the smell. It doesn't take long to check all the rooms, find them empty but turned over. I hit speed dial on my phone and step into the kitchen, not quite sure whether it's been ransacked or the mess is all my own. My call is answered on the second ring.

'Karen? Hey, it's me. Con.'

'Hey, Con. Good to hear your voice.' The background noise of wherever Karen is makes me wonder if she can hear anything at all. Compared to the utter silence in the cottage, it makes me feel strangely off balance.

'Good to hear you, too. Listen. Someone's broken into the cottage. Looks like they were searching for something and didn't find it.' I wander from the kitchen to the living room as I speak, not seeing anything I didn't already notice.

'Shit. You want me to call in the police for you?'

'They're not exactly my favourite people right now. And I reckon I know who did this is. Those two Neanderthals who jumped me outside the pub. They're long gone anyway.'

'Yeah, Diane told me all about that. The bloody cheek. Still not sure why you didn't just tell the custody sergeant who you are.'

I climb the stairs again, check the bedroom and bathroom a bit more thoroughly. Outside, I can just make out the car's bonnet where I reversed into the field gate. Better get back to Lila and let her know everything's OK. Except that it isn't. Not really. On the other end of the line, I hear the noise fade as Karen finds herself a quiet spot.

'It's complicated, K. And the fewer people round here know about me the better. Thing is, I reckon that's all going to go to shit now.'

'You think?' Karen barks a short, mirthless laugh.

'Yeah, fair enough. Look, can you do me a favour? Well, maybe a couple?'

'Sure thing, boss. What d'you need?'

'First off the two idiots who jumped me. You couldn't find out what's happening with them, could you? I don't even know their names, let alone whether they were charged with anything. This mess looks horribly like payback to me.'

'I'll track 'em down and email you all the details, OK? You be

56

careful though, Con. Don't think Diane'll be too happy if you end up taking another six months off.'

'I'm not—' I stop myself. I'm still not sure if I'm going back at all, but Karen doesn't need to know that. Not yet, anyway.

'Whatever. You said two things? What else is there?'

As I continue picking my way through the devastation, I tell Karen everything I know about Lila. It's pitifully little; I only caught her surname in passing as she was talking to Amy before we left Plas Caernant. I don't know how old she is, whereabouts in Ukraine she's from, anything about her at all, really.

'So why's she interesting to you, this Lila Ivanova?' Karen asks as I make my way back down into the kitchen. 'How do you even know her?'

'She was in the same cell as me at Aber nick.'

'Say what? Aren't we supposed to be in some kind of pandemic?'

'I know, right? Think one of the constables fucked up. The thing is, she turned up here yesterday. She needs help, but I reckon she's here illegally, probably trafficked. Almost certainly being used as a drug mule, so she might know things that could help with Cantre'r Gwaelod.'

Karen's silent for a while, which hopefully means she's scribbling down notes. When she speaks next, I don't hear what I was expecting.

'That file the boss gave you on the operation. It's safe, right?'

For a moment I almost panic, but if I'd let that confidential briefing go missing, I'd be so far out of a job it would hurt. Which is why I took it with me to Plas Caernant.

'Not my first rodeo, K.' Although now she's mentioned it, I worry that whoever broke in and ransacked the cottage might have been looking for that. Except that how would they know? No, Con. You're getting paranoid.

'I have to go. Looks like I've got a road trip coming up.'

'Road trip?' Karen asks, then adds, 'Forget it. I'll call you later, when I've managed to dig up some info.'

'Thanks, K.' I hang up, shove my phone in my pocket and go back to the door. The wood around the lock is splintered where someone's given it a good kick. In London it would have multiple bolts and the frame would be reinforced with steel, but out here in the middle of nowhere half the folk don't even bother locking up when they go out. I'm still going to be out of pocket fixing it, and anything else that's been broken. At this rate, I'll have to go back to work just to pay for the damage.

I close the door as best I can, then start picking up the clothes that have been strewn about the yard as I make my way back to the old Volvo. The early sun glints off the glass, making it impossible to see inside until I'm up close and putting the key in the lock. My bag is on the back seat where I chucked it, so the briefing notes for Operation Cantre'r Gwaelod are safe. But the passenger seat is empty.

Lila is gone.

8

'I'm sure she'll be back soon enough. Poor thing was probably scared half to death when she saw someone had been to the cottage. Thought they'd come to drag her back to wherever it was she'd escaped from.'

I'll say one thing for Gareth Caernant; he's a good man. I spent the better part of an hour searching for Lila along the clifftop coastal path and down to the shingle beach. I even went into Llantwmp, spoke to Cerys in the pub and Myfanwy in the little grocery shop that mostly serves the caravan parks. Nobody had seen her. By the time I got back to the cottage, Gareth had arrived with a local joiner in tow, and the two of them were fixing the door. Now he's helping me tidy up the mess.

'You've let Amy know to keep an eye out for her?' I ask, for perhaps the tenth time. It's my fervent hope that Lila's decided to walk back to Plas Caernant. That's the last place she must have felt anything like safe, after all. The pessimist in me knows better than to hope.

'She'll phone me the minute Lila turns up, Con. Don't worry yourself.' Gareth reaches out a comforting hand, then stops himself. Given that we're both standing in the small living room, and have been in each other's company for quite some time recently, it all seems a little foolish.

'I guess it saves me an eight-hundred-mile round trip. Still need to find out who broke in here and why, though.' I set to rearranging the cushions on the sofa, and discover my laptop slipped down the side of the arm where I was last using it. 'They weren't burglars, that's for sure. Even if they did neck the last of my good whisky.'

'You say "they", Con. Would I be right in thinking you suspect someone already?'

'Well. The two idiots who jumped me outside the pub seem the most likely.' I open the laptop and power it up. 'Wouldn't be all that hard to work out where I lived, if they wanted to. Ask around the village for an English girl with red hair.'

'I suppose so. Would you like me to ask Sergeant Griffiths about them?'

I remember the surly custody sergeant who insisted on locking me up even though it was obvious I'd done nothing wrong. Well, obvious to me. 'No, it's OK, Gareth. I have my own sources and I don't want you dragged into this any more than you already have been. Whatever "this" is, of course.'

The laptop finally churns itself into life, asking for my fingerprint to let me see what's inside. Nothing much that would have been any interest to anyone. A few emails that are borderline NCA confidential, I suppose; the half-hearted first few chapters of a thriller I thought I might write while on sabbatical; lots and lots of photographs of the coastline, the mountains and forestry tracks around Llantwmp. I'll run a deep scan on it later, just to make sure nobody's managed to get in and plant some malware or tracker app, but it seems very unlikely. Whoever broke in wanted to mess things up. They'd either have taken the laptop or broken it if they'd seen it, so they can't have been looking all that hard.

'You'll come back to the hall, of course,' Gareth says.

I look up swiftly from the screen. 'Excuse me?'

'Well, you can't stay here. Not on your own. What if they come back while you're sleeping?'

I'd not really considered the possibility. If this was Slaphead and Greasy Rat looking for a little payback, I'd say they've had it now. Any normal person would move on, secure in the knowledge that their justice had been served. Nothing quite like shoving a whole box of sanitary pads down the toilet until it's good and blocked to say 'Hah, gotcha!' But of course, going to all the trouble of tracking me down isn't normal. Trying to jump me outside the pub in broad daylight isn't normal.

'Thank you, but I don't want to be an imposition. I'll be fine here.' Still, I look around the living room, suddenly seeing shadows where there were none before.

'Don't be silly, Con. Geraint will have the door fixed fine this afternoon, but I'll have him put locks on all the windows too and that'll take a day or more. Probably have to order stuff in from Swansea or somewhere. Your room's all made up at the hall, so stop worrying about it. You'd be better off putting that great detective brain of yours to finding that poor young girl. She must be frightened out of her wits.'

He's right, of course. It's no great hardship moving in to Plas Caernant for a couple of nights either. But I can't help thinking if I leave this cottage now, it will be a break in the continuity, the routine I'd built up here. I'd found somewhere I could just be me. And maybe dream of being a successful novelist rather than a worn out detective, true. The cottage was never my home, but in the months I've been stuck here I've grown rather fond of it. Now that's been ruined, and if I leave here with that final memory, I might never come back.

Karen's call comes through as I'm packing the last of my stuff into the back of the Volvo. Gareth's already gone, Geraint the joiner with him. Part of me wants to say sod it and just stay.

'Hey, K. How's it going?' I say as I climb into the driver's seat and close the door behind me, as much to get out of the wind as anything.

'Busy. You know how it is. Got some information for you I thought you might want to know soonest. You driving?'

'Ah. Not exactly.'

'Well, you can write this down, then. The two blokes you put in Bro . . . Broo . . . I'm not even going to try to say that. The hospital, right?'

I thought of all the words around here, Bronglais would have been the easiest to pronounce. I didn't grow up in the East End of London though, so what do I know? While Karen's talking, I reach onto the back seat and drag my bag over. Fishing around in it for pen and paper, I come out with the Operation Cantre'r Gwaelod briefing. It's only printed on one side, so fair game as far as I'm concerned.

'Let me guess. Released without charge.'

'Got it in one. They were never even processed. Straight to the hospital and then discharged once they'd been treated for their injuries. Nice job you did on them, by the way.'

I can hear the irony in Karen's voice, but also a certain amount of praise. It doesn't surprise me that Slaphead and Greasy Rat got off scot free, but it pisses me off all the same.

'So, you're telling me there's no record of the incident? No log from the squad car that picked us all up?'

'Oh, there's a log. Female arrested on suspicion of common assault. Victims sent to Bron . . . Brow . . .'

'Bronglais, Karen. It's not difficult to pronounce. You should try getting your mouth around Cwmystwyth or Llanfihangel y Creuddyn.' I bang the back of my head against the top of the seat in frustration at the news. 'So we don't even have names for them, is that what you're saying?'

'Nothing in the police record, which is shoddy even by my

standards. Should've been statements taken at the very least. Seems when they decided to let you go without even a caution, they reckoned the whole thing could just be forgotten. Like I say, shoddy.'

'Damn. I was hoping to be able to track them down. Maybe pay them each a visit.' I'm guessing Cerys in the pub will probably know, or know someone who does.

'Oh, ye of little faith. We're the National Crime Agency, Con. It's not that easy to escape our all-seeing eye. Your local bobbies might not have been interested, but the hospital keeps records. Two men admitted to A&E with injuries sustained in a fight. Released once they'd been treated. Karl Peterson, 42, and William Kendall, 35. Both have addresses in Cardigan. Is that where the woolly jackets come from?'

'Nah, it's named after the seventh Earl of Cardigan. They say he wore one while leading the charge of the light brigade, but that seems unlikely.'

'Seventh Earl? He some relation of yours or what?'

'Probably. If I dig deep enough. Who knows? But seriously, K. These two goons, Peterson and Kendall. They got any previous?'

'I was getting to that. Kendall's clean apart from a caution when he was a teenager. After school fight got a bit out of hand. Peterson on the other hand? He's done time for GBH and a couple of minor drugs offences. Kept his nose clean since he got out five years ago. Parole has him working on a trawler out of Fishguard. Wait, is there really a place called Fishguard?'

I can't help smiling. 'We're going to have to get you out of the city, you know. Maybe you should come visit. See the delights of Wales.'

I can't tell from the silence that follows whether Karen's considering it or is utterly appalled by the idea. Maybe both.

'Anything about Lila Ivanova?' I ask.

'Yeah. No. Nothing yet. I've had a word with the Ukraine Embassy, but it'll take more than a few hours to come up with something based on just a name. The boss is very interested in talking to her though, if what you say about her being a drug mule is right.'

I let a silence stretch out along the line.

'You still there, Con?' Karen asks.

'Still here, yes. There might be a bit of a problem though. She's done a runner.' I bring Karen up to speed on events. 'She took quite a fright when she saw the cottage had been broken into. I'm hoping she's trying to make her way back to Plas Caernant on foot.'

'Plas Caernant?' Karen does a good line in astonished. 'The Grail place?'

'Grail . . . How do you know about that?' I'd assumed it was a secret, but now I think about it, Gareth never actually said as much.

'Old girlfriend of mine. She's obsessed with all that conspiracy bollocks. You know, Baigent and Lee? Holy Blood and Holy Grail? The Cathars and the Merovingians and the Priory of Sion?'

Karen's sudden enthusiasm and knowledge of a subject I know nothing about makes me think the girlfriend in question is perhaps not quite as ex as she's saying. I've never really pried too deeply into Karen's private life, figuring she'll share what she wants when she wants. Hard enough being a black lesbian police officer without everyone poking their noses into her business.

'Let's pretend I don't know anything about any of those things you just said. Plas Caernant's where my landlord lives. I took Lila there yesterday. I was . . .' I'm about to launch into a long-winded explanation, then realise it's not really necessary. 'It's complicated, but my best guess is she'd go back there if she felt threatened.'

'OK. You want me to ask the local police to be on the lookout for her, just in case?'

It's tempting, but then I remember that they let Slaphead and Greasy Rat go after they'd locked me in a cell, and handed Lila back to her 'boyfriend'. 'I'd rather not have them involved at all. Best I get out there and find her before anyone else does. Take her as far away as possible. Once she's safe, I'll run the idea of her talking to Diane past her.'

A thought occurs to me as I speak. 'Wait, the boss knows about Lila? You told her?' I should have picked up on this earlier. I'm out of practice.

'Hard not to when she's watching over your shoulder as you look up the contact for the Ukrainian Embassy. Is it a problem?'

Is it? I'm not really sure. On the one hand, Lila could be the breakthrough Operation Cantre'r Gwaelod needs. Someone who's been on the inside and wants desperately to get out. Trading her freedom for revealing a few secrets is what we do, and someone like Diane Shepherd would know exactly how to find Lila the papers she so desperately needs. On the other hand, it's Lila. The young woman who came to me for help, whose life has been destroyed by the kind of horror and misfortune I can't even begin to imagine. Helping her should be unconditional, shouldn't it?

'Let me find her first, then we can worry about that, eh?'

'Sure, Con. I've sent all the details in an email. I'll let you know as soon as I hear anything more, OK?'

I drive the back roads slowly to the hall, peering into the trees as I go for any sign of Lila. It's been that long since she disappeared now, she could have walked all the way back to Aberystwyth, although I can't for the life of me think why she'd want to. She took nothing from the car when she left. My bag was untouched, and she hadn't even looked for any money. There was a few quid in change for the parking meters nestling in the little cubbyhole in front of the gear lever, and it's still there. She's got the clothes on her back, admittedly some of which are mine, and nothing else. Christ, how scared must she have been to take off like that?

When I pull up outside the hall and kill the engine, I don't immediately get out. My phone's pinged en route, and when I check it I see that Karen's emailed me all the details about Greasy Rat and Slaphead. Or Karl Peterson and William Kendall as I'm going to have to start calling them now. Peterson's rap sheet is as impressive as Kendall's lack of one. What brought such different people together, aside from a desire to rape the first woman they see? As I scan down through the details, I notice they both work for the same company, Erinka Fisheries. Something to do a bit of a web search on later, I think.

I catch movement out of the corner of my eye as I'm scanning the details on my phone screen. For a moment I think it's Lila, escaping from the rhododendron bushes that surround the gravel driveway on this side of the house, but when I look up I see the grey-bearded face of a deerhound. Is it Gelert? Given the way he saunters up to the car and peers through the window at me, I suspect it probably is. I open the door enough for him to shove his face in, give him a scratch behind the ears.

'Don't suppose you know where she's gone?' I ask. There's no reply, other than a wagging tail and a loud fart. I wave away the aroma with my free hand. 'Thanks for that.'

I push the door open wider and clamber out. Gelert stands close, leaning against me as I grab my bag and laptop. Then we both go around the back of the hall to the servants' entrance and the short corridor to the kitchen.

'Think you've got a friend there.' Amy stands over the stove, stirring something that smells a lot better than the dog. She lifts up the spoon and takes a taste, sprinkles a little salt into the pot and then pushes it to the back of the hotplate, hauling a kettle into its place. It's years since I've cooked on an Aga, and this kitchen brings back too many conflicting memories. Tea is a good one though, so I pull out a chair and sit down.

'I'm so sorry about the cottage,' I say, as I accept a warming mug. 'I'll pay for any damage, of course.'

'Nonsense, dear. From what Gareth says, there's only the lock broken anyway.' Amy shakes her head, takes a drink from her own mug. 'I don't know what the world's coming to. First you're attacked. Then someone breaks into your home.'

I open my mouth to correct her, then decide now's not the time. Right now, I don't know where home is. Certainly not Harston Magna where I grew up. Not even my tiny flat in London, although I'm not going to be able to keep up with the rent on it much longer so it wouldn't much matter if it was. But the cottage isn't my home either, even if until recently it's the place I've felt the most at home in a long while.

'I do hope that Lila is all right,' Amy says.

'You were very kind to her.'

'What are we if we can't be hospitable to people in need? And besides, she's had such a horrible time. I could scarcely believe some of the things she told me.'

I almost hit myself for being so forgetful. It was only this morning that I saw Amy and Lila sitting here at this very table, nattering away like old friends. I have no idea how long they'd been chatting by the time I came down.

'What did she tell you? She wasn't really all that forthcoming with me.'

Amy sighs, stares into the distance for a while before bringing her focus back. 'How she came from school after there was a big explosion, and her home didn't exist anymore. But then, it got worse. She has an aunt and uncle in the west of Ukraine, apparently. She was trying to get across the country to ask them for help, but a lot of people were fleeing the fighting at the same time. She skirted around the subject a bit, but from what I can piece together, she fell in with a bad crowd. Lost what little money she had, and ended up . . . Well, best I can describe is modern day slavery, isn't it?'

'Did she say how long she'd been here? In Aber?'

Amy shakes her head. 'No. But I got the impression she's not been here long. Dragged around by that man of hers. What did she call him, Kevin? No—'

'Kieran.'

'That's it, yes. Kieran.' Amy puts her mug down and stares straight at me. 'You should find him. Put him behind bars where he belongs.'

I hold her stare. Up until that moment, I was undecided about what I was going to do with my life. I've been hiding away, avoiding people so that I could avoid the question. But Lila's brief appearance in my life has forced me to come to a decision. It's time to get back in the saddle.

'Oh, I will,' I say. 'You can trust me on that.'

9

I hadn't expected to be having supper with Gareth and Amy two nights in a row. We eat in the kitchen again, and I get the feeling Amy is enjoying having someone to cook for other than her husband. Either that or they have some secret that allows them both to dine like, well, lords every day and yet remain fit and slim regardless. It's more food than I'm used to, for sure.

Conversation is muted. I can't help but notice how Amy glances every so often to the chair where Lila sat the night before. I can see the question forming in her mind each time, but she stops herself from raising the subject.

I'm staring at a plate still half full, wondering at what point I can politely stop eating before I explode. Thankfully, I feel a gentle nudge at my lap. Looking down, I see the grey-haired head of the old deerhound, Gelert, mournful eyes gazing up at me in silent supplication.

'He really likes you,' Amy says. 'Although it might just be because you've got a plateful of food and he already knows that begging doesn't work on either of us.'

I reach down and play with his ears and he leans his great head even more heavily into my lap, slow tail thumping the floor in his pleasure.

'We never had dogs, when I was growing up. Not at the hall, at least. My aunt had a succession of Labradors though.'

'Didn't your father have gundogs?' Gareth asks.

I shake my head. 'He can't stand shooting. I think it was something to do with my grandfather, but I never got the full story. Whenever we went to Newmore, it was always for the fishing. I think all the shooting rights over the land have been leased to one of the neighbouring estates.'

Gareth shrugs, and I take the moment of distraction to bring my knife and fork together on the plate in an admission of defeat.

'Oh, dear. Did I give you too much?' Amy asks.

'It was delicious, really. I've just never had a big appetite. Meals were always something to endure when I was growing up, and it's always grab what you can and run when you're on the job.'

'Never mind. I'm sure it won't go to waste,' Gareth says. 'Gelert's always happy to help with the washing up.'

I look down at the dog again, surprised at how something so large can be so docile and gentle. 'It's a strange name, Gelert. Is it Welsh? Does it mean anything?'

'You don't know the tale of Gelert? Well, of course you don't, or you wouldn't ask.' Gareth picks up his wine glass and takes a good mouthful, savouring the taste before he swallows. 'Well, see now. If you go north, up into the mountains of Snowdonia, you'll come across the little village of Beddgelert. Gelert's Grave. There's a mound there where it is said the remains of Prince Llewelyn the Great's faithful old hound lies.'

Every time Gareth says the dog's name, it twitches slightly, but its head is firmly wedged between the underside of the table and my lap now, and it's not going anywhere until I stop scratching it behind the ears. Either that, or whenever it's had whatever's left on my plate.

'There's a sad tale of how the poor beast died,' Gareth continues, leaning back in his chair. 'Legend has it that Llewelyn, on returning home after a hunting trip, found his infant son's cot knocked to the floor and lying empty. The hound, Gelert, was covered in blood. Llewelyn instantly assumed the worst; that the dog had gone mad and savaged the baby. Taking his sword, he slew the poor beast in his rage. Only once the deed was done did he discover the unharmed infant, hidden away in the blankets pulled from the upturned cradle. And close by, the body of a wolf that had somehow managed to find its way into the room. Faithful Gelert had fought and killed the wolf to defend the child, and his reward was to be killed by his master.'

I have a lump in my throat, even though I know this is just a silly old legend. I'm about to say something, but clearly Gareth isn't finished yet.

'As you can imagine, Llewelyn was distraught beyond belief at what he had done. He buried the dog in a manner befitting the noblest of warriors, but he could never forget its dying cry. They say that until the day he died, he never smiled again.'

The room falls into an eerie silence, and Gelert – the living, breathing Gelert – shoves his head deeper into my lap as if he has understood every word of the tale. I've read some of the Welsh folklore since coming here, same as I've tried to learn some of the language, but I'd not heard that tale.

'But can it be true? I mean, it's just a legend – right?'

Gareth laughs. 'No, of course it's not true. Beddgelert is really named after an old Celtic saint, Celert. The legend of the faithful hound slain by his master is an old story pressed into service to encourage tourism to the area in the nineteenth century. It's a good name for a deerhound, all the same.'

The old dog finally decides he's had enough of my lap, or that he's not getting my leftovers quite as easily as he'd hoped. He shuffles backwards away from me, then wanders around to where Gareth sits at the head of the table. Lord Caernant hasn't finished his food either, and he scoops up a morsel with his finger before letting the dog lick it clean.

'Gareth, dear. Not at the table.' Amy's chiding is so gentle I almost laugh, but Gareth does as he's told. I imagine this must be how normal couples behave, particularly couples who have been together as long as these two. It's such a stark difference to the bitter lack of any relationship between my own parents, I almost mourn for the childhood I never had. How much nicer it would have been to have grown up somewhere like this. How different my life might have turned out.

Plas Caernant might be ancient, tucked away in a steep-sided valley, but it still has broadband and WiFi. Geographically speaking, Wales, and Ceredigion in particular, is the arse end of nowhere. It's surprisingly well-connected, though. I'm back in the guest room above the kitchen where I slept last night, only this time I have my laptop on my knees and a fresh notebook lying on the bedspread beside me.

Having promised the lady of the house that I would see Lila's tormentor put away, I need to start thinking about how I'm going to do that. So far, I have a name. Only a first name, for that matter. Kieran isn't a particularly common name, which helps, but there's only so many times I can ask Karen to search the NCA database for me before the wrong people start to notice. I might be acting like a detective, but I'm not sure I'm quite ready to commit to re-joining the team. I know Shepherd wants me digging into this; there's no other reason she would have given me the Cantre'r Gwaelod briefing notes. But she wants my involvement unofficial, unsanctioned, unrecorded. That's why she warned me off at the same time. How well she knows me. I should be annoyed at being played, but I can't help admiring her skill.

It doesn't make this job easy though, and I need to tread carefully with the local force, too. There's something not right when I get thrown in a cell and my attackers are let off without their names even appearing on the system.

I know I should be focusing on the mysterious Kieran, but I

can't help my thoughts from coming back again and again to Slaphead and Greasy Rat. I've no direct evidence that Peterson and Kendall were the ones who broke into the cottage, but I can't imagine why anyone else would. The timing's too coincidental for my liking. The only other possible explanation would be someone looking for Lila, but how would they have known she'd come to me? Nobody knew she was there except for Gareth and Amy, and it's hardly likely they'd have talked to anyone. No, it's far more likely my two attackers came looking for payback.

I bring up the details on them that Karen sent me and read through them more thoroughly this time. There's almost nothing on William Kendall beyond his employment history and the hospital records. No permanent damage to his testicles, more's the pity. He's been working for Erinka Fisheries for two years, and while the dossier I have on him doesn't tell me what exactly it is that he does he must have been working on the boats when he first attacked me. He had that classic seaman's stance that made my kick so much easier to aim.

Karl Peterson has worked for Erinka for much longer, in between periods of incarceration. That surprises me when I see it; most employers would let a man go if he ended up in jail. Does he have a family tie to the business? Sure enough, when I search the internet for more details on the company, there's an Erik Peterson listed as one of the directors. According to their website, they operate lobster boats along the Cardigan Bay coast, and also deal in wholesale supply of seafood to the continent. Something about that name rings a bell, and it isn't until I've scrambled around through the briefing notes Shepherd gave me that I find it. Erik Peterson's name is on a list of wholesalers who regularly bought crab and lobster from a boat named Teifi III, registered in Cardigan and found with twenty kilos of finest Colombian cocaine in among the shellfish, back in 2010. The company was called Deheubarth Trading then, but the address is the same as for Erinka, a warehouse in Fishguard.

I stare at my notes and at the screen for a long while, trying to find anything but coincidence in the connection. There are a dozen other names on the same list as Peterson, though. A dozen different buyers and wholesalers. There's no clear suggestion he was involved with the drug smuggling; he certainly never faced any charges. And yet I can't shake the niggling feeling that this connection is more important than it looks. Karl Peterson, Greasy Rat, presumably related to Erik in some way, did time for drugs offences. Is he part of the organisation that Operation Cantre'r Gwaelod is trying to uncover? Just my luck to be dragged into it like this.

I'm still trying to get my head around everything, when a hollow thud distracts me. Looking up, I see the door open, but no face appears. For a second, I wonder whether Plas Caernant has ghosts. Then I see a grey muzzle as Gelert pushes his way into the room, tail wagging.

'You meant to be up here?' I ask as he leans his head on the bed beside me. I have to stifle a yawn, and a quick glance at the clock on my laptop tells me it's far later than I'd realised. I close it down, shuffle my notes and the briefing paper together and shove them all in my bag, watched all the while by those doleful eyes. He follows me to the door, then out into the corridor as I head off to the bathroom, and I fully expect him to have gone by the time I've got myself ready for bed. Sure enough, the corridor is empty when I'm done. Just him saying good night, then.

Except that when I step back into the bedroom, there he is, curled up in a surprisingly tight ball on the floor at the end of my bed. He thumps his tail a couple of times, but otherwise makes it clear he's going nowhere.

'OK.' I relent all too easily, tired after a long and traumatic day. I need sleep, not an argument with a stubborn canine. 'But if you snore, you're out.'

10

I'm up bright and early the next morning, feeling refreshed and ready to go. It's only when I swing my legs out from under the covers that I remember my nocturnal visitor. Gelert is fast asleep on the sheepskin rug, but he wakes swiftly, tail thumping a good morning to me. I pat him gently on the head, then make my way to the bathroom. As far as I'm aware, he neither snored nor farted in the night. The perfect sleeping companion.

'Still no sign of Lila?' I ask as I step into the kitchen, faithful hound at my heels. Amy is making enough porridge to feed an army, but she shakes her head in answer.

'Nothing, I'm afraid. Gareth's put word out around the estate. Sure she'll turn up soon enough. She found you once, she'll find you again. Now sit you down, Con. Porridge is almost ready.'

I'm still full from last night's supper, so the thought of yet more food makes me queasy. 'Just a coffee would be great, thanks. Need to get going soon. I'm going to take a little trip down the coast to Fishguard. See what I can find out about the two lads who attacked me. They both work for a company based down there.'

Amy moves the pot to the side of the hotplate and turns her attention to me. 'Is that wise?'

'Probably not, but I have to do something. I'm almost certain it was them who turned over the cottage. The more I can find out about them, the better position I'll be in if they have another go.'

'But shouldn't you go to the police? I mean, I thought you were the police.'

I shrug. 'It's complicated. Technically, I'm still a detective, but I'm on sabbatical. And besides, the local police haven't exactly gone out of their way to impress me.'

'You can't think Dyfed Powys Police is corrupt now, surely?' Amy's shock isn't faked.

'Not all of them, no. But there's always some coppers on the take, whatever the force. Believe me, I've seen it.' My old boss in London, DCI Gordon Bailey, for instance. Currently serving at Her Majesty's pleasure in an open prison somewhere in Essex. Should have banged him up in the Scrubs with the lifers for what he did.

'But what about Lila? Aren't you going to look for her?'

'Yes, of course. But I need to tread carefully there.' I can't exactly tell Amy about Operation Cantre'r Gwaelod, but maybe a little context might help. 'You know I work for the NCA, right? The National Crime Agency?'

Amy nods. 'You're the Feds, right? Our equivalent of the FBI?'

'Something like that. It's a nationwide agency, and we're not just police. We've people from all walks of life. My boss was in the army before she joined the NCA. A general, no less.'

That gets me a raised eyebrow and a noise that I think indicates a mixture of admiration and approval.

'We investigate crimes that span the whole nation. Overseas, too. A lot of modern day slavery, sex trafficking, drugs. All that stuff you hear on the news. I hope I'm wrong, but I think Lila might be mixed up with a gang of interest to my team. That's why she ran as soon as she saw trouble. Why she's so hard to find. These are dangerous people, especially when they think they're being crossed.'

Amy's holding a hand to her throat, the horror written across her face, and I fear I've gone too far. I don't really know much about her, apart from the fact that she was at St Bert's with my aunt. Somewhere along the line she met Gareth, married him, and ended up here at Plas Caernant. She's not stupid, not naive, but she isn't exactly street-smart either. And this little corner of Wales is far from the sort of thing she might have seen on *Crimewatch*. Except that it isn't, really. The dark underbelly is everywhere, just better hidden in some places than others.

'I'll be fine, Amy. Don't worry. I'm not going to go and cause a ruckus. All I want to do is see where they work, maybe ask a few questions. Anything more serious, I'll leave to my colleagues.'

She looks at me with an expression I've seen on Aunt Flick's face so often I almost laugh, but at least she's stopped clutching her non-existent pearls.

'Well, be careful, won't you? I'd hate to have to tell Tittie you'd been hurt.'

Now I can't help myself laughing. 'Tittie?'

'I . . .' Amy's face reddens as she realises what she's said. 'It's what I've always called her. Don't you?'

I might try it the next time I see her, but only if she can't reach me. 'Heavens, no. I call her Aunt Flick.'

'Flick? How strange. I guess it makes sense. Felicity, Flick, Tittie.' Amy shakes her head, composure regained. 'Just promise me you'll be careful, OK?'

It takes longer to get to Fishguard than I expect, even though I've been there before. The road follows the coastline south along the edge of Cardigan Bay, and while it's better than most of the inland roads in Wales, it's still lacking in places to overtake. When my car was new, it would have had little trouble dealing with the tractors, elderly Land Rovers and surprisingly large trucks that make up most of the traffic. But somewhere in the two hundred thousand miles on the clock it's lost a few horses. One near miss with an oncoming HGV is more than enough to decide getting there alive is better than getting there quickly.

I've plugged the address I have for Erinka Fisheries into my phone sat nav. I'm expecting it to take me to the ferry port, where boats head daily over to Ireland. Instead, it directs me to what must be the oldest part of the town, judging by the stone-built warehouses and tiny harbour. A sluggish river flows out through tidal mudflats speckled with wading birds and small, beached dinghies. The lobster creels that line the road to the quay remind me of the drug smuggling racket Operation Cantre'r Gwaelod is investigating, but the neat stacks of plastic crates and all the other paraphernalia I have no name for suggest this is more about shellfish than cocaine. As I pull into a parking space beside a small cafe, I can see only one boat moored up, a couple of fisher-men hauling nets on board. It must have a shallow draft to get out to sea at this tide.

A note pinned on the cafe door says '*Back in ten minutes*' although there's no indication as to when those ten minutes began. The place doesn't look totally abandoned, so with time to kill, I decide to stroll the last hundred yards to the quay where the boat is moored. Painted in various shades of matt black and rust, her stern bears the name, *Anwen's Favour*. Both fishermen ignore my approach, busy getting all their gear stowed away. A rust-streaked old Transit van has been backed up close to the gangplank, back doors wide open. I glance casually into it as I pass, and see heaps of nets, more fish boxes and creels piled up to the roof.

'You looking for something, love?'

I turn to where the voice has come from and see that one of the fishermen has stepped off the boat onto the quay. He's short and broad, with a face like a piece of leather left in the sun too long. His spiky black hair is beginning to go grey, but I wouldn't want to hazard a guess at his age.

'Not really, no. I was just on my way to Haverfordwest. Stopped for a coffee, but the cafe isn't open, right now. Thought I'd stretch my legs.'

He shrugs. 'That'll be Siân popped into town for more milk. She'll be back soon enough.'

'Thanks.' I turn back, making a vague wave towards the bay. 'You heading out today? Looks like you've missed the tide.'

'Ach a fi. Should have been gone out an hour ago. Still waiting for the last of my crew.' He leans into the Transit and pulls out a couple of lobster creels. They look heavy to me, but he hefts them as if they're made of air, handing them up to his companion. 'If he's not here by the time I've got this lot loaded, I'll be setting off without him.'

'I'll not distract you then.'

'It's never a distraction when a pretty woman gives you the time of day.' The fisherman – should that be lobsterman? – reaches in and grabs more gear, swinging it up to his mate with an ease born of long practice. I do my best 'pretty woman' smile, even if the compliment's not exactly welcome.

'What is it you catch? Lobsters? Crab?'

'Whatever the sea will give us, see?' He hauls another two creels up onto the boat. 'But it's mostly the lobsters we're after. That's where the money is.'

'I've heard they're very good, the ones you catch around here. Do you sell yours locally?'

The lobsterman shrugs again, then steps past me to shut the Transit doors. He doesn't lock the van, which is a bit surprising if he's just about to head out to sea. 'Most of my catch goes to a local wholesaler. They pay a half decent price, though more would always be better, mind. If you want fresh lobster and crab, you need to get down the harbour at dawn, see. Not here, but New Quay or Aberaeron. Maybe Aberystwyth if you're that far north. Or you can go and see if the wholesaler'll sell you some.' He points up the hill towards the bulk of the town. 'Erinka Fisheries. Ask for Karl and tell him Captain Jenkins sent you. He'll see you right.'

I nod my thanks, but the lobsterman has already turned away, climbing back onto the boat as he shouts something in Welsh to his mate. Along the shore road, I can see the cafe door standing open, so I walk back in search of a coffee.

Siân turns out to be a middle-aged woman who could easily be the lobsterman's sister, given her features. She scowls at me until I remember my mask, then smiles as I apologise. I order a latte to go, confirming my status as an outsider, but redeem myself by also buying a couple of freshly baked Welsh cakes.

I'm almost at the door on my way out when I notice someone walking along the shore road towards the quay. He has that half-skip, half-run of a man who knows he's late. I assume he's the third member of the lobster boat crew, finally turning up for work. I'm about to step out into the daylight when something about him registers and I pause in the doorway. He's closer now, all his concentration on the boat, so he doesn't notice me shrink back into the cafe. I'm just in time, as he glances at the open door on the way past, giving me a clear view of his face. I hold my breath for a moment, hoping he won't stop and come in.

It's Slaphead, or William Kendall to give him his proper name.

The last person I need to bump into.

He doesn't even break his stride, hurrying on towards the boat. I let him get a bit further along the shore road before I go to my car and climb in. I don't relax until I've closed the door and hit the central locking button.

Sitting safely, I watch as Kendall reaches the quay. My new friend the lobsterman stands at the top of the gangplank, arms crossed over his chest. I'm too far away to hear anything, but it's obvious from Kendall's body language that he's grovelling, obvious that the captain is giving him a verbal six of the best with the cat-o-nine-tails. Finally he relents, stepping aside to let Kendall aboard. Black smoke billows from an exhaust at the stern of the boat as they cast off.

I pop the lid off my coffee, pull out one of the still-warm Welsh cakes from the bag lying on my lap. Both are delicious, and I savour them, thinking, as I watch the boat navigate the narrow channel out into the bay.

11

My phone beeps an incoming text as I watch the boat round the point and disappear. A message from Karen, back in London, asking if I'm up for a chat. I take another sip of coffee then hit speed dial. She picks up on the first ring.

'Hi, K. How's it going?'

'If you don't count Billy Latham chewing the walls every time your name's mentioned? Sweet. You need to come back, Con. If only for my sanity.'

I laugh at Karen's joke, but there's a note of desperation in her voice. Detective Sergeant Latham hates me, I know. He was best mates with another DS I worked alongside for a while, who turned out to be on the take and got himself shot dead for the sake of it. Not my fault, of course, but you try telling Billy Latham that. He doesn't like that I come from a posh background, either. Or, at least, that I come from a posh background and rejected what he assumes to be a nice, cushy life.

It's complicated.

But you can see him flinch every time my name's mentioned, and I'd bet good money my name's being mentioned a lot right now.

'Might be a while, K. I'm still trying to work out who turned over the cottage, and I need to find Lila, too.'

'Yeah, about that.' Karen's voice carries an unmistakable edge of uncertainty.

'Is there a problem?'

There's a pause, the line silent for long enough I risk another sip of coffee. I'm about to take a bite out of the second Welsh cake when Karen speaks again.

'I'll send everything over to you in an email, but if we're talking about the same person, then she should be dead.'

'Lila?' Despite the coffee and Welsh cakes, my stomach goes cold. 'How so?'

'Well, according to the Ukrainian Embassy, there was a Lila Ivanova living in a town whose name I'm not even going to try to pronounce. Somewhere near Crimea, I think? It's a bit sketchy getting full details from the area, but her whole family were killed when bombing destroyed their house and half the street. Official report says the whole family. Lila included.'

'That's pretty much what she told me. Except that she was at school at the time. I reckon she must have fallen in with the wrong crowd, ended up being trafficked here for sex work or being a drug mule. Both.'

Karen makes a noise that sounds like a strangled gasp. 'Christ, I know people are animals, but . . .' She trails off and I can picture her slowly shaking her head.

'What is it?' I ask, even though I suspect I know.

'If it is the same girl, then she's been missing for five years now.'

'Shit. No wonder she's paranoid. I'd be a basket case if that happened to me.' I cast my mind back five years, imagine what I've done over that time. What's been done to Lila. 'I'll find her, K. And when I do, I'll make sure she's looked after. Properly.'

'Yeah, I know you will, Con. If you can.' Karen pauses a moment and I know there's worse to come. 'Thing is, when her family were all killed in that explosion? She was only thirteen.'

'Jesus. Thirteen?' I do the maths. 'So, she's only what – eighteen, nineteen now? If it's her. That could be right, you know. I mean, she comes across as older, but then you would, wouldn't you? If you'd survived what she must have been through.'

'Yeah. And Diane's getting excited about the possibility of her being a witness, you know? If she really is who she claims to be, then that ties in with Cantre'r Gwaelod. There's Russian and Ukraine links we've only the very barest intel on.'

I notice that for all she can't pronounce Bronglais Hospital, Karen seems to have mastered Cantre'r Gwaelod, even if it does sound strange in an Essex accent. I guess she's heard it said enough times.

'Have you got anything else on Lila? Local address, maybe?' I remember the sheet of paper the young woman had lifted from the custody sergeant's desk with my details on it. That's how she found out where I lived, after all. There should have been something similar for her.

'We put in a request, but according to Sergeant . . . Hang on a minute.' I hear a noise of shuffling papers on a desk, and then Karen's back again. 'Yeah, sorry. Sergeant Thomas. Not sure if that's his first name or surname, to be honest. Anyway, Thomas says there's no record of any young woman in the cells the same day as you. Mind you, they don't seem to have any record of you either, so there's a surprise.'

'Lila lifted my sheet before it could be entered onto the system. I'm guessing hers was "lost" when someone tipped off her handler and he came to fetch her. We thought there might be a leak in Aber nick, didn't we? Guess this proves it.'

'Yeah, well. Means we've drawn a blank at this end. Sorry.'

'No worries, K. I'll just have to see if I can dig something up the old-fashioned way.'

'Well, keep it low key, eh? And try not to get yourself into any more trouble.'

'Thanks for the vote of confidence. I'll let you know how I get on.'

'Where you headed now?' It seems like an innocent enough question, but I can hear Diane Shepherd's voice echoing in Karen's words. I'm suddenly all too aware of the enormous leeway I'm being given here, and the potential for cocking things up badly. What is it that Shepherd wants from me? Is it something as simple as plausible deniability? Or am I meant to be the ace hidden up her sleeve? It would be nice to be told.

'Going to have a quick look at the place where my two attackers work, Erinka Fisheries. Not sure if it'll turn anything up, but you know me.'

Karen's voice is a picture of cynicism. 'Yes. I do, Con. That's the problem.'

The drive up to Erinka Fisheries' modern-looking warehouse and offices takes me through the town of Fishguard, all two streets of it. I turn into a soulless industrial estate, much like a thousand others spread across the country, then park across the road from the entrance to a compound surrounded by the kind of heavy-duty metal fencing more suited to a company making Hi-Tech components for the arms industry than one selling lobsters and crabs. It looks well kept, too, despite the collapse of the UK seafood industry after Brexit. Clearly, they're doing something right.

A small line of socially-distanced workers queue up towards a burger van at the road end, and a quick glance at the clock on the car's dashboard tells me it's past noon already. I'm still full of Welsh cake, so I settle back in the seat and check my phone for Karen's promised email.

There's very little information about Lila Ivanova beyond what Karen told me on the phone. Nothing as useful as a photo, for sure. I hastily read through what there is. It's possible there are two Lila Ivanovas with similar Ukrainian backgrounds, both tragically affected by the war there, but then again, it seems unlikely. How many Lila Ivanovas can there be in Wales? So, either the Lila I met is the one whose family were killed by a stray bomb, or she's someone who has adopted the real Lila's identity. It doesn't really matter which is true. She's a young woman who has been coerced and abused. She needs help, she sought out my help. She might also be able to help us.

There I go with the "us" again. Is this what you really want, Con? To be back in the thick of it? Not as if I'm being given much choice.

I put my phone away and pop open the car door, ready to pay a visit to the offices tacked onto the edge of the warehouse. I want to see if I can winkle any information out of the receptionist, when movement at the end of the road makes me pause. A large SUV turns the corner and heads towards me, shiny, expensive and new. I can't make out the faces behind the windscreen, but there are definitely two people in the front. By the driving, I assume that the car is going to carry on past me. But at the last minute, it pulls in to the kerb opposite where I've parked. There's a pause while the passenger says something to the driver, then climbs out. With an unnecessary roar of engine and chirrup of tyres, the car accelerates away, leaving the passenger at the gates to Erinka Fisheries. He stops for long enough to raise a questioning hand in the direction of the departing vehicle.

That's when I recognise him.

Karl Peterson, otherwise known as Greasy Rat.

He shrugs and heaves a backpack onto his shoulder, then saunters up to the office. In moments he's disappeared inside. I slowly pull the car door closed again, watching to see if he comes out. I don't want to run the risk of bumping into him, and I curse myself for assuming he would be on a boat somewhere like his mate, Slaphead. Then I remember the captain of *Anwen's*

Favour this morning, telling me I could get fresh lobster from this very place, and to 'ask for Karl and tell him Captain Jenkins sent you'.

Idiot, Con. You've been away from the job too long.

There's little point hanging around here now. I pull my phone out and slide it into the holder stuck to the dashboard, set it into hands-free mode as I start the engine. I've wasted enough time in Fishguard chasing down my two assailants.

I need to get back to looking for Lila.

12

Aberystwyth's a funny little town. Huddled between two steep-sided hills like the nest of some giant carrion bird, it's literally the end of the line, furthest you can go before you fall into the sea. I heard one description of it as being the perfect refuge for the unambitious man, but I think that's probably being unfair. Somehow, stuck away in the arse end of nowhere, it survives. Thrives, even. Of course, it has the university to keep people coming, and the National Library of Wales sat at the top of the hill like some great white monument to past ideals. Bronglais Hospital, where Greasy Rat and Slaphead had their injuries treated, is the other main source of employment, along with the Welsh Government building across the road from the police station where I'm headed. Again. At least I'm in my own car this time, and visiting rather than staying.

The light's fading, and a cold wind brings with it the damp taste of impending rain. I hurry into the nice warm reception area, glad I phoned Gareth and asked him to speak to the custody sergeant, Ben Griffiths, and set up a meeting. After what happened to me before, I didn't really want to involve the local police with my enquiries in case word got back to the person I was asking about. But Gareth assures me Sergeant Griffiths is as honest as the day, albeit permanently grumpy, and he's left word at the front desk to show me through as soon as I arrive.

'Well, now. If it isn't our little detective constable.' He looks up from a desk more cluttered with paperwork than any I've seen in a long while, and motions for me to take a chair.

'Thanks for agreeing to see me,' I say. 'And sorry about the other day.'

He peers at me over the top of some half-moon spectacles. 'Gareth Caernant and I go back a long way. If he says you're sound, then I trust his judgement on that. Even if you've done nothing so far to convince me.'

Permanently grumpy doesn't really do it justice, but I bite down on the first retort that comes to mind. 'I wish I didn't have to. No offence intended, but I'd be happier if we'd never met.'

'You know, if you'd told us straight away that you were with the NCA, let us know why you were staying in the area . . . Well, none of this need have happened.'

I shake my head, trying to find the right words. I've been dodging this all winter, but eventually I'm going to have to make my mind up. 'I'm not on active duty. Don't think sabbatical is the right word, but it's not exactly furlough either. Until those two idiots jumped me outside the pub the other day, I wasn't really thinking about myself as a police officer.'

Something in Sergeant Griffiths' expression shifts. He's gone from belligerent custody sergeant to sympathetic old-timer, with little more than a change in posture. He really should have been an actor.

'Look, I've heard what's happened to you. Down in London. First your boss getting killed, then your mother dying like that.' He shudders, even though I'm the one picturing Detective Inspector Pete Copperthwaite's brains plastering the wall behind his chair, my mother laid out in a two-thousand-year-old stone sarcophagus.

'I can understand why a person might want out,' he continues.

'All that and the press hounding you like you're some kind of celebrity.'

'And yet trouble keeps finding me, even when I run away and hide.'

The sergeant tilts his head in acknowledgement, so I take my cue to continue. 'Which brings me to why I'm here. Why I wanted to speak to you direct rather than go through the normal channels.'

'Your unwitting cell mate?' he guesses.

'Lila Ivanova, yes. I was hoping you might be able to tell me something about her.'

A slight frown creases his brow. 'Is that what she said her name was? That's not what she told us.'

'You don't have her arrest sheet.' I'd meant it as a question, but it comes out as a statement.

'I don't, no.' The grumpiness is back in the sergeant's voice. 'I assumed she took it along with yours. Not exactly a glowing testimony to the professionalism of my colleagues, but there you are. As it happens, I processed the young lady in question myself, and the name she gave me was Lillian Vance.'

'What was she arrested for in the first place?'

'She was found sleeping rough at the back of the railway station. A few people had complained a woman matching her description had been begging in the town centre, too. The weather's not kind at the moment, so we put her in a cell for the night to keep her from freezing to death. That would have been much more paperwork, if we'd found her body in the morning.'

'You didn't charge her, in the end.' Again, it's not a question. I know they didn't, but I want to see the sergeant's reaction. Something between anger and irritation crosses his face, although it's hard to tell from his resting grumpiness.

'No. Not worth the effort of prosecuting something like that, so we let her go in the morning. Least that's what I was told. My shift ended not long after you were picked up by his lordship.' He pauses, as though considering something. 'Might I ask you a question, Detective Constable? Why the fascination with this young woman? What is she to you that you're so interested in her?'

'Gareth . . . Lord Caernant told you that she turned up at the cottage I'm renting?'

The sergeant nods.

'She came to me as a last resort. So desperate she'd throw herself on the mercy of a total stranger. I'm not the sort of person who can ignore that, Sergeant Griffiths.'

He stares at me for a long time before nodding once in acceptance of my explanation.

'And now she's disappeared again, I hear. We haven't seen her, if that's what you're here to ask me.'

'I didn't expect you to, no. I was hoping you might remember the address she gave when you brought her in.'

The sergeant gives me a look I've seen a hundred times before from a hundred other weary officers. I try my best smile on him, and with a sigh he reaches for a slip of paper, scribbles something down and hands it over.

'It's a council estate. Not the best part of town, I'd be the first to admit. Aber has its share of . . .' The sergeant pauses as if searching for the right word. I know what he wants to say, but his sense of self-preservation is well tuned.

'Folk on benefits, unfit for work, a few refugees sent as far from the centre as possible?'

'Your words, not mine. But you're not wrong. There's always a few fall between the cracks. Miss Lillian Vance would appear to be one of them.'

'Does the name Kieran mean anything to you?' I ask, watching the expression on the sergeant's face. But he's too much of a professional to give anything away. Or maybe there's nothing for him to give away.

'Should it?'

'Lila . . . Lillian, whatever. She told me she was running away from her boyfriend, Kieran. He'd roughed her up a bit too, by the look of her when she was in the cell here. Are there any Kierans among the local underclass? Petty criminals, minor drugs, that sort of thing?'

Sergeant Griffiths doesn't answer straight away, which makes me think he's considering the question rather than dismissing it out of hand. 'No one springs to mind,' he says finally. 'But I can ask around if you'd like me to. We don't have much of a plain clothes presence here, mind.'

'It's OK. Like you say, it's probably not worth the effort trying to track her down. Sure, she came to me for help. But then she ran away. Best I move on, right?' I push back my chair and stand, noting that the sergeant doesn't do the same. He's looking at me with an expression that says eloquently how little he believes I'll ever move on. Damn him, he's good. I've only met the man twice now, and he's got my measure to a T.

The street lights are on when I leave the police station, and the last hurrah of the setting sun paints the undersides of the clouds as it sinks into the Irish Sea. The weather's turned cold again, a wind whistling in from the west. I wonder about the lobster boat I saw this morning. Is it still out there in the bay, hauling up pots? I hope not, even if Slaphead does deserve an uncomfortable night on choppy waters.

I'm not surprised the address Sergeant Griffiths gave me turns out to be the same estate I followed the 4x4 into, even if the actual housing block is not the one it stopped outside. As I park close to the front entrance, my old Volvo fits in fine with the random collection of cars along the kerbside, nothing less than fifteen years old, many missing crucial parts such as wheels. I'm not planning on being here long, so hopefully mine will still be in place when I get back.

The address is on the top floor of a squat three-storey building, its communal staircase open to all. I'm surprised it's not messier, just a few neatly tied up bin bags on the ground floor waiting to be put out for collection. The walls are damp, speckled with black mould, but there's no graffiti, no stink of stale urine, and no evidence of drug use where I'd expect to see it on the landings. Someone's even put a couple of pot plants on the first floor windowsill, although they don't look like they're enjoying the position much.

There's a deathly quiet about the place as I climb to the top floor, no noise of televisions from behind the closed doors of the flats, no muted conversations or voices raised in argument. I don't know why, but the quiet gives me a deep sense of foreboding.

I approach the door to the flat Lila claimed was her home. There's a door buzzer, but the clear Perspex cover where a name should go is empty and there is no light to indicate it is working. I press the button anyway, listening for a noise inside that doesn't come. I'm reaching up my hand to knock when a voice behind me makes me freeze.

'You're wasting your time. Nobody lives there any more.'

I turn slowly, letting my hand fall to my side. Across the landing, the door to the neighbouring flat is open and an old woman stands staring at me. I can't understand how I didn't hear her open the door, or, indeed, how she heard me. She's speaking through a mask, and belatedly I realise I'm not wearing my own. I make a show of taking it out of my pocket and putting it on before I speak.

'Are you sure?'

'Do I look stupid? Course I'm sure.' She shifts her position slightly, still blocking the open doorway. Not that I particularly want to go in.

'I was looking for a woman called Lila, or maybe Lillian?'

'And who might you be, then? Debt collector? You don't look like a dealer.' The old lady leans forward and peers at me, her nose wrinkling as she scowls, hand holding her mask in place. 'You police?'

'No, no and no. I'm just looking for Lila. I was trying to help her get away from her abusive partner.'

That gets me a snort that might be derision or might simply be the old lady clearing her throat. 'Good Samaritan, are you? Wasted in these parts, mark my words.'

It strikes me then, what I hadn't immediately noticed. She's not Welsh, this old woman. Her accent's almost RP, with just an edge to it that hints of an adult life spent away from the posh people she grew up around. How she ended up here, in a council flat in Aberystwyth, is a tale that might be worth listening to, but I'm not sure I'm in the mood for that kind of distraction.

'Well, I'm sorry I disturbed you. Guess I'll have to look somewhere else. If you see her though, maybe tell her Con's looking for her. If she wants it, the trip to Burntwoods is still on.'

The old lady's scowl deepens for a moment, then she straightens up. Not that it makes her tiny frame much taller. She reaches for the elastic and unclips her mask, as if that will make hearing me easier. 'What did you say?'

'That's where I was going to take her. Burntwoods. The Downham Trust. You know it?'

'A lot of folk know about the Downham Trust. They run a shelter out near Devil's Bridge.' The old lady peers at me again. 'But very few people know about Burntwoods. And that's a long way to take someone to get them away from an abusive relationship. Who are you?'

There's two ways this can go, I reckon. Either my connection with the Trust makes me an ally, and I'll be invited in for a cup of tea and a blether, or this old woman's already deep suspicion will make her clam up completely, and I'll get nothing from this visit at all. Time's marching on, but this is really my last chance of tracking down Lila, so I might as well be friendly.

'Con Fairchild,' I say. 'I'd offer to shake your hand, but these are strange times, and I never really got the hang of the elbow bump.'

She eyes me with deep suspicion, then glances past me to the closed door of the other flat. 'There was a young woman there, but she wasn't around for long. Don't think I ever got her name, but she was foreign. Could tell that from her accent.'

'When was this?'

The old woman switches her focus back on me as she unhooks the other ear of her mask and folds it neatly into one hand. 'You're not infected, are you?'

I got myself tested after being in the cell with Lila, and that came up negative. On the other hand, I've been out and about far more than usual in the past few days. 'Don't think so. Certainly haven't had any symptoms.'

She shrugs, then with a little flick of her head turns away and heads back into her flat. 'Had my vaccine already, anyway. Come on, then. I'll put the kettle on and you can tell me all about yourself.'

13

Her name turns out to be Isobel Brady, and she's lived in Aberystwyth for fifty years without catching so much as a hint of a Welsh accent. Some people are like that, breezing through life completely unchanged by their surroundings where others blend in with chameleon skill. She leaves me in her tiny living room while she makes tea, and I have to suppress my detective's urge to scan the room for clues to her identity. By the time she shuffles back in with a tray, I've only managed to glean that she'd been married, sometime in the early 1970s, if the faded colour photographs are anything to go by. I can only guess that Mr Brady is long gone.

'What brought you to Aberystwyth, then?' I ask as she pours the tea into elegant china cups.

'I came to the university to study English Literature. Met my husband-to-be. Dear Jonathan. He was a postgrad supervisor. Very handsome, you know. Fairly swept me off my feet. But my family didn't approve. Cut me off. Didn't even come to the wedding.'

'I'm so sorry. That must have been heartbreaking.'

She shakes her head slowly. 'I was glad to get away, if I'm being honest. My father was a . . . difficult man. The only reason I stayed as long as I did was to try and help my mother. She finally managed to escape from him about a year after my wedding. The Downham Trust helped her. That's how I know about Burntwoods.' She takes a sip of tea, peering over the cup at me. 'How do you know about it? You don't look like someone who'd suffer an abusive relationship.'

'My sister – half-sister, I should say. She ran away from her father, ended up at Burntwoods. I tracked her down.'

That gets me a raised eyebrow. 'Really? You must be good.'

'Good?'

'At finding people. You're a private detective, aren't you? I've been trying to work out what your game is, and that's the only answer that fits.'

'No, I'm not a private detective. I was a detective, technically still am, I guess. But finding Lila has nothing to do with that. She came to me for help, but then something scared her and she ran away. From what I've found out, her life's been pretty miserable these past five years. She's fallen in with a very bad crowd and I'd like to get her away from them. The boyfriend, Kieran, especially.'

The slightest of flinches crosses Mrs Brady's face as I mention the name. She's heard it before.

'Well, as I told you earlier, there's been nobody living across the way in months. A crying shame, given the waiting list for council houses.'

'Who was the last person to live there, then?'

'Let me see.' She cocks her head to one side as if that will make the memories come into sharper focus. 'There was a couple of young lads, for a while. Don't think they were an item, not gay you understand. Although sometimes it's hard to tell these days. Darren and Edward, that was their names. They were polite enough, but always coming and going. Sometimes they'd disappear for days, a week even. Then they left one time and never came back. Must have been a month, maybe six weeks and I was about to get in touch with the council about it, but a gang of them turned up one day. Let themselves in, lots of boxes. Well, I thought it would be nice to have some new neighbours, but they didn't stay. Just locked the place up and left.'

'And that was it?' I have a niggling feeling I know what's going on across the landing, and if the local police have been ignoring it, then the NCA won't be quite so lax. 'How long ago was this?'

'A year, maybe? No, longer. It was summer time, but not last summer. Nothing happened last summer. Must have been eighteen months then.'

'And no one's been living there since? But I thought you said there'd been a young foreign woman.'

'Oh, she never stayed there, but she'd turn up for a night sometimes. Sort of the opposite of Darren and Edward, I suppose. It was never more than a night though, maybe two. Then the man would turn up and fetch her back. That would be the Kieran you mentioned.'

'You said you never got the young woman's name, right? Can you describe what she looked like? What both of them looked like?'

'Well, let me see.' Mrs Brady takes another sip of her tea, then carefully places the cup and saucer down on the table in front of her. 'She was a little taller than me, but then I suppose most people are. Skinny, underneath those baggy clothes she always wore. You know the things I mean? I used to call them track suits, but I don't think she was ever an athlete.'

'What about her hair?' I recall Lila's ash-blonde curls once she'd showered and used almost all of my shampoo.

'Oh, that was always changing, but I could tell it was her. She had cheekbones like a model, you know? And the most piercing blue eyes. Not that she ever looked at anything but her feet most of the time, poor thing.'

It sounds like Lila, certainly. And she gave this as her address, so she had to have known it. 'What about the man, Kieran? What did he look like?'

'Him? Yes, well. He's tall. At least as tall as you are. Broad, too. Arms like he spends a lot of time in the gym. Dark hair, cut short. You know that way people do it nowadays, with a trimmer all over? I keep well away if I hear him coming. Nasty brute of a fellow.'

'What makes you say that? Just an impression, or have you seen him hurt people? Hurt Lila?'

'I grew up with a controlling father, dear. I know the type even if I don't see the bruises. The way he put his hand on her shoulder.' Mrs Brady lifts up her own hand to demonstrate. 'Thumb and forefinger around her neck like he could squeeze the life out of her, if he chose to. Dare say he could.'

I think back to when I first saw Lila in the cell. Was it really only a couple of weeks ago? She was showing the bruises then, so perhaps this old lady's appraisal is spot on. It doesn't bode well though, if Lila's run away before only for him to come and fetch her back. How many times can she do that before he stops her permanently? I need to find this Kieran, find out as much about him as I can.

'I don't suppose you know what his surname is, do you?'

Mrs Brady raises an eyebrow at this. She starts to shake her head, but then stops as a thought occurs to her. 'Now that you ask, it's possible that I do. There was one time he came and I was caught out on the landing. Normally I'd stay well away, you know? Never a good idea to draw attention. But here's the thing. There was a young lad with them. His driver, you might say, although he didn't look like any chauffeur I've ever seen. Nobody ever said much, but the young lad called him Mr Johns, if I remember right.'

'Kieran Johns.' I say the name out loud even though I know I won't forget it. Mrs Brady looks very pleased with herself now, her initial suspicion diminished by the fact that I've not strangled her or tried to steal anything. I need to make my excuses and escape before she starts telling me her entire life history. Instinctively, I reach for my pocket and the stack of business cards I keep there. Except that I've not had any with me for months, and they'd identify me as an NCA detective.

'More tea?' she asks, giving me the perfect opportunity to decline.

'Actually, I need to go. You've been very helpful, Mrs Brady. Thank you.' I stand as I speak, pat my jacket pockets, then smile. 'You wouldn't have something I could write on, would you? I'd like to leave you my number, if you don't mind. Just in case Lila turns up again.'

I briefly consider seeing if I can't pick the lock on the flat across the landing, but Mrs Brady insists on standing at the door as I leave. She watches me all the way down the stairs, and I'm sure if I glance back as I walk to my car I'll see her peering out through her living room window. I don't look up though; I'm too busy checking to see I've still got all four wheels and none of the tyres have been slashed.

Slipping my phone into the dashboard cradle, I tap the screen to call Karen on Hands Free. By the time it's connected and she's answered, I'm driving away from the council estate and heading south towards the seafront.

'Hey, Con. How's it going? You on your way back home yet?'

I know that by home she means London, and that she's only half-serious. I can't remember exactly when it was that Karen and I became firm friends, but some time in the months after my mother died she started calling me Con, rather than Detective Constable or the oddly public school 'Fairchild'. I've not been close to many of my colleagues over the course of my career. The last true friend I had was more of a mentor, and he got a bullet in the head for his troubles.

'Soon, K. Soon. Meantime, I need you to run a name for me. Please. See if anything pops up?'

There's a pause long enough for me to realise I've taken the wrong lane again, and now I have to navigate the town's bizarre one-way system. I imagine Karen's either firing up her computer, checking to see no one in the office is watching, or trying to think of a way to tell me she's not my personal assistant. Eventually, I hear the sound of her heavy sigh even over the five cylinder rumble of the Volvo's elderly engine.

'Go on, then. What's the name.'

'Surname Johns, first name Kieran. Likely to be part of the local drugs trade. I ran his first name past the only honest copper in town and it didn't ring a bell though.'

'Only honest copper?' K's laugh crackles across the airwaves. 'You make it sound like the Wild West.'

'Yeah, well it's got that frontier feel to it sometimes.' As if to confirm my claim, I have to wait for a tractor to rumble past before I can turn out into the next street. I swear, one of these days I'm going to be stopped by some farmer walking his sheep to market.

'Nothing showing up on the PNC,' Karen says as I plan yet another change of route to avoid getting stuck behind the tractor. You can walk from one side of Aber to the other in half an hour, but sometimes it seems to take twice that in a car.

'Nothing?' I consider what Mrs Brady told me, and my suspicions about the flat. Have I got it all wrong? Has she got it all wrong?

'I'll do a deeper search on the name, but it'll have to wait till tomorrow.' At her words, my gaze flicks across to the clock on the dashboard and I'm surprised to see how late it's getting.

Tea with Mrs Brady might have been pleasant enough, but it's eaten up time.

'No rush. I'll see what I can turn up on Google. You never know.'

'Why the interest? I thought you weren't getting involved with Cantre'r Gwaelod?'

Karen's question brings me up short. I've been concentrating so hard on finding out about the two idiots who trashed my cottage and looking for Lila that I've not really stopped to consider how close I'm coming to trampling all over an active NCA operation. Then again, if Kieran Johns isn't on our radar and the local police haven't heard of him either, then chances are he's got nothing to do with the local drugs trade at all. Yeah, right. You don't believe that do you, Con.

'I think he might be Lila's abusive boyfriend. Handler. Whatever.' I tell Karen all I've learned so far, which is to say not much at all. 'Chances are he's taken her back, or she's gone back willingly. Well, I doubt willingly is the right word, but you know what I mean.'

'Yeah. Seen enough abusive relationships on the job. Never as easy to escape as people think.'

Over the line, I hear the sound of someone coming into whatever room Karen's working in, and her voice goes louder as she leans into her handset. 'Gotta go. I'll give you a call in the morning, OK?'

'Sure. Take care.'

'You too. And be careful. If this bloke's true to form, he's not going to take kindly to your interfering, right?'

I'm about to answer, but then I hear a voice in the background saying, 'Who you talking to?' It's faint, but I can tell who it is simply by the tone. Detective Sergeant Billy Latham is pissed off about something. Nothing new there, then. I catch Karen's breezy 'No one important', and then the line goes dead.

14

Karen's parting words stick with me as I finally break free of the gravitational pull of Aberystwyth's one-way system and escape south along the coast road. If I manage to track down the elusive Kieran Johns and it turns out he is as manipulative and possessive as I've painted him to be, then I'll need to tread very carefully. There's also the small matter of his having no entry on the police national computer, no criminal record. That strikes me as strange. My instinct is the flat across the landing from Mrs Brady is being used as a store house for drugs, and possibly a place for people to stay if they're needing to keep a low profile for a while. If Lila is being used as a drug mule, that would explain her knowing the address. Why else would a perfectly good council flat be sitting empty? Too many questions and not enough answers.

It's almost completely dark as I reach the turning that will take me inland to Plas Caernant. I've an open invitation to stay there as long as I like, and it's very tempting to fall back into that routine of being looked after. But I'm a grown woman. I can take care of myself. Have been for quite a while. I know that the locks have been changed on the cottage door now; Gareth gave me a key before I left this morning. The windows have all been fitted with locks too, and the place is far more secure than it was. Still, there's a gnawing sense of unease in the pit of my stomach when I think about sleeping there alone. It's so remote, at least half a mile away from the nearest house. Nobody would know if I was attacked again.

Stupid, Con. They're not coming back for you. Slaphead's on a boat out in Cardigan Bay somewhere. Greasy Rat's not going to come on his own. They had their fun, made their point, and if I give in to the fear then they've won. No way I'm going to let that happen.

I've slowed for the Caernant turning, hand reaching for the indicator stalk, when I make up my mind. The toot of horn and flash of lights behind me as I speed up again is a timely reminder to pay attention. Five minutes and a quick call to Amy to let her know what I'm doing later, that same car toots again and roars off towards Llantwmp as I turn across the road and onto the steep drive to the cottage.

A newly fitted more powerful security light bathes the entire yard as I park the car; another useful feature that goes some way towards calming my nerves. The clouds from earlier have blown away, the wind dropped and even through the glare of the spotlight I can see pinprick stars filling the night sky. Grabbing my bag from the back seat, I lock the car and then let myself in to the cottage that has been my home for almost a year now, expecting it to feel alien and changed.

It doesn't. Apart from the light smell of disinfectant hanging in the air from where the cleaners have been through, it's almost exactly as it was two days ago. Along with the new lock, the joiner has fitted two deadbolts, top and bottom on the door, which seems a little bit like overkill to me, although I'm almost certainly going to slide them home before I go to bed.

The kitchen and living room are both tidier than I've seen them in a while. I curse my own stupidity when I open the fridge to find it more or less empty. I should have done some shopping when I was in town. There are tins in the cupboard, dried pasta and the makings of a meal. I'll have to go to Llantwmp for milk in the morning, but that's OK. I could do with the exercise.

I carry my cobbled-together meal to the living room and switch on my laptop before I fetch myself a glass of wine. Suitably fortified, I bring up the browser window and start to search for the elusive Kieran Johns.

It takes a lot less time than I thought it would. But as I scan through the results, I rapidly discount the half dozen or so people who seem to share that name. Two hits are for obituaries, and not the same death unless that particular Kieran Johns died twice, five years apart. There's a brief history of a Reverend Kieran Johns who looked after the parish of Llantwmp in the late nineteenth century, but I doubt he's still hanging around these parts. I discard two more reports mentioning the name, as both have the man in his late seventies. That Kieran John was a town councillor in Aberaeron for many years. I read far too much about him before noticing that he's John, not Johns. I'm sure Mrs Brady said the man at the flat was called Mr Johns, but I can't discount that she might have misheard. Or, indeed, made the whole thing up. Well, it's not as if I've anything better to do this evening.

I work my way through the entries, sipping wine and shovelling in the occasional mouthful of pasta, until I've scrolled down at least a dozen pages. It's surprising how many people share what I'd taken to be an unusual name, but so far none of them seem a likely candidate for the man Mrs Brady described. Putting the plate to one side, I click on the image search for the name, and look at the faces that appear. Again, it's a lot of old men, black and white photos clearly taken in a previous century, engravings lovingly scanned. There's even a series of photographs of the church in Llantwmp and a gravestone leaning at a jaunty angle. I scroll and scroll, until my eyes start to lose focus. Image after image of nothing important, certainly not what I'm looking for.

And then something registers.

I stop scrolling, stare at the screen and try to work out what it was that I saw. I go back a bit, then forward, then stop. There it is. A photograph of a small group of people at what looks like a country fair. When I click the image to enlarge it, I get a clear look at the elusive Kieran Johns for the first time, and I have to say Mrs Brady was spot on. It wasn't him that caught my attention though, but the young woman standing beside him. Johns has an arm around her that could be loving, but seems more possessive to me. I've absolutely no doubt this is the man Lila was running away from, because there she is.

Her hair's different. Tidier for one thing, but a mousy brown rather than the blonde I remember. She's better dressed, too, and her face looks fuller, older somehow, although that's probably clever make-up. There's no mistaking those piercing blue eyes. I click through to the website where the image has come from, and find a Young Farmer's report on the Aberystwyth Country Fair from the summer before last. It reads a bit like the society column in a tabloid newspaper, only these celebrities are very much Z list or lower. Lila isn't named, and neither are most of the others in the photograph, but helpfully the caption identifies Alwyn Kieran Johns for the world and posterity. And even more helpfully, it tells me the name of his family's farm, Penparc Uchaf. Strangely enough, I don't even need to put it into the map search to know where it is, either. I've seen the wrought iron sign as I've driven past the farm entrance every time I've been to town. It's only a few miles up the coast from here. We're almost neighbours.

Back in the kitchen, I screw the cap back on the wine bottle and shove it in a cupboard out of sight after only one refill. Tempting though it is to numb myself before bed, I don't much fancy the hangover in the morning. Especially if I have to go down to the village before breakfast to get milk. I spend another hour idly searching for more information about Kieran Johns, or Alwyn Kieran Johns as I now know his real name is. I'll have to ask Karen to run that in the morning, although our systems are clever enough to bring up variations like that.

It's still early by city standards when I finally close down the laptop with a yawn. Out here in the sticks I've reverted to my childhood pattern, following the rhythms of the day. I rose at dawn this morning, so I've every reason to feel tired now. I check the toilet still flushes properly after my tiresome uninvited guests shoved a boxful of sanitary towels down it for a laugh, then I wash and get ready for bed, all the while trying to think calm thoughts. When I go to put my phone on the charging stand beside the bed though, I notice my hand is shaking. All of a sudden, a tumble of memories floods through my mind like a dam burst after months of rain. Pete Copperthwaite sat in his chair, a hole in his forehead and his brains on the wall behind him; Dan Penny casually murdered, right in front of me; the close stench of the man who attacked me outside the Danes Estate in London last year, blending seamlessly into Slaphead and Greasy Rat outside the Black Lion; a ginger-haired boy tossed out with the garbage in an Edinburgh back street, his heart ripped from his skinny chest; my mother's pale corpse laid out in a stone sarcophagus meant for me.

Without knowing how I've got there, I'm in the darkest corner of the room, knees hugged to my chest, shivering like heating's never been invented. A little part of my brain knows what's happening, tells me in the voice of my Aunt Felicity that it will pass, I just have to give it time. It's a very quiet, timid part of my brain, drowned out by the panic that wants to take over. Deep breaths, Con. You've got this.

And I have.

Eventually.

It takes far longer than it should before I have sufficient control of my limbs to even think about moving. At least the corner gives me leverage, and something to lean on when I finally manage to stand. I'm shaky still, but it's a jittery, adrenaline-rush shaking now as my body swings hard in the opposite direction of the panic attack. Slowly, awkwardly, I pull my clothes back on. There's no way I'm going to be able to bend to lace up my boots. I sit for a while until the room stops spinning and my thoughts settle. Keeping still only lets the madness catch up with me though, so I finally tie loose knots with shaky fingers, grab my phone off the nightstand and half-walk, half-run back downstairs.

It's not the first time this has happened to me since my run-in with the Reverend Edward Masters a year ago. If I'm being honest, it's the real reason I'm still living in a cottage in the middle of nowhere. I'd thought I was getting better. It's been months since I last had an attack, and they'd been getting milder, more easily shrugged off as nothing to worry about. What happened just now has put the lie to that, and I'm not so stupid as to miss the connection between this relapse and my stepping back into my old role as a detective.

In the past, I'd go for a run, as hard and fast as I could manage until I either felt like being sick or actually threw up. I know, that's not a healthy kind of purging, but what do you expect me to do? Therapy? I tried that and my therapist quit after three months. Drugs? Get real. It's too dark for a run now, even if a fat moon has risen over the sea. I still need to keep moving though, stay one step ahead of the thoughts. I can't do that cooped up indoors, so I pull on my coat, check the head torch is still in the pocket, and step outside into the night.

★ ★ ★

It's one of those calm, clear nights when I begin to understand how people can get so excited about telescopes and searching the heavens for particular stars. Growing up, I never cared much for being outside after dark, and as an adult I had London's street lamp glare to dampen any astronomical curiosity. Looking up was more likely to result in a face full of bird crap, and anything bright enough to twinkle was probably on its way to Heathrow. Out here, at the end of the world, it's different.

The moon has moved towards the low clouds lurking on the horizon, its bright disc reflected in a blurry line on the almost calm sea. I can see the dull glow of Aberystwyth to the north, Llantwmp a lesser pollution inland and south. Further away, the lights of Aberaeron and distant New Quay mark the sweep of Cardigan Bay, but looking straight up, the sky is black, like an opera cape sprinkled with diamonds.

My fear seeps away as I move from the house and out across the fields. The sheep are either sleeping or used to me by now, as they barely move when I pass by. The light of the moon makes my head torch unnecessary, and as I approach the clifftop I can hear the sound of waves far below, gently lapping at the rocks.

There's a bench a few hundred metres along the path, dry for once. I sit down, huddled into my coat for warmth, and stare out to sea as my heart begins to slow and my thoughts become less fractured. I've been using the pandemic as an excuse for my hermit-like solitude, but I know there's more, much more to it than that.

I recall the conversation with my aunt, many months ago, when she first told me of a place I could go to unwind. I'd managed to hide the panic attacks from everyone at work. Or at least, I thought I had.

But Aunt Felicity knows me too well and wasn't so easily fooled. Or maybe she heard me crying in my sleep those times I retreated from London to stay with her, when the bright lights and bustle of the city got just that little bit too much for me. She must have spoken to Gareth Caernant first, then somehow found out who my boss was, and who his boss was. Just like Aunt Flick to go straight to the top, and I imagine she and Diane Shepherd would have got on just fine. That would explain why, completely out of the blue, I was offered six months' compassionate leave with a possible extension to a year's sabbatical, right at the same time as the cottage became available.

Strange that I've never really thought about it until now. It's surprising how easily we can lie to ourselves, and more so how readily we accept our own lies. I'd not planned on being here more than a month. The pandemic made it easier to stay, but I have to admit this little corner of Wales has got under my skin. It was all going well, until I let myself start thinking like a detective again. All going fine until Slaphead and Greasy Rat decided my being rude to them in the pub couldn't go unchallenged.

The memory of their attack threatens to bring back the panic, which makes me angry at being so weak, which only makes things worse. I stand up, walk about some more, lean against the low stone wall that stops the sheep from falling off the cliff, take deep breaths. Come on, Con. Pull yourself together.

I could scream, that might help. And it's not as if anyone would hear me. Except the sheep. I push myself upright again and stare out to sea.

And that's when I see the boat.

It's too dark, and too far away to tell if it's the *Anwen's Favour*, and anyway why would it be? There must be hundreds of similar craft working these waters. I can't hear the noise of its engine either, although it is leaving that faintest of luminous wakes in the moonlit sea. It takes me a while to realise what's wrong with the whole situation, but then it hits me; the boat has no running lights. I can't see even a glow from the lit interior of the wheelhouse. Running dark.

My senses suddenly on edge, I watch as the boat makes its slow way towards the cliffs. It's hard to tell in the darkness, but it seems to have come from further out in the bay and is heading towards Aberystwyth. Except that it's surely coming too close to the shore for that, unless it's picking up lobster pots at the base of the cliffs. Do they do that at night? Without lights?

As it comes ever closer, I begin to hear the motor chugging away. The boat's moving slowly, the calm sea rolling it gently from side to side. Too dark to see properly. Is it my imagination, or does it sit lower in the water than it should? Then the moon slips behind the clouds that have begun to mass on the horizon with a promise of more rain, and if I hadn't been staring all along, I wouldn't be able to see the boat at all.

I walk closer to the cliff edge and peer down, trying to make out where it's going, but I lose track of it, and the sound of the engine fades away into the general noise of the waves. The breeze picks up, finding all the gaps in my coat. What the hell am I doing, out here in the middle of the night? At least the sight of the boat has been enough of a distraction to break the cycle of bad thoughts that sent me out here in the first place. I might not sleep tonight, but I won't be climbing the walls either.

I take one last look at the sea and the few remaining stars, shove my hands in my pockets and retrace my steps to the cottage.

15

I see Pete Copperthwaite in my dreams, but unlike the times before, where he's been draped in his chair with his brains over the wall, this time it's a younger, fitter version. Almost happy. How I remember him when I first moved from uniform to plain-clothes and he took me under his wing. When I wake up, it's with memories of better times, not the bitter hangover of my panic attack. It's still horribly early though, and I'm almost tempted to laze around in bed all morning.

The good mood lasts until I'm out of the shower and getting dressed. My phone buzzes one of the few programmed ringtones I know I can't ignore. I almost drop it in my rush to answer the call, catching it at the last moment.

'Up early. That's good.' Diane Shepherd doesn't waste time on pleasantries. 'I hear you're pursuing your own angle on Operation Cantre'r Gwaelod.'

'I . . .' I hesitate to answer. Not because I'm surprised she knows what I'm up to, but because she's usually got her finger firmly on the pulse and that's not what I've been doing at all. Have I?

'Keeping the local police out of the loop's a bold move, but probably wise. We've always suspected there's a leak somewhere, and the fewer people who know what you're up to the better.'

'But I'm not—'

'I need you to come to Carmarthen. I'll be there at . . .' Shepherd's voice goes distant and I can just about make out her asking someone when they're due to arrive '. . . call it one o'clock. Probably shouldn't meet at Police HQ. Not if you're undercover. Anywhere else you can think of?'

I can't, really. I've hardly been anywhere since I came to Wales. I'm also not meant to be working, undercover or out in the open. What's Karen been telling everyone back at base?

'How about the Botanical Gardens? They're a bit of a ways out of Carmarthen, but if you're driving, you'll go right past.'

Another conversation muted by the rumble of tyres on tarmac a long way away, then Shepherd comes back. 'Botanics is fine. See you at one.'

I'm about to announce, with more than a touch of sarcasm, that I'll be wearing a red rose and carrying an umbrella. Fortunately, Shepherd hangs up before I can get the words out. I drop my phone onto the bed, and carry on drying myself from the shower. It's only when I make it down to the kitchen that I remember there's no milk. Not much in the way of food, either. Probably better to pick up something on my way to Carmarthen, then. It'll only take me an hour from here, but there's no harm in getting there early.

I make sure the house is properly secured before I leave, and once again take my bag with my laptop and the briefing papers with me.

There's not much in Llantwmp for breakfast, so I carry on to Aberaeron – a little way down the coast. The car park overlooks the harbour, and as I sit with a styrofoam cup of barely drinkable coffee and a soft bacon roll from a nearby cafe, I stare out at the seagulls, clamouring around the boats. The tide's in, and a fairly large trawler is tied up to the quayside, unloading boxes. I can't see the name on its bows from where I'm sitting, but I don't think it's the same lobsterman that put out of Fishguard yesterday. Not that I'm any great expert.

I flick through my texts and emails on my phone while my coffee cools enough to drink. There's a message from Karen, warning me that the boss wants a word. Too late, K, but thanks anyway. The rest of it's inconsequential stuff, although there's a nice email from Izzy letting me know she's enjoying herself in Edinburgh and has made friends with a Detective Sergeant Harrison of my acquaintance. Detective Sergeant? When did that happen? Maybe I should give her a call.

I'm tapping the contacts icon to find Janie's number when, out of the side of my eye, I notice someone moving away from the quay towards the main street. I don't know what it is that made the movement register. When I see who it is, though, I immediately switch the phone off and drop it onto the passenger seat.

Greasy Rat. Also known as Karl Peterson.

He walks like a man who doesn't want to draw attention to himself. Which is precisely what drew my attention to him in the first place. He has a duffel bag slung over his shoulder, one of those army surplus numbers that are probably made in a sweatshop factory somewhere in the Far East, and have never been part of any military kit anywhere. From the way he keeps hefting it, the thing's filled with something heavy. He looks around furtively as he hurries to the main street, and I quietly emerge from the car to follow. Call it a copper's instinct. Or maybe I'm just naturally nosey.

There aren't many people around this early in the morning, so I keep back to avoid being seen, and almost miss him as he runs across the road to where a Range Rover sits waiting, a little waft of steam billowing from its exhaust as the engine idles. Black paint, blacked-out windows, a number plate that identifies it as being less than a year old. Close to six figures on wheels there, which doesn't quite square up with the Karl Peterson who strode into the Black Lion in Llantwmp a couple of weeks ago. It's not the car that dropped him off in Fishguard yesterday either; that was a BMW and not cheap.

And here's me thought the seafood industry was in crisis.

Peterson dumps his bag in the back, then climbs into the front passenger seat. The car sits for a few moments, then indicates and pulls out into the road, heading north. I watch it as far as I can see, past the town boundary. Then I pull out my phone and text the registration number to Karen. Might as well find out who Greasy Rat's rich friend is, after all.

The National Botanic Garden of Wales lies a few miles east of Carmarthen, in a little place called Llanarthne. I remember reading about it at school, and being amazed by the massive glass dome of a greenhouse that was the central attraction. I'm not much of a gardener, but I visited once because I needed to get out. It wasn't as impressive as I'd expected, but that might have had more to do with lockdown and a global pandemic than the gardens themselves.

Old habits die hard, so I arrive a good hour early to scope out the place. I never specified exactly where in the gardens I was to meet up with Shepherd, and presumably Billy Latham since he seems to be her shadow these days. I glance at my phone every so often as I walk around the walled garden, pretending I'm interested in the plants when watching the few hardy visitors is far more interesting.

They're mostly old couples, stopping every so often to point at a plant and discuss it at great length. A young woman is pushing a pram slowly along the narrow paths, and I watch her for a while to try and work out what she's doing. She walks the inner circle around the centre of the garden until she's completed a circuit. Then she moves to the next circle out and completes another circuit. The garden isn't laid out sym-metrically, so her route isn't immediately obvious, but she seems to be trying to work her way around every single path. And all the while, she pays no attention whatsoever to the plants on either side, instead focusing her attention on the baby. There's a story behind that, I'm sure. Perhaps she needs to get out of the house, or maybe wheeling the pram is the only way to get the child to sleep? Maybe she has a meeting with someone important and arrived an hour and a half early to scope out the place. Who knows?

I'm so mesmerised by her performance, I almost don't notice the buzz of my phone as a text comes in. I glance at it, confused that it's from Karen but that it says to meet at the entrance to the Great Glasshouse. Of course that's where Shepherd would go, but why on earth is Karen telling me? It becomes obvious as I approach the main entrance to find three people waiting for me, Shepherd, Latham and Karen herself. That would explain why she never responded to my text requesting a search on the Range Rover registration number.

'Hey, Con. Good to see you.' She's the first to speak, her smile broad and genuine. It's been months since I last saw her, and I'm surprised at how that makes me feel.

'Interesting choice of meeting place,' Shepherd adds, glancing around. She's not much of a one for smiling at the best of times, but at least she's not scowling at me like DS Latham.

'There's a small cafe inside.' I point towards the entrance to the glass house. 'Or we can go to the Stable Block. There's more space there. Probably better for social distancing and all.'

Latham doesn't quite manage to suppress his snort of derision at this, and I can see Shepherd's face tighten.

'Billy, why don't you go and wait in the car?' she suggests, with a tone that is more irate mother than boss, and which musters the tiniest slivers of sympathy in me for the detective sergeant. It can't be easy working closely with someone like Diane Shepherd. Not when you're a fool and she doesn't suffer them gladly. Latham's scowl is saved for me as he walks off.

'A shame he hates you so much. He's a good detective otherwise. Shall we?' Shepherd waves in the direction of the stable block and we walk over, finding a table in the courtyard far enough away from the few other visitors here that we won't be overheard. Karen goes off in search of coffee, leaving me and the boss alone again.

'This Ukrainian woman you think might be a drug mule. Any luck in tracking her down yet?'

I bring my boss up to speed on where I've got in the search for Lila, which is to say not very far at all. She listens intently until I've finished, which makes a change from most of my interviews with male detectives.

'So, the flat on the council estate she gave as her address. You didn't go in, I take it?'

'No. I might have done, if it hadn't been for the old lady who lived opposite. The lock didn't seem up to much.'

Shepherd nods once. 'No, it's as well you didn't. If it is what you think it is, then they'd know if someone had been in there. I'm more concerned about the fact that you telling me is the first I've heard of it. We don't have your man Johns on our radar at all, either. He's what? A farmer, you say?'

'I don't know anything much about him, but I did find a photo online. Coverage of a local agricultural show the summer before last. He had Lila with him.' A thought occurs to me. 'If they were an item then, that's borderline child abuse – she's only eighteen now.' I pause. 'That's if she's the Lila Ivanova we think she is.'

'Too many unknowns. I don't like this haphazard way of conducting an investigation.' Shepherd pauses a moment as Karen returns bearing a tray. Coffees all round, and some warm

Welsh cakes. Bless her, how did she know I've not eaten since my solitary bacon roll for breakfast?

'You keep on treating this like it's an active investigation,' I say through a mouthful of crumbs. 'Like I'm back at work.'

'Aren't you? You certainly seem to be making a lot of use of Karen's time, and our databases.' Shepherd picks up one of the Welsh cakes and looks at it suspiciously before putting it back down again. 'I wouldn't want to think you were using NCA facilities for personal reasons, Detective Constable.'

There's a moment where I consider telling Shepherd about last night's relapse. The panic attacks were why I took time off the best part of a year ago, after all. Why she agreed to me taking time off and hasn't pushed too hard about me coming back. At least until now. But of course I'm too damned stubborn to admit that, not even to myself. Not fully. And here's neither the time nor place for that conversation.

'I don't know if Lila is connected to anything. I've no proof she's even here illegally. I only have what she told me, which might have been a sob story to get me to help her. If she's telling the truth though, then I'd like to find her. Find out how she ended up in Aberystwyth in an abusive relationship with some unknown farmer. How she's stayed alive all this time. If any of that information is useful to Cantre'r Gwaelod I'll let you know, of course.'

Shepherd picks up the Welsh cake again, sniffs it, then takes a bite. Her eyebrows arch in surprise and she chews for a moment before speaking again. 'Not bad, for a cafe. Seriously though, Con. We do need you back on the team. I need you back on the team. It's unorthodox, I know, but you're in a good position right now, and we're hitting too many obstacles and dead ends. Every time we think we're getting somewhere with this organisation, they disappear only to pop up somewhere else. They've either got someone at Dyfed Powys feeding them key intel, or they've found a way to hack our secure coms network. You've read the briefing I gave you, right? You know the whole operation's hanging by a thread. We don't come up with something, and soon, then it's going to get shut down. That's months, years of hard work down the drain, and you know how much I hate waste.'

As if to underline the point, she shoves the rest of the Welsh cake into her mouth and washes it down with a swig of coffee.

I'm backed into a corner.

I can't find Lila without picking up my old job again. And I can't deny there's a puzzle here that needs solving. I don't care too much about Operation Cantre'r Gwaelod's future; that's something for the high-ups and bean counters to worry about. I do care about modern-day slavery, trafficking young girls for sex work, using them as drug mules.

'I'm not on the books?' I ask, and Shepherd smiles like a snake.

'Far as I'm concerned, Detective Constable Fairchild is on extended leave. Nobody knows you're here.'

That's not quite true, but it's good enough. Guess that's me back at work then.

16

Penparc Uchaf Farm sits closer to the cliffs than I realised.

I'm tempted to drive up to the farmhouse and pretend to be a lost tourist so that I can have a snoop around the yard, but I don't want to bring too much attention to myself. Not if Diane Shepherd wants me to be her unknown ace in the pack. Instead, I log into Google Maps and zoom in as close as I can get before the resolution turns too fuzzy. This part of the country's not as well covered as some more urban areas, but it's still good enough to make out the house, a collection of old buildings forming a courtyard close by, and a set of more modern buildings at a short distance. Three vast steel-roofed sheds that you could fit the entire farmyard inside. It would be one way to get them out of the rain.

Without access to the full suite of data I'd have at NCA headquarters, I can't easily work out the farm boundaries and who the neighbours are, but it occurs to me that I know someone who might be able to fill me in. Much like Harston Magna back home, Plas Caernant is the centre of what was once a vast estate of many farms. Most of them have been sold down the years, but Gareth still has a fairly large landholding, including the farmland that surrounds my cottage. The sheep I failed to disturb on my nocturnal stroll last night belong to my nearest neighbours, Dai

Young and his wife Ellen, who rent Twmp Farm and live in the farmhouse a half mile down the hill. I've not had much to do with them beyond the occasional hello as I'm walking to the village, but if anyone's going to know about the local farming scene, it's them.

I'm no stranger to farmers. Growing up where I did, it was hard to avoid them. There may have been a couple of teenage crushes I'd be embarrassed to admit to now. For example, I spent a fair amount of time hanging around the home farm at Harston Magna, especially at harvest time. Northamptonshire is good arable land though, and this part of Wales doesn't much lend itself to crops. Livestock farming seems to involve a lot more mud and worse, so I pull on my heaviest walking boots before taking the short trek down the hill.

A couple of filthy sheepdogs greet me as I approach the house. They're not aggressive, seemingly more intent on herding me towards the door than keeping me away. Somewhere in the back of my mind I know their names, but they don't spring to mind immediately.

Ellen Young greets me at the door. Like her dogs, she's not aggressive but I can see the suspicion in her eyes as I approach. It looks like she's in the middle of baking, judging by her stained apron, rolled-up sleeves and the smudge of something that might be dough on one cheek. She pauses in wiping her hands on a teacloth and shrugs when I ask her about Penparc Uchaf.

'I know the place, but not well, see? Didn't grow up in these parts. You'd be best talking to Dai. He'll have known Kieran from his young farmer days. They're all as thick as thieves round here, playing the rugby and getting drunk after.'

'Is he about?' I ask, aware that Ellen Young and I are much of an age. Is her calculating look born of worry I might steal her man? If so, she needn't fret. He's really not my type.

'Said he was going to trim the hogs' feet. Can't be far off or these two would be with him.' Ellen waves her free hand at the dogs, still circling and pacing. The ceaseless motion is disturbing. 'You could try the pens, round the back of the old barn.'

'Thanks.' I start to turn away, but Ellen stops me with a question of her own.

'What you want to know about the Johns for, anyways? Has it something to do with the cottage being done over? That was shocking.'

How much should I tell her? I don't know if Ellen is a gossip, how wide her circle of friends is, who might talk to whom. On the other hand, she already knows I'm asking about Kieran Johns, so if it's going to get back to him there's nothing I can do about that now.

'I met a young woman who said she knew him. She was in a bit of a bind, and I said I'd help her out, but now she's disappeared. Thought I'd find out a bit about Johns before I approached him. I know some of the local farmers can be a bit touchy about us.' I see a frown of confusion on Ellen's face. 'English folk. Non-Welsh speakers.'

The frown smooths away almost instantly. 'Oh, some people can be devils that way. Even when you've come down from the north like me. Aberystwyth's not too bad, with the university and everything, but some of these rural communities are very parochial.'

'I've not had too much trouble, really. Cerys at the Black Lion's always friendly, and Lord and Lady Caernant never seem to stand too much on ceremony.'

Ellen smiles. She turns slightly, looking back over her shoulder towards what I assume is the kitchen, then faces me again. 'I'm sure Dai will be along any minute. He's usually in for his tea about now. Why don't you come in for a cuppa and we can wait for him in the warm?'

'Are you sure?' I shove a hand in my pocket and pull out my mask.

Ellen waves it away. 'Sure, you'll be fine. I've not been anywhere to catch anything lately, and they've started vaccinating people now. Come in, come in. I'll put the kettle on.'

The kitchen is wonderfully warm after standing outside in the yard. I sit at a cluttered table while Ellen sets about filling the kettle and putting it on the hotplate of the large Rayburn that dominates the room. When she bends to open the oven door, the air is flooded with the intoxicating scent of fresh-baked Welsh cakes. As if summoned by the aroma, the back door bangs open and Dai enters. He's wearing the greasy overalls and mucky boots uniform of farmers the world over, and as he pokes his head in from the back lobby he jabbers something in Welsh that I don't have a hope of understanding. Ellen says something back, then nods her head in my direction. Only then does the young farmer notice me.

'Ah, I'm sorry, Miss Fairchild. I didn't see you there.' Dai rubs his hands on his overalls which only has the effect of spreading the muck even more. For a moment, I think he's going to offer one hand to shake, but he seems to remember himself in time, staring at his palms. 'I'll just go and have a quick wash, now.'

By the time he comes shuffling back into the kitchen in his socks, cleaner if not exactly clean, the tea is made and Ellen has poured me a mug.

'Miss Fairchild wanted to know about Kieran Johns, up at Penparc Uchaf,' she says as she hands a mug of tea to her husband.

'Please, call me Con. Miss Fairchild sounds like some kind of primary-school teacher.'

'Con?' Ellen asks as she proffers the plate of Welsh cakes,

fresh from the oven. I take one and bite into it. Realise that the ones I've been buying from cafes near here are a pale imitation of the real thing.

'It's short for Constance. And that really does make me sound like a primary-school teacher. I prefer Con. Do you know Mr Johns, then?'

Dai is already tucking into a Welsh cake, so it takes him a while before he can answer.

'Alwyn?' He shakes his head, sugary crumbs falling to the wooden tabletop. 'What do you want to know about him for? Or do you mean old man Johns? His father?'

'Is he Kieran too?' I can't imagine Lila having much to do with someone who must be at least as old as my own father.

'Kieran's something of a family name with the Johns. The old man's Tegwin Kieran, I think. I've always known him as Johns Penparc though. That's how we tend to refer to folk around here. Ask people about Dai Young and they'll think you mean the rugby player. Say Dai Twmp and they'll know exactly who you mean.'

I nod sagely, even if I'm only half sure I understand. 'Let's assume it's the younger Johns. You called him Alwyn?'

'Alwyn, that's right. What do you want to know about him?' Dai slides another surreptitious Welsh cake off the plate.

'Anything, really. His name came up recently and I'm trying to find the person who mentioned him.'

'Woman was it?' Dai shakes his head slowly. 'Don't think I've ever seen him with the same one on his arm more than twice. Goes through them like some farmers cull their ewes. Anything not quite right, and off they go. Always young, too. Maybe a bit younger than they should be, if you take my meaning.'

'You don't think much of him, then?'

'Oh, as a businessman he's canny enough. Must be or they wouldn't have those posh barns and all that expensive kit now, would they? I'm never sure how much of that's to do with Alwyn though, and not his old man. Johns Penparc is a bit of a legend at the market, see. Always pays the best if he likes the look of what you're selling. Never shy with the luck money when you buy from him either.'

'He's a sheep farmer, then? Like you?'

Dai's laugh brings crinkles to the skin around his eyes. There's an openness about him I've not seen in a while.

'He's a farmer, surely. But not like me. I can't afford to swan about in a brand new Range Rover. And no disrespect to his Lordship, but the barns here aren't exactly state of the art.'

'How big is the farm, then? Must be a fair few acres if they're making good money.'

'It's big, that's for sure. Seven, eight hundred acres maybe. A lot of that clifftop land's not the best, mind you.'

'And they raise sheep? Cattle too?'

'The old man has a pedigree herd of Welsh Blacks. Shows them at the Aber Fair and Builth every year.'

'Builth?'

'Builth Wells? The big agricultural show, see. He's won a fair few prizes for them. But I don't think Alwyn's quite so interested. He's more of a dairy man. Spent a lot of money on a new automatic milking parlour a couple of years back. Couple of million, some of the lads at the rugby were saying.'

I can't help but raise an eyebrow at that. 'Two million pounds? Where'd he get that kind of money from?'

Dai shrugs as if such sums aren't as impressive as I think. 'From the bank, same as any of us, I'd guess. Doubt there's a farm anywhere between here and the border isn't in hock to one of the big banks. It's the only way to survive, see?'

I don't, but then I don't know much at all about farming, it seems. My detective's brain is beginning to see a few patterns in the disparate bits of information, though. I'm sorely tempted by just one more of Ellen's excellent Welsh cakes, but I need time to think about some of the things I've learned today. I drain my tea, then place my hand over the empty mug when Ellen offers me a top up.

'No, thank you. You've been very helpful, but I should probably be going. It'll be getting dark soon.'

That seems to be enough of an excuse, or they want rid of this strange English woman who's descended upon their domestic calm, asking odd questions. Outside it is indeed getting dark, low clouds overhead threatening rain. The two dogs circle around, unsure of me as I wave goodbye and walk across the yard to the track. For a moment, I wonder if they're going to follow me all the way to the cottage, but a sharp whistle from Dai has them scurrying home. I hold up a hand in a wave of thanks, but don't bother turning to see if my neighbours are on the doorstep watching me leave. It's been a strange kind of day, a strange few days after months of barely talking to anyone, but all I really want now is to get back to my little cottage and the lonely solitude of my thoughts.

17

The terrors wake me this time, the loud bang of the gun that ended Dan Penny's life echoing in my head as I sit bolt upright. Disoriented, it takes long moments for my heart to stop thudding away like a steam engine, my memories to reassemble themselves in the correct order. My back is clammy, the draft from the ill-fitting window sends shivers across my skin until I pull the duvet around me and sink into the pillow.

I lie for a while staring at the dark shapes on the ceiling and let the room expand around me until it no longer feels like the claustrophobic confines of a stone sarcophagus. I will my heart rate to slow, for sleep to come back. It doesn't work, and bitter experience tells me that it won't. After a while, I get up, dress in warm clothes and stout walking boots, grab my phone and wander out into the darkness once again.

It's not as clear as last night, the moon already set. Heavy cloud hides most of the stars, and I have to use my head torch a couple of times to get across the field to the clifftop path. There's a stiffer breeze throwing a heavier swell against the rocks far below as I walk to the bench and take a seat. No boats out at sea, or at least none in view.

By the time I've reached my bench, I've walked the worst of the terror out of me, but I'm still jittery. I shove my hands between my thighs to stop them trembling, then pull them back again to wipe the moisture from my eyes, rub at my nose. Christ, it's like being a teenager all over again. My body doing its own stupid thing no matter how much I want it not to.

I really thought I'd been getting better, so the last couple of nights have come as a shock. And a disappointment. The small part of my mind that is still rational can't help but see a correlation between my first few tentative steps back into the career I used to love and the return of the psychological hang-up that forced me to take a break from it in the first place. Correlation isn't causation, of course, but that's not much consolation when you're this close to hysteria.

The wind plays with my hair as I stare blindly out into the dark. A year ago, when I last had a haircut, it was so short I must have looked like a pencil. If the therapist I consulted hadn't quit so soon after taking me on, he'd probably have told me I was overcompensating, trying to rid my body of all connection to the horror that had been visited on it by the Reverend Edward Masters. There might even have been a grain of truth in that, but I also quite liked the mousy brown wig I'd adopted as a disguise, and shaving off all my flame-red hair made wearing it a lot easier. Made me less obviously me.

Trying to be someone else. The laugh that bursts from me sounds flat and foreign, out here at the edge of the world. I reach up and tuck an errant lock back under my woolly hat, marvelling at how long it's grown now. I can't remember the last time I had to use a scrunchy to keep it under control. School, probably.

Shivering at the cold, I shove my hands deep into my coat pockets, pulling in on myself for warmth. Stupid, really. There's a warm cottage a couple of hundred metres away, a kitchen that will give me a cup of tea if I ask it nicely, or a nip from the bottle of Penderyn Welsh whisky I picked up in Carmarthen on the way back from my meeting with Diane Shepherd. Tempting though all of those things are, I remain stuck to the bench, staring out at the black sea. Something is preying on my mind. Well, to be fair, lots of things are preying on my mind right now, but there's something in particular that my subconscious has noticed that I've clearly missed. Something that's keeping me up at night, I'm sure.

My mind scrolls through the options. Is it Lila? It's only a day or two since she ran, but when I try to picture her, the image that comes is not of her in the car as we approached the cottage. Instead, it's of her wide-eyed wonder when Gareth took us both down to his subterranean chapel and invited us to drink font water from the Holy Grail. What he claimed was the Holy Grail.

Another laugh forces its way past my lips, a little less bitter than the last one. Since that episode, I've looked up the wooden goblet online. It's one of many claiming the dubious title of Holy Grail, and even the most earnest believer would have to admit that they couldn't all be genuine. That's not to say there isn't a rich history surrounding the Estate, and extensive local mythology too. It's just that most of the stories date from the latter part of the eighteenth century. Either that, or from a time before anyone had heard of Jesus Christ.

Lila, though. She was like a child in that chapel, even though when I'd first seen her in the police cell she looked older. Careworn, even. My first instinct had been that she was an addict, and I've no doubt she's used in the past. She more or less confirmed she'd been a drug mule, too. But then, there she is in a photograph from an agricultural show, dressed like she'd fit in pretty much unnoticed at my old boarding school and hanging on the arm of a man who's almost twice her age. What the hell is her story? Who is she, really? And where has she got to?

I'm still trying to make my mind up, aware that this particular jigsaw is missing rather more than half its pieces, when the details that have been evading my conscious mind finally break through.

Voices.

I can hear voices.

At first I think I'm imagining it. The wind comes in gusts, and it's only in the lulls between each blow that I hear anything at all. Mostly, there's the crash and rumble of waves on rocks, a constant background sound. But every so often, I catch something else. Snippets of a conversation just too faint to make out. Not the actual words, but the cadence is there. Speech.

And now that I'm concentrating, I can make out other noises, too. The occasional hollow clunk, like an oar tapping the side of a boat. There's someone down there, at the bottom of the cliff.

My eyes have adjusted to the near total darkness as much as they are ever going to, but even so it's nerve-racking as I cross the footpath. It's a long way to the sea, and there are nasty, jagged rocks tumbled around the base of the cliff. As I get closer I take the sensible option and crawl on hands and knees to the edge before peering down.

There's something eerily luminescent about frothing waves. I don't know, maybe it's actually luminescent; there's certainly not enough light from the overcast sky to make it glow that way. My stomach clenches as I focus on the churning waters and see how far away they are. For a moment, it's like everything is slowly spinning. Is this what vertigo feels like?

Slowly, the world begins to steady. I'm lying flat on my stomach. For a moment, I can hear nothing but the wind ruffling my hair about my ears, the splosh and crash of the waves far below. I strain to listen over those noises, and then I catch it again, a creak of wood on wood and something that might be a low-muttered whisper. Again, I can't make out actual words, but the sound gives me a space to focus on, and finally I see it.

The boat is perhaps twenty metres off the base of the cliffs. Painted dark, and low to the water, it's almost impossible to make out much detail, but I'd say it's a decent size for something that can be rowed. How anyone out there can see where they're going is beyond me. They must know these cliffs intimately to even contemplate coming out in these conditions. On a moonlit night, with a good powerful torch, maybe. But now? It makes no sense.

No legal sense.

For a moment, I think I've lost it in the darkness. Then an oar catches the water and sends up a cascade of white foam. A moment later, there's that harsh, guttural voice again. I don't need to hear the words to understand the urgent tone. Someone is trying very hard not to be seen, even here in the dead of night. And that can only mean they're up to no good.

It's rained during the day, and the damp begins to seep through my jeans and coat. The chill has crept up my body without me noticing. A great spasm of a shiver runs through me and my teeth start to chatter. I doubt whoever is in the boat can hear me if they didn't notice my earlier manic laugh. Given the height of the cliff and the dark clouds overhead, it's even more unlikely they can see me, but even so, I shuffle backwards onto the path before clambering to my feet. My legs are stiff and cold, my arms weak as if I've been working out for hours. There's not much I can do about the boat except maybe put in a call to the marine authorities in the morning. Right now, I don't even know who that might be. Coast guard? Fisheries department? Karen will know.

Hands shoved deep into my coat pockets in search of any last vestiges of warmth that might be there, I turn my back on the sea and begin the careful walk back home.

Which is when finally I notice that I'm not alone.

18

Two indistinct shapes walk side by side along the path towards me. Their casual, unhurried gait suggests they haven't seen me yet, and I've no idea what they're doing out here. We can't all be suffering from panic attacks and night terrors, can we? At least I have the excuse my cottage is only a couple of hundred metres away. It's a good mile and a half to the next nearest house.

I freeze, knowing that any movement will alert them to my presence. It's only a matter of time before they reach me though, and not much time at that. They've come from the direction of the village, following the track up from Llantwmp beach. If I want to get back to the cottage I need to go past them, and now I'm over the initial shock of finding them out here, it's fairly obvious they're here for the same reason as the boat down below. Something I don't want to be caught witnessing.

There's nothing to hide behind, except for the bench. I take a chance, crouching as I cross the path as stealthily as possible and squat down. I make out the sound of their boots on the gravel path, the soft rustle of clothing barely audible above the breeze. When I hear them talking, I hold my breath.

'Hate these dark nights. So much easier when the moon's out.'

'Easier to be seen too, mind. Don't want to draw any more attention to ourselves now, do we? You know the boss isn't happy with all the nuisance you've been making of yourself lately. It's the first rule, isn't it? Keep your head down in the run up to a job, right?'

For once, I'm glad of the almost total darkness as the two figures walk past. They're concentrating too much on the path immediately ahead of them to notice me, but even so I don't even dare look up as they pass. I don't need to. One of them is Greasy Rat, for sure. He only spoke to me briefly at the pub, but I'd know that voice anywhere. It has a distinct North Wales edge to it, that odd mixture of Welsh and Scouse the locals disparagingly call Gog.

'Bitch put me and Billy in Bronglais, didn't she. Only fair we mess her place up.' Greasy Rat's nasal whine is even worse when he's actually whining.

'Not her place though, is it? Belongs to Lord Snooty Caernant, doesn't it? That's trouble with a capital T. No wonder the boss is so mad.' His friend is local, but clearly not Slaphead.

'He's always like this when there's a new shipment coming in. That little whore of his running off, see? That's put him in a bad mood, too. Surprised he took her back. Usually grows tired of them when they reach her age. And it's not the first time she's done a runner, is it?'

The conversation carries on, drifting out of earshot as the two men continue their slow walk along the clifftop path. I stay frozen to the spot, breath silent and shallow. Slow minutes tick by before I even think about moving. Long after their footsteps have faded away.

But that doesn't stop my mind from racing through what I've just heard. What Dai and Ellen Young told me earlier, too. What I've pieced together from all the fragments of information gathered over the past few days. The boat below, silent and dark in the water; the men up here, keeping an eye on the clifftop path in the witching hour of a dead, moonless night; the narrow coves and long-disused jetties hidden along this remote stretch of the Ceredigion coast. It doesn't take a genius to work out what's going on, and I've a briefing paper back at the cottage in case I need reminding.

I finally stand up, my bones creaking, and grimace at the pain that cramps my cold muscles. The path is empty now as far as I can see, which isn't very far at all. I pull out my phone, ready to call someone, anyone, but who? There'll be a desk sergeant on duty at Aberystwyth nick, but I've a feeling that's something these people already have covered. I could call back to base, maybe wake Karen or speak to whichever poor sap's on the night shift in London. But there's not much they could do right now, and do I really have enough information to go on? Snippets of overheard conversation that might or might not refer to me, to Lila, and the things I've been looking into over the past few days. Or it might be Greasy Rat and his friend going for a night stroll quite innocently. Just like me, unable to sleep.

Aye, right, as my friends in Police Scotland might say.

My thumb hovers over the screen, ready to wake my phone, when it occurs to me that it will light up like a beacon in this dark night. What if Greasy Rat and friend are looking back this way? No, I need to find out a bit more of what's going on here before I call in the big guns.

Slipping my phone back into my pocket, I set off in pursuit.

It takes only moments to find what I'm looking for, creeping along the clifftop as silently as possible. The path starts to dip, and I remember the many times I've walked this way. A narrow track zig-zags a steep descent into a cliff gully. As I peer through the scrubby gorse bushes clinging to the rocks, I see the pinprick lights of a dozen or more head torches down at sea level.

134

Voices drift up on the air, again too distant to make out what's being said. I can't see well enough to be sure, but it looks like the boat has been pulled up onto the narrow shingle beach and is being unloaded. It brings to mind childhood stories of smugglers on the Devon and Cornwall coasts. Rum and tobacco brought in under the noses of the excisemen. There could be rum and tobacco here, but my guess would be more likely cocaine and heroin.

Any contraband will surely have to be carried up the track and off to wherever they have a vehicle waiting, presumably in one of the nearby fields. But as I watch, the line of head torches snakes along the base of the gully for only a few metres before, one by one, the lights go out. At first I wonder if they've switched them off to avoid being seen, but then it dawns on me that there must be a cave down there. I can't think how I've never noticed before, in months of idly walking these clifftops and coves. Unless this is one of the coves I've not yet explored. There are a few along this stretch of cliffs that are a lot scarier in the daylight than the darkness, accessible only with ropes or a death wish.

Another sound echoes over the endless rush of waves, a sudden shriek of alarm cut short as if someone has fallen and been caught. A light flares, brighter than the head torches. It briefly illuminates a small huddle of people, clustered around one of them dangling over a narrow ledge in the cliffside. The drop isn't far, but it's onto sharp rocks and rolling waves. In the dark, the fall would be fatal. I watch as the hapless climber is hauled back onto the ledge, and then the brighter light swings up towards me as if whoever is holding it has sensed my presence. I freeze, even though I'm hidden. I feel the beam pass over my face, the glare temporarily robbing me of my night vision. Too late, I realise that it was never directed at me, but at someone on the clifftop path behind me. Someone with their own torch, who has signalled their accomplices below.

'Well, well. What have we here? A little birdie hiding in the bushes.' The voice is far too close. I can't believe I've been so caught up in the events below that I've forgotten about Greasy Rat and his friend, patrolling the path. Now I'm trapped between them and an almost certainly fatal fall. Stupid, Con. Really stupid.

I rise to my feet and turn slowly, hoping there might be some way to overpower them, or at the very least push them aside so that I can make a run for it. I have my torch in my hand, and I click it on, even as I shield my face from the glare of the two beams of light pointed at me. If I can dazzle them enough, then maybe I can slip past. But in my panic, I fumble with the switch and the beam misses their faces. Instead, it gives me a clear view of the nasty-looking guns they are both aiming at me.

Christ, but I hate guns.

'Well now. If it isn't the karate kid herself.' Greasy Rat's thin face breaks into a broken-toothed leer. 'Looks like Christmas has come early this year.'

19

I curse my own stupidity all the way down the steep path to the narrow pebble beach. I should have called in as soon as I saw these two bastards walking the clifftop path. I should have gone straight back to the cottage as soon as I saw the boat. I should have done everything differently, and now I'm well and truly fucked.

Way to go, Con. Out in the dark and chances are nobody will notice you missing for days.

It takes so much concentration, simply negotiating the track to the bottom of the gully, that I can't think of any sure way to escape. But once we step out onto the shingle, shifting danger-ously underfoot, I start to look around in the hope of finding something, anything, I can use. There's nothing, short of grab-bing a handful of briny pebbles and flinging them at one of my captors. Satisfying as that might be, the other one would simply shoot me where I stood, and it's a slow, dangerous climb to get back out of here.

Brilliant.

At closer range, I can see now that the boat is actually quite large. There must have been at least two oarsmen, probably more. Maybe, an electric motor. The vessel has been hauled onto the beach with what looks like an ancient iron winch. The rope from its bow is taut under the strain, but thick and well secured. There'll be no hurried pushing the boat out and leaping on board, leaving my captors helpless on the beach. I don't much fancy my chances with night swimming either.

'What's going on here?'

An unfamiliar voice looms out of the darkness, followed shortly by a man I've never met but who is nevertheless unpleasantly familiar. He's a little older than his photograph, a bit more weather-beaten. Perhaps the wind and the cold have chapped his cheeks that ruddy colour, or maybe they've always been like that. Either way, Kieran Johns is every bit as tall and broad as I'd imagined. Standing immediately behind him, Slaphead squints into the torchlight shone by his fellow smugglers. I should be terrified. I am terrified, really. And yet as my brain reels at the possibilities and recriminations, searches for a way out of this situation born of my own stupid curiosity, I can't help but notice not a single person in this entire group is wearing a mask. I guess if you're going to break one rule, might as well ignore them all.

'Found this one snooping on us. Up there, in the bushes.' Greasy Rat flicks his torch beam up towards the cliff top, but before it's even halfway there, Johns has reached out and grabbed him around the wrist. I take a little solace in the anguished yelp of pain that escapes from Greasy Rat's lips. The sudden violence of it brings home just what a desperate situation I'm in, and I have to fight the waves of terror that threaten to drown me.

'Stop waving your light around like it's a fucking rock concert.' Johns' voice is not what I'd been expecting at all, and quite out of keeping with his size and bulk. High pitched and almost feminine; I can't imagine how he would command any respect sounding like that. And yet Greasy Rat clearly defers to him, as does the other man. Both point their torches at the beach, leaving the big man to shine his light in my face.

'You.' He reaches out with a massive hand and grabs my head like I'm a breeding ewe and he wants to inspect my teeth. 'What are you doing, spying on us? You're not with the police now, are you?'

Given that his thumb is pressed hard into one cheek, fingers into the other, I figure it's a rhetorical question. I pull away from him, or at least try to until the squeeze of his hand gets too painful.

'She's the one who jumped me and Billy outside the pub,' Greasy Rat says.

'This?' Johns jerks his hand to swivel my head round, almost breaking my neck in the process. The pain is like a hot knife in the base of my skull, but it gives me a focus. Something to keep the fear at bay. 'This put you both in the hospital? Well now, that changes things.'

He finally lets go. A couple of other people have moved close enough that I can see their figures in the low glow of the downward-pointed torches. I'm too busy getting my breath back to take in much detail, but they seem a mismatched bunch. An odd assortment of clothes and boots. Illegal immigrants being shipped in, or part of the local smuggling scene? I'm too preoccupied to tell.

'You have a name, Spy?' Johns asks.

'Going to put me on your Christmas card list?' I realise as soon as the words are out that I should have kept my silence.

'English, is it? Well doesn't that just take the fucking biscuit?'

I'm concentrating on his face, which is a mistake. The punch comes from nowhere, slamming the air out of my lungs as it connects with my stomach. I fall to my knees, and puke out the remnants of my supper.

'Hefin, your gun.'

Out of the corner of my eye, I see Johns extend a massive hand towards Greasy Rat's friend. There's a moment's pause, and then the man hands over his weapon. Johns checks it like he's used guns many times before, pulls back the slide and clacks a round into the chamber.

Fuck. This is really happening.

Damned if I'm going out on my knees. I spit the last of the vomit out of my mouth and push myself upright. Johns is still fussing with the gun as I stand, and the light from his head torch illuminates the people standing close to him. I almost gasp when I see one of them, staring at me with wide eyes. Well, one wide eye. The other's swollen shut in a misshapen lump.

Lila.

She opens her mouth to speak but I stare her down, shake my head just enough for her to stop. No reason for both of us to die tonight, and who knows? She might be able to escape again and tell the world what happened here.

'You kill me,' I announce, 'and there's a whole ton of shit going to fall on your head.'

'Do I look like I care?' Johns finally stops fiddling with the gun, raises it and points it straight at my head. It's not the first time someone's done that to me, so I guess he's disappointed when I don't weep, piss myself or beg for mercy. 'You should. Police know I'm looking for you. I go missing, you're the first person they're going to come calling on. And not your friendly local bobbies either. Not the ones you pay to look the other way. It'll be the untouchables who come and turn your farm over. Be interesting to see what they find there.'

A flicker of uncertainty clouds Johns' eyes. Either that, or the batteries are running low on Greasy Rat's torch.

'You're bluffing.' Johns takes a step forward and presses the barrel into my forehead. The metal is cold, and I swear I can smell the gun oil. It reminds me of Harston Magna, my grandfather showing Ben how to properly clean a shotgun. It hits me then that I'll never see my brother again. Will my family find out what happened to me, or will my disappearance be a mystery that haunts them for the rest of their days? I blink, my eyes suddenly wet. Not at my impending death but for those who'll mourn me. I close my eyes slowly, so as not to let the tears show, and a strange calm settles over me as I wait for the trigger pull.

'No. She's not.'

I snap my eyes open again as another voice speaks from further away. I sense more than see the shuffling as someone pushes through to the front. 'Put that gun down, Alwyn, before you hurt yourself.'

Johns doesn't immediately comply, but this close to the business end I can see his finger move from the trigger. He turns away from me, and for an instant I wonder if I could wrestle the gun off him. And then what? I've had some basic firearms training, but the main lesson I learned from that was never to get anywhere near a gun.

'Do as I say! Damn you, boy!' My unlikely saviour steps into the light from Greasy Rat's faltering head torch, and I know instantly who he is. Alwyn Kieran Johns clearly takes after his father, Tegwin. The old man is a little shorter and less broad than his son, but he has that same cruel face, lined and leathery from years of working outdoors and close to the sea. He stares at me with eyes like black pits, and his posture oozes contempt. For me, for his son. For the entire world.

'Karl and Hefin found her snooping,' Alwyn says by way of explanation, raising his free hand up towards the clifftops.

'I'm not stupid, boy. And I'm not deaf. I know where she came from and what she was doing.' Tegwin turns to face me now. 'Who do you report to? You're not Dyfed Powys. Certainly not fisheries. Must be National Crime Agency then. Fucking Feds.'

He hawks and spits onto the shingle, points to the men who

found me. 'You two. Bring her. And mind you don't put a mark on her.'

I'm still alive, that's the important thing. That's why I do as I'm told, following the older man as Greasy Rat waves his gun at me. I need an opportunity to escape, but so far nothing has presented itself.

We enter a cave that narrows until there's only space for one of us at a time. If I didn't know better, I'd think it was a dead end, but after a few metres it opens up again into a much larger cavern, part natural, part hewn by pickaxe and muscle. It's lit by permanent electric bulkhead lamps, and the ground is laid with concrete, its rough surface sloping towards the seaward end in what looks like a loading ramp. I can hear the lapping waves echoing up ahead in the darkness. There must be another entrance to the cave, accessible at low tide.

Before I can get much of a look at anything, I'm bundled across the way. A short tunnel leads into another cavern, drier than the last. This must be a temporary holding area, given the haphazard piles of boxes and crates. Shiny film-wrapped bundles are almost certainly drugs. It's a shame I'm being taken at gunpoint to somewhere I doubt I'll ever leave, as it seems I've inadvertently stumbled upon the very thing Operation Cantre'r Gwaelod has been trying to uncover. Bloody typical.

I've a reasonable sense of direction out in the open, but it's hard to keep hold of as I'm marched along seemingly endless narrow tunnels. There are bulkhead lamps fixed to the wall at intervals, looping cable stretching between them and occasionally clipped to the stone. Unlike in the cavern, they're not switched on here. I can only see by the soft illumination from the head torches, but I think we're going north and inland. Well, obviously inland or we'd be in the sea, but north I'm fairly sure.

The darkness plays havoc with my sense of time, too, and

how long we have been walking for. It soon becomes apparent that this tunnel is part of a larger network. We pass several junctions before we finally emerge into another cavern, and then out into fresh night air. I'm impressed with Tegwin's fitness. For a man his age, he seems to have no problem with the climb, or with negotiating the tumble of rocks in a small coomb that masks the entrance to the cavern. I guess he's been doing this all his life and knows the place like the back of his hand, which makes me wonder how long these tunnels have been here, and how they've been kept a secret all that while. I can't dwell too much on such questions as he's setting quite a pace, and only stops when I go over on my ankle and let out a sharp cry of pain.

'Nobody will hear you. We're too far away, and besides anyone living close knows better than to pry. Shame you don't have that same sense of self-preservation now, isn't it?'

He gives me hardly any time to protest that I wasn't trying to raise the alarm and am actually in some considerable pain before he sets off again. Hefin's gun in my back forces me on, but I can't help limping as I go.

The dell is only a few metres in from the clifftop, I discover as I reach its edge. We're in a field of sheep, an old dry stone wall marking the boundary. Tegwin climbs over it with ease, and I'm suddenly very afraid. I know what's coming, and frankly the bullet would have been preferable. Hefin must have sensed my hesitation, as he grips my arm. Before I can do anything, Greasy Rat has grabbed me on the other side. Together, they force me over the wall and onto the path that runs between it and cliffs.

'My family have been smuggling on this coast for generations.' Tegwin stands too close to the edge for comfort, but far enough away from me that I can't use that to my advantage.

'We've had our ups and downs, over the years, see? But we've never been outwitted by the excisemen. And certainly not by some woman.' The way he spits out the last word almost makes me laugh. Of course he's a male chauvinist prick. Why wouldn't he be?

'Now, Alwyn. He's not the brightest lad. Hard working, true. And he'll not shirk from getting his hands dirty, if necessary. But see, now. If he'd shot you in that pretty little face of yours, we'd have had to be very careful disposing of your body. And people would come looking for you, too. You had the right of it there.'

Off in the distance, I can see a dull glow lighting the underside of the clouds. Aberystwyth, if I'm not much mistaken. Is that where I'll end up?

'But you like to go walking at night, I see. Out along the clifftops to watch the stars. These paths are so very dangerous, mind. Especially when the rain's been on. Isn't that so, lads?'

I struggle now, but the two men have a tight hold on me. And then Hefin kicks my ankle, right where I just sprained it. The pain is sudden and overpowering. My body failing me just when I need it most.

'Terrible tragedy,' Tegwin says as he leans out and peers down. Somehow, I know this is one of the highest points along this part of the coast. 'Tripped and fell to her death.'

And without another word, they fling me into the night.

20

Everything hurts.

My head pounds like I've been on a weekend hen do with my sister-in-law Charlotte's celebrity crowd. The impossibly dry mouth and throat that feels like one of those cracked, empty riverbeds you see in programmes about climate change suggest maybe too much whisky and karaoke. But neither of those help explain the fact that I can hardly move. I try, of course, but every tiny twitch of muscle brings its own bright star of pain, and I have absolutely no strength at all.

What the hell happened?

I try to gather my thoughts, but they're elusive, fragmented. I don't remember karaoke, but I do remember the sea. Darkness. A cliff. A man screaming in terror as he plunged to his death. A man?

I open one eye, just a slit, and gaze up at a fairly standard institutional ceiling tile. Moving my eyeball enough to look further around takes too much effort, and the light hurts too, so I close it again.

'Urgh.'

It isn't the word I want to say, but it's about all I can manage. My neck is stiff, but warm, and as I concentrate on that I begin to sense my surroundings. I'm in a bed, my neck's in a brace, there are quiet machine noises, the smell of disinfectant, a tannoy message too far away to hear the words. A hospital.

'Hey. You awake?'

I know that voice, try to raise my head to see the person who has spoken, regret it instantly. Moments later, I sense a shadow above me, crack open my eye again and see a familiar face, half smiling, half deeply concerned.

'K?' I can just about manage that, although it might sound like I'm trying to impersonate some small bird.

'You are awake. That's brilliant, Con. Stay there, I'll fetch a nurse.'

I close my eye again, wondering at the beautiful idiocy of Karen's words. It's not as if I'm going to get up and walk out while she's gone. It's possible I might have fallen asleep for a moment, because she's back very quickly, accompanied by the promised nurse.

'You're awake then. That's good,' is about all she says as she fusses about checking my vitals and the drip plugged into my arm. Finally she finds the control to raise the bed so that I'm sitting a little more upright, and then offers me small sips from a plastic cup of water. I say water, but it's more like some kind of magic potion as far as I'm concerned. It not only helps with the sore dryness of my throat and mouth, but gives me strength enough to clear my thoughts a little more. There are so many questions I want to ask. 'Where am I?' is the one that makes it out first.

'Hospital,' Karen says, as if the nurse and the bed and all the other paraphernalia around me weren't a clue. Something in my expression must convey my irritation more eloquently than words, as she quickly elaborates. 'Bron . . . Brongle Ice? You know, in Aberystwyth?'

It doesn't hurt quite so much to move my head now, and when I look past Karen towards the window I can see the roofs of houses and beyond them the sea. The nurse looks pointedly at her watch, then speaks to Karen in a voice that brooks no argument.

'Five minutes. No more. I'll go and let Doctor Cairns know

the patient is awake.' And without another word she leaves the room.

An awkward silence stretches after her departure until I realise it's eating into my allotted time.

'How . . . get here.' My voice croaks like I've been smoking sixty unfiltered Gauloises a day since turning twelve.

'Couple of walkers found you washed up on the beach near your cottage. You were pretty battered and bruised, Con. What happened to you?'

The beach? Washed up? That doesn't make sense. On the other hand, it's painfully clear I've had a blow to the head, so maybe it was all hallucinations.

'Don't . . . remember . . . much.' I flex my hand, lift my arm weakly and point to the cup of water. As I do so, I'm hit by a flash of memory. Darkness. Flailing. Scrabbling at something. Falling. The rifle shot crack of breaking bone as an arm smashes into rock. This arm. That was real. That happened. And yet as I roll my head slowly over to look at both my arms, I can see no damage to either. I strain to lift my head and peer down the bed, but my legs are hidden away under hospital blankets. I can feel them though, and wiggling my toes hurts like hell. How am I not broken into tiny pieces?

'Here. Let me sit you up a bit more and you can try for yourself.' Karen operates the bed again, a noisy electric motor whirring away as I'm raised into a more upright position. I'm so weak I can scarcely hold the cup, let alone lift it to my lips, so she helps me with that too. Bless her. The water's sweet and soothing and once again brings me much needed energy. Still not enough to keep my head upright, so I let it flop back into the pillows.

'I should probably let Diane know you're awake.' Karen puts the cup down and pulls out her phone, then pauses, no doubt wondering whether it's OK to use one in this ward. No, not ward. I'm in a room of my own. 'You mind if I pop out to make this?'

'Not going to run off.' I manage a smile, which seems to relax Karen a little. She's on edge about something and I've a niggling worry I might know what. 'K?' I ask, before she can leave the room. She stops, nods.

'Yeah?'

'Thanks. For coming, for watching over me, you know.'

She shrugs. 'Boss's orders. She's been chewing up the furniture ever since you were found. Be nice to have her calm down a bit.'

I know there's more to it than that, but her words more or less confirm my suspicions, too. 'How long?'

Karen's face drops as if she's doing a death knock, and I feel a bit bad for pressing her on the matter.

'You were unconscious when they found you on the beach. Doctor told me she didn't think you'd make it a day, you were that cold. Guess you're made of tougher stuff than the rest of us, eh?'

'How long, K?' I try to make the question sound more urgent this time, but frankly it's an effort to get any sound out at all. Karen doesn't answer immediately, which in a way is all I need to know.

'They found you first thing, two days after we met at the Botanic Gardens, but it took a bit longer to get an ID. You . . . you weren't wearing anything when they found you. Wasn't until someone mentioned your red hair and the landlady at the pub heard about it. Put two and two together. Your friend, Lord Caernant, confirmed who you were, told your aunt and she called us. We'd been trying to contact you for a couple of days by then, but you were already in here, hooked up to every machine they've got.'

'You're babbling, K. I'm fine. Well. I'll be OK. Just tell me how long I've been here.'

Karen bites her lip in a manner that might be cute if I wasn't so exhausted. If my head didn't hurt so much. If the random, disconnected fragments of weird, horrifying memory didn't keep throwing themselves at me. Finally, she makes up her mind and tells me what I both do and don't want to know.

'It's been a little over two weeks, Con. You've been unconscious for fifteen days.'

Diane Shepherd appears early the next morning. I don't know what they're giving me through my IV drip, but it dulls the pain enough for me to rest. Unfortunately, it also scrambles my brain a bit, which isn't all that helpful given how fractured my memories already are.

'You look like you've been in a car crash,' is the first thing Shepherd says, which is about par for the course with her. No 'Hello, Con – how are you?' or any other niceties.

'I feel like I've been in a car crash. Or maybe gone ten rounds in the ring with . . .' I stop speaking when it occurs to me I can't remember the names of any boxers. Shepherd doesn't comment.

'We need to know what happened. Establish a timeline of events. I understand you went to speak to Dai and Ellen Young at Twmp Farm, asking about one of their neighbours. Where did you go after that?'

I look around the room to try and cover up the fact that my brain is moving particularly slowly. It's a nice room, away from the bustle of most of the hospital. Karen's stepped outside, and the door's closed. Just me and the boss.

'I . . . I went home. To the cottage.' I do my best to replay the scene in my head, all too aware that there are sizeable chunks missing. 'I had supper, did a bit of work, then went to bed.'

Shepherd nods as if checking my account off against something she already knows. 'So how do you think you ended up on the beach a little more than twenty-four hours later?'

'I don't . . . What?' My sluggish mind catches up. 'Twenty-four hours? I thought I was found the next morning.'

Shepherd shakes her head. If she's not careful it'll fall off at this rate. 'No. We met you on the Wednesday at the Botanics. I was expecting a call back on the Thursday, didn't push it until the Friday because we all know you're not the most reliable when it comes to answering your phone?'

'I was found on Friday morning, then.' I have no idea what day of the week it is now.

'Half past five. A couple from the caravan park out walking their dog. Bloody lucky they found you when they did. Another hour and you'd likely have been dead.'

I stare at the ceiling tiles for a moment. Something about Shepherd's words rings untrue. I wouldn't have been dead because I'd already died. But that makes no sense.

'Did you maybe go for a night walk along the cliffs again?' Shepherd asks, and there's another question unspoken behind that one.

'What do you . . . ?'

'I know you were having bad dreams. Worse than that. Night terrors and panic attacks, wasn't it?' And now I detect a softening in Shepherd's voice, a genuine concern. She's ex-military, she understands about PTSD better than most. That's why she's been so accommodating this past year, giving me the time and space to heal. 'You should have told me it wasn't getting any better, Con. We could have arranged for more therapy.'

Because the first lot went swimmingly. 'I didn't try to kill myself, if that's what everyone's thinking.'

'But you were walking the clifftops at night. That path's dangerous enough in the daytime, especially if it's been raining.'

Knowing Shepherd, she's walked it already. Probably forced poor old DS Latham to keep up with her the whole way from Twmp to Aber in the teeth of a howling gale.

150

'What's so funny?' she asks, and I realise I've let an idiot grin slip onto my face at the thought. Damn, I used to be better at hiding that sort of thing.

'Nothing. Just that you've got it all wrong. I didn't jump and I didn't fall. I was pushed.'

It takes a while to tell the story. Partly because I can't seem to get it all in the right order, partly because my throat is still as raw and dry as salted cod. I have to pause every so often to sip water and gather my thoughts, which is a bit like trying to eat jelly with your fingers. I'm exhausted by the time I get to the point where I'm thrown off the cliff, and the memories are getting more and more disjointed. There's something important happened then, but I can't think past the moment I realised what they were doing. I let my eyes close for a moment in a vain attempt to see into the past. Shepherd says nothing, or maybe I fall asleep. The light doesn't seem much changed when a sudden thought wakes me again.

'Greasy Rat.'

'I beg your pardon?'

'Greasy Rat.' I flail around for a name. 'One of the two men who jumped me outside the pub. Peterson, that's it. Karl Peterson.'

'What about him?' Shepherd asks.

'He was there. Had a gun.' There's something else, but still the memory's too slippery to grasp. 'He was there, and so was the other one, Slaphead. Only he stayed behind in the caves, I think. And the old man, Johns.' I can't stop the shudder from running through me as I see his face in my mind, but nothing else, as if that horrible visage has burned itself onto the back of my eyes. An image of my murderer preserved forever, as those old Victorian detectives believed.

Shepherd takes out her phone and taps at the screen, either oblivious to or unconcerned about the danger it might pose to the sensitive hospital machinery. She gives it one final tap then slips the handset back into her jacket pocket. 'I'll have someone bring Peterson in for questioning, Kendall too. That really should have been done as soon as you turned up on the beach.' She shakes her head in obvious irritation. 'Maybe I'll get some of our own officers on to shaking them down a bit, not leave it to the local boys.'

'And Johns?'

'Yes, Johns . . .' Shepherd stares at the wall behind me, as if the answer to her conundrum might be written there. Then she dismisses whatever thought she was having with a minimal shake of the head, stands up and carefully places her chair back under the window where it came from. I want to ask her what she means by her words, but I'm too weary, my head too full of conflicting memories.

'You need to rest, Con. You've had a brush with death and a nasty blow to the head. It's going to take time for it all to come back to you. Maybe some of it never will.'

'Are you going to—?' I start to ask, then can't think of which question is most important. There are so many it's overwhelming.

'Don't worry about that. We've got it all in hand now. Karen will be staying in town for the foreseeable future. Reckon I'll probably be here more than I'd care, too. We'll keep you up to speed with any developments.'

If I wasn't so tired I might have argued the point, but as it is I can hardly keep my eyes open any more. She's right, too. There's nothing I can do except rest and hopefully get better. Work on proving her wrong about my missing memories. I look up, intending to thank her and wish her good luck, but I must have fallen asleep again without noticing, as she's nowhere to be seen.

21

It's another four days before they'll let me out of the hospital, by which time I'm just about climbing the walls. Or at least I would be if I wasn't so damned tired and weak. Karen seems to have appointed herself my liaison, keeping most of my unwanted visitors, such as the local police, away. She lets Aunt Felicity in though, and the three of us spend a happy afternoon chatting. Well, they spend a happy afternoon chatting and I drift off to sleep.

You'd think that would be a welcome thing. I'm well looked after by NHS Wales, nursed slowly back to some semblance of strength with nothing I need to do other than stare out the window towards the sea, eat the tiny amounts of food I can manage, and sleep. Despite everything my fractured memories tell me, I have no broken bones. Even my skull shows little sign of the blow that must have rendered me unconscious for so long. There's only the constant, dragging exhaustion, and a weakness that makes visits to the bathroom feel like climbing a mountain. At least when I'm awake I'm not troubled by nightmares as my memories try to reassemble themselves. Ironic, really, considering it was bad dreams and panic attacks that got me into this mess in the first place.

Leaving the hospital feels strange. I try my best to thank

everyone who's looked after me, but I'm still as weak as American tea, so Karen arranges for a car to pick me up at the front. What she doesn't tell me is that the car is an ancient Rolls Royce, driven by Lord Caernant himself. I'm surprised that neither Gareth nor Amy have come to visit me, but as his lordship tells me at least half a dozen times on the trip back to Plas Caernant, he hasn't stayed healthy all his life by going anywhere near hospitals. I suspect there's a little more to it than that, but I don't press the matter.

I'd thought I'd go back to the cottage, even if I've not really got the strength or stamina to live at the top of that hill right now. The doctors say I'll make a full recovery, in time. If I behave myself. I'm doing my best, but it's not easy. Aunt Felicity suggested I go back to Harston Magna and convalesce under her care. There's an undeniable logic to that, but I'm not done with Aberystwyth yet and I don't believe it's done with me, either.

'We've put you in the same room as before, dear,' Amy says as I step into the kitchen, Karen following me with a couple of bags. 'Thought that would be easiest. As long as you can manage with the stairs?'

'Stairs are fine. Thank you, Amy. But you didn't need to go to all this trouble. I'm sure I'd be fine up—'

'I won't hear of it. Now's not the time for you to be alone.'

I'm about to protest that I wouldn't be alone, since Karen's been my shadow pretty much ever since I woke up in a hospital bed, but the words spark a thought that I need time to follow, so I say nothing. I'm saved from any further awkwardness by the arrival of Gelert, the deerhound. Unlike everyone else, he doesn't treat me any differently from the last time I was in this kitchen, shoving his huge head into my crotch with that innocent overfamiliarity all dogs have. I give the ruff of his neck a good scratch, and he shows his appreciation with a groan of ecstasy followed by a loud fart. Wagging his tail with obvious pride only serves to waft the aroma around the kitchen, but as everyone else covers their noses and makes noises of complaint, I'm transfixed by another strange fragment of memory. Or is it hallucination?

I'm lying half-paralysed on a beach somewhere, cold and broken. The sand is rough under my cheek, salt water stinging in my eyes. Breathing hurts, but I can't feel anything below my waist. Only a rhythmic push and tug as waves lap at me. One arm is twisted underneath me, broken so badly even thinking about moving it is agony. The other, miraculously unscathed, reaches up past my head. I flex my fingers, dig my hand into the beach and try to haul myself up, out of the water. Even in this flashback, the anguish is vivid as I fail. The understanding settles over me. I didn't die in the fall from the cliff, but now the cold and the sea will claim me.

And then this old grey muzzle is in my face. Licking away the salt, pulling me from danger, lending me his warmth while he howls for rescue to come. I stare into his calm, clouded eyes, and the look he gives me is all innocence even as he thumps his tail on the floor again. I think he rescued me, but that can't have actually happened. Can it?

'How about some tea?' Amy's question shatters the moment. When I look up, she's already putting the kettle on the hotplate. Having walked from the car, through the house to where I'm standing now, a sit down feels like a very good idea, so I pull out a chair and settle myself.

'We were so worried when you went missing,' Amy says as she fetches teapot and mugs. 'What with that poor young girl and everything.'

'Lila? Has she been found?' Another image flowers in my mind. I'm surrounded by darkness, men wearing head torches that blind me. But when one turns, his light plays on a group a little way off, Lila among them. Bruised. Terrified.

'No, no. It's just the way she disappeared. And she was such a poor little thing. I do hope she's all right.'

I have my doubts, but keep them to myself in front of Lord and Lady Caernant. It's only once we've had our tea, and Karen's helped me up to the room, that I have a chance to quiz her.

'Kieran Johns. Has anyone spoken to him? Have we searched the farm? I think he found Lila, or one of his men did and took her back to him. She was there, K. I saw her.'

Karen's eyes widen at my outburst, but she has the presence of mind to first check the landing outside, then close the bedroom door firmly before replying.

'First, Con, you need to slow down a bit, right?' She puts my bag on the end of the bed and then leads me to the ancient armchair by the window. The burst of energy that got me this far has fizzled out as quickly as it came on. Mentally, the surge of clarity has fogged over too, as happens a lot right now. I wish I could say the lucid times were lasting longer than the befuddlement, but I'm too addled to be sure. Christ, it's so frustrating not being able to hold a thought for more than a few moments.

'OK. Here's the situation.' Karen pulls the rather-less-comfortable chair out from in front of the dressing table, twirls it around and sits so close that out knees almost touch. 'Cantre'r Gwaelod's a bust. The operation's been closed down.'

I open my mouth to say something, then close it again without comment. Mostly, I'm surprised at how easily Karen says Cantre'r Gwaelod, when she struggles with Bronglais and Aberystwyth.

'It's not your fault,' she says, mistaking my inability to form coherent sentences for either outrage or embarrassment. 'Truth is, it was always going to be a difficult one. When you had your . . . accident?' She looks unsure of herself. 'Whatever it was . . . that kind of put the nail in the coffin for Diane. Don't think she's completely given up, but the team's working on a couple of things that have been given higher priority.'

'What's this got to do with Lila?' I ask.

'It's more what it's got to do with Kieran Johns. Both of them. They've got no form, Con. Nothing on the system apart from a couple of speeding tickets. The old man's what they call a pillar of the community, right? He's got connections.'

'But . . .' I can see that horrible, evil face in my mind. The utter lack of anything resembling a soul.

'We searched the farm, anyway.' Karen's voice breaks through, and I see the worry on her face. For a moment, I think she's going to reach out and take both my hands, but she stops herself.

'You . . . You did?'

'Well, not me. A team went in the day after we found you on the beach. Given what you'd already told us about the younger Johns, we had to follow that up.'

'And what did they find?' I ask the question even though I know the answer already.

'Nothing, Con. They found nothing at all.'

Karen stays in Lila's room. K's offer to go back to whatever soulless hotel she's been staying in before sounds half-hearted after Amy insists. Of course, she already knows more about Plas Caernant than I do, thanks to Karen's mysterious ex, with the thing for Celtic mythology and Grail legends. At some point in the afternoon, while I was fast asleep with Gelert keeping watch at the end of my bed, she cadged a lift up to the cottage from Gareth, and brought my old Volvo down, along with a rather better selection of clothes than the hospital had to offer.

Supper in the kitchen is a quiet affair, perhaps in deference to my fragile state. I can't manage much to eat, and I'm steering well clear of alcohol. Even after spending much of the day asleep, I'm struggling to stay awake as I listen to Karen and Gareth prattling on about Merlin, Bran the Blessed and other names that spark glimpses of memories. As they talk about sacred springs and magical cauldrons, it's as if I'm in a great cavern deep underground, surrounded by warmth as my broken bones are knitted back together and my torn muscles mended. Did that really happen? Or is it my damaged brain spinning new tales out of the old ones my host is telling. It all seems so real, and at the same time impossible.

'How would you like to see the Holy Grail?'

Gareth's question cuts through the dream state I'd drifted off into as effectively as if someone had poked me with a sharp stick. I'm suddenly hyper-aware, in that horrible way I often am when woken with a start.

Karen's expression is inscrutable. When Gareth looks over at me, I can only muster a weak smile. Amy plays her part, of course.

'Gareth, are you sure?' she asks. I know now that this is a well-rehearsed routine. How did I not see it before? I guess it was my first time, and I'd drunk rather more cocktails and wine than was perhaps wise.

'I would be honoured,' Karen says before the offer can be withdrawn, her gaze flicking nervously in Amy's direction.

'What about you, Con? Feel up to another visit?'

I'd thought that maybe I was too tired, but I realise that I do. 'It would be lovely to see it again. Yes.'

And so we follow the same route through the oldest part of the house, down into the basement. Perhaps because this is my second visit, and I'm not quite so much in awe of it, I notice other details as we descend. The lime plaster and whitewash on the walls give way to stone at the bottom of the steps, bringing another flash of memory. Glancing up, I expect to see bulkhead lights and looping cables, but the short passage to the chapel doors has only a couple of ceiling-mounted bare light bulbs. They cast shadow patterns on the rough-hewn rock that look like entrances to other tunnels. Only, as I walk past, these melt away to reveal nothing more than the uneven surface where ancient miners have chipped away the rock.

Karen's gasp of astonishment drags my attention back to the chapel, where Gareth has opened the doors and turned on the lights. It's a delight to see her so amazed, although it puts me in mind of Lila's reaction and that makes my gut churn. All of a sudden, I have to hurry to the nearest pew and sit down. Maybe coming here was a mistake.

'I think you and I both know it's not the real Grail.' Gareth's words echo across the small chapel. When I look up, I see him and Karen by the open cupboard door. 'Even so, you can have a drink from it, if you'd like.'

Karen holds the old wooden bowl as if it's someone's newborn infant. She glances over at me, then carefully hands it back to Gareth.

'No, thank you. I . . . It's OK.'

If Lord Caernant is upset, he doesn't show it. He has that same wistful smile on his face as he carefully wipes the bowl, places it back in its hidey-hole and locks the cupboard. I can't help but notice how his gaze strays over to the font, then comes to rest on me.

'Not so impressive a second time, Con?' he asks as the two of them come to join me and I heave my tired body to its feet.

'Quite the opposite. This chapel is astonishing, and I say that as someone who's never been all that comfortable in churches. I'm just tired, still.'

Gareth nods, his eyes darting once more to the font before he indicates the chapel door. 'It's getting late. Perhaps another time.'

I'm not entirely sure what he means by that, but I'm too tired to puzzle over it for long. We all file out of the chapel, and make our slow way back up to the kitchen. Amy greets us all with a smile that drops a little as she looks past me to where her husband is bringing up the rear.

'You look all done in, dear,' she says to me. 'Perhaps you should get some rest.'

Once again, the clock says it's later than I'd thought, and I am dog-tired so it's not hard to persuade me. I thank everyone for their kindness, then head for the door that leads to the back stairs. As I pass the Aga, Gelert gets up and pads along behind me.

My shadow.

'I should probably turn in, too,' I hear Karen say, and she follows me and the dog. As I turn to open my bedroom door, her phone rings. She stares at the screen for a moment before answering. I don't get much of the conversation hearing only her side, but by the way she looks at me, I can tell that it's something to do with my situation. I wait until she's hung up, even though I can hear the siren call of my oh-so-comfortable bed.

'Your old mate, Sergeant Griffiths.' Karen slides her phone into her pocket as she approaches. 'Seems they've found a body washed up on the beach that matches the description of one Karl Peterson.'

A flash of images arc across my mind at the name. A face, astonishment and terror writ large. My hands gripped tight around the sleeve of an old, denim jacket. How is that even possible? I snap out of it, a jolt of energy making me stand straight and pull the half open door closed.

'We should—'

'Get some sleep, Con. We should get some sleep. There'll be a post-mortem tomorrow morning. You can help with the identification then.'

22

I hadn't thought I'd be back at Bronglais Hospital so soon. Karen drives me in my old Volvo, moaning all the while about how horrible it is. I'm not a good passenger at the best of times, but I'm also not in any fit state to drive yet, although I am feeling a lot stronger than yesterday, when I felt stronger than the day before. Slow progress is better than no progress, as my aunt would tell me.

The hospital mortuary is much like any number of places I've visited in the course of my career; there's only so many ways you can store a dead body, after all. The young assistant who greets us tells me his name is Edgar, but doesn't offer a surname. Or maybe that is his surname. It doesn't appear he's been told about my condition, as he leads us along shiny corridors, jabbering away in such highly accented English it might as well be Welsh for all I can understand. At least he uses the service lift, rather than forcing me to test myself on the stairs.

When we reach the examination theatre, Mr Edgar asks us to wait. I think he says he's going to fetch the boss, but there's no time to ask him to repeat himself before he's bustled off again. I'm a little too out of breath for questions, anyway.

'He seems nice,' Karen says, her tone just about neutral enough for me to consider whether or not she's being sarcastic.

I don't reply, partly because I'm having to breathe too deeply for easy speech, and partly because there's a single examination table in the middle of the room and it's occupied. Whoever's laid out there is covered with a white sheet, but that's never stopped me before. I assume it's the body we've come to see anyway, and convalescence has made me impatient.

'Shall we?' I cross the room to the table, wishing I'd taken up Gareth's offer of a walking stick. Nothing hurts, particularly, it's just that any movement tires me to the point of needing to sit down or lean on something. And it feels a little disrespectful to slouch against the examination table.

'Shouldn't we wait?' Karen asks, even as she follows me. In answer, I pull the top corner of the sheet away. Beside me, Karen lets out a little gasp of surprise, her hand flying to her mouth. I hope she's not going to be sick, but I'm too preoccupied with my own flood of memories.

The man on the table is the same person I last saw at the top of the cliff, even if weeks in the water at the mercy of fish have left his nose little more than gristle and turned his beady eyes into ragged holes. Something clicks in my brain at the sight of him, and another piece of the puzzle falls into place.

They fling me bodily from the cliff top, Greasy Rat and the one called Hefin. But I don't just go meekly to my death, do I. Not a chance. I scratch and grab, and get a hold of Greasy Rat's sleeve that I'm never going to let go. We teeter there for horrible seconds, his weight perfectly counterbalancing mine. And then the old man, Tegwin Kieran Johns, looms out of the darkness into the yellow circle cast by Hefin's head torch.

'Useless bastard.' His words are flat, cold, completely lacking in any kind of emotion as he shoves Greasy Rat hard in the back.

Sends both of us flying to our deaths.

'Couldn't wait, eh?'

I snap back to the present with a little yelp of surprise. Partly at the dreadful realisation of what happened, partly at the unexpected voice. A short, middle-aged woman in a white coat approaches us from the door.

'Sorry. He was just lying there. Mr Edgar left us.' As though that's any explanation for peeking at cadavers.

'Ed's heart is in the right place. He can be a bit brusque though.' The woman extends a strong, callused hand to shake. 'Sally Harcourt.' She nods at each of us, in turn. 'I'm the pathologist.' Her glance comes to rest on me. 'You must be the famous Constance Fairchild.'

I opt for a half smile.

'So, you've come to see our drowned man,' Harcourt says, once I've introduced her to Karen. 'The sea can be cruel to a body, can it not?'

She strides around the examination table, then rolls the covering sheet back to reveal the rest of Karl Peterson in all his battered glory.

'You've already examined him, I see.' I point to the Y incision across his mottled chest, neatly stitched up now, presumably by the absent Edgar.

'This morning, yes. Not that I can tell a great deal from what's left of him. The sea doesn't leave much in the way of forensic evidence.'

'You called him "our drowned man",' Karen says. 'Is that an accurate description of his cause of death?'

Harcourt looks at Karen for a moment, then turns to me. 'I like her. Perceptive.' She shifts her focus back to Karen again. 'No, Detective Constable. He didn't drown. Or at least, I don't think he did. His lungs were full of water, but they were also full of holes where he'd been bashed and mangled on the rocks. The sea washed him pretty clean, as you can see. But the damage to his head and neck are what most likely killed him. And I'd stake my reputation on them happening before he went into the water.

163

Likewise, the major fractures to his arms and left leg. He looks very much like someone who's—'

I'm falling into the darkness, one hand still gripping tight to Greasy Rat's sleeve. His momentum takes him out and over my head in a wide arc, so that when we reach the first outcrop on the way down, he hits first and cushions the blow of my impact.

'Fallen off a cliff.' My interruption brings the slightest of furrows to Harcourt's brow, but it disappears almost instantly.

'Exactly so. How did you guess?'

'Two things, really. First, there's a long stretch of coastline here with paths along dangerous cliffs. It's all too easy to lose your footing if you go too close to the edge.'

'And second?'

'I was there with him when it happened.'

The silence that follows my words is almost total, before it's broken by the clatter of doors being bashed open by a gurney. Edgar, the assistant, stops when he sees us all standing around the examination table.

'You . . . were there?' Dr Harcourt asks. Beside me, Karen reaches out and places a hand on my arm. I'm staring down at Karl Peterson's broken body, but at Karen's touch I get another flash of memory. I close my eyes, seeing the whole thing play out again in excruciating slow motion.

'He went head-first. The rock must have caved in the back of his skull. Snapped his head forward into his chest so quickly it would have broken his neck.' I feel the wind being driven out of me as I smash into his chest and the two of us bounce off the rocks, back into the void.

'That's not a bad description of his head and neck wounds, actually,' I hear Dr Harcourt say, but her voice is distant, far removed. I'm out over the sea, tumbling, Peterson's dead body running ahead of me as we both plunge to our doom. Is that how I survived? His life paid to save mine? It seems kind of poetic justice, given how he was the one throwing me off the top in the first place.

It feels a bit pathetic, but by the time we've finished talking to Dr Harcourt and taken the service lift back to the ground floor of the hospital, I'm so knackered I need a sit down.

'Want to get a coffee?' I ask Karen, nodding my head in the direction of the small reception area and the uninspiring vending machine tucked away in the corner. I wouldn't normally even consider spending more time in a hospital than was absolutely necessary, but Karen seems to understand the situation.

'Sure. Grab a seat and I'll see what I can find.' She points me to a small round table with a couple of plastic chairs. They look uncomfortable as hell, but my legs are so tired from standing in the cold mortuary they're actually trembling. A numb bum is better than an ungainly and embarrassing collapse. The car's parked down the hill too, and that's a steep slope to negotiate at the best of times.

'There you go. Doesn't look much, but it tastes OK.' Karen puts a cardboard cup down on the table in front of me before pulling out the other chair.

'So, that's definitely your man Peterson down there on the slab?' She takes a sip of her coffee. I sniff mine, surprised at how good it smells. A shame Karen didn't bring any biscuits.

'It's him. And yeah, I know he didn't have much in the way of identifying features left, but the clothes he still had on when they fished him off the beach are the same I saw him wearing that night. Same jacket he had on when he attacked me outside the pub, too.'

'Odd that he didn't have any ID on him, don't you think?'

I sit back, shuffling to try and find some way of easing the pressure points. 'Not really. He and his mate were out on the clifftops in the dead of night making sure nobody stumbled onto what was happening down below. You wouldn't go on an undercover assignment with your warrant card in your wallet, would you?'

'Point taken.' Karen seems to remember something. For a moment, I think it might be a relevant piece of information, but she shoves her hands into her jacket pockets and pulls out two plastic-wrapped packages. 'Almost forgot. Chocolate or blueberry?'

I'd have preferred biscuits, but I'm not going to turn down any food in my current state, especially not something as sugar and fat rich as a chocolate muffin. For a while we eat in silence. I'm busy licking my fingers and dabbing at the wrapper when Karen speaks again.

'Seeing him down there? Peterson.' She tilts her head slightly in the direction of the basement mortuary. 'Did that bring back more memories, then?'

I lick the last of the chocolate from my finger and wipe it on a paper napkin. 'It's odd. I get flashes, but they're all jumbled up. I see things that don't make sense.'

'How do you mean?'

'Well, when I saw Peterson, for instance. I remembered falling, how he hit the rock first, cushioned me a bit, I guess.' Reflexively, I reach for my left arm with my right hand, touch my bicep under my jacket. 'But I also have a very vivid image of my arm shattering, and then I was in the air again.'

'But your arm's fine. You only had bruises, no breaks.'

I shrug. 'Yeah, I know. And that's what my brain's been telling me, all along. But Peterson was there. Him and another man. Think his name was Hefin.'

'Heaven?'

'Hefin. H E F I N. They pronounce a single F as a V in Welsh. It's not an uncommon name around here.' I shake my head. 'It's not important. What is important is that Peterson and Hefin threw me off the cliff.'

'Why?'

'Because that way it would look like an accident, K. It worked too, didn't it? Everyone thinks I either threw myself off in despair or I was so wrapped up in dark thoughts that I didn't notice how close I'd got to the edge.'

Karen looks a little uncomfortable at the suggestion, which makes my point for me.

'I was out wandering the clifftop path in the dark, it's true. But I had my head torch with me, and I was mostly sitting on a bench and staring out to sea.' As I talk, more memories slide into my head. Karen stops looking at me like a sympathy case and starts to take more notice when I tell her about the boat and the people being offloaded and led into the caves.

'It's like a warren down there. They must have led me past a dozen different junctions. Christ, folk have been smuggling goods along this coastline for as long as there's been taxes. They're still at it only what they're bringing in has changed.'

Karen pulls out her phone, then appears to notice the 'No Mobiles' poster drawn by a small child and blu-tacked to a nearby pillar. 'We need to speak to Diane. Get someone in to help you reconstruct your memories.' She shoves the phone away and stands up. 'And we need to go back and search those cliffs again. Properly, this time.'

I agree, although as I push myself laboriously up from my chair, I realise it'll be a while before I'm in any fit state to act as a guide. 'Back to the car, then.'

Karen offers me an arm to lean on, then changes her mind. 'Why don't you stay here? I'll bring the car to the front. Nobody'll complain if I'm only parked a minute. If they do? Well, I'm not undercover – so I've got my warrant card. Should see off any local traffic wardens, right?'

I nod once, although I'm not sure, and settle back into my chair. Karen gives me a cheerful 'back in a jiffy' and disappears.

My coffee cup is empty. I sit and stare at the few other people in the waiting area for a moment, then shove my hand into my pocket, instinctively reaching for my phone. Except that it's gone, of course, along with the clothes I was wearing that fateful night. Strange that the sea left Karl Peterson his jacket, T-shirt, trousers and underpants even after they'd been together three weeks, but it ripped off all my clothes in a day.

I hear the front door swish open again, start to stand, expecting to see Karen waving for me to hurry up before she gets me a ticket. What I see instead turns my blood as cold as the sea.

Three familiar men have entered the hospital together.

It's only because they've headed straight to the reception desk that they've not clocked me.

As quickly as I can, I duck back behind a fake pot plant. There's a copy of the *Cambrian Times* on a nearby bench, so I snatch it up and open it wide. I don't see what's printed on the pages – I'm too busy watching the three men, the oldest of whom is leaning close to have a word with one of the receptionists. The other two have turned around, one looking at the door with a bored expression on his face, the other staring at his fingernails. I'd recognise them both anyway.

Hefin, who threw me off the cliff. Alwyn Kieran Johns, who pressed a loaded gun to my forehead. And the older man with them, the one in charge, who coldly planned it so my death would raise no suspicions. As if it's something he's done many times before. Who thought nothing of sending Karl Peterson over the cliff with me, just because he was holding things up.

Alwyn's father.

Tegwin.

23

Karen finds me ten minutes later, hiding in the toilet. I'm not entirely sure how I got there.

When did I turn into such a gibbering wreck? I was never in any danger from those three men. Not really, not here in a busy hospital. Having them see me still alive might have even worked in our favour, panicked them into doing something stupid. And yet the instant I saw the old man, I was paralysed with fear.

I'm still shaking, wobbly on my feet and needing Karen's support to make it from the toilets and out to the waiting car. As predicted, there's a traffic warden eyeing it suspiciously when we arrive, but a quick flash of warrant card and quicker explanation elicits sympathy from the woman. As I buckle my seatbelt, she wanders off to rebalance the scales.

'Stick to the left lane, or you'll get trapped,' are the first words I utter once we've left the hospital behind. The terror that gripped me has subsided now.

'What was that about, Con?' Karen asks as she negotiates the one-way system.

'I don't know, K. I just froze. The moment I saw him. Tegwin Johns. All I could see was that same look on his face when he pushed Karl Peterson off the cliff and me with him.'

169

'Jesus.' Karen shakes her head. 'What do you think he was doing there? At the hospital, I mean?'

I'd not really given it much thought, but then my brain hadn't been working properly so that's hardly surprising. My mind scrolls back. 'He was talking to the receptionist about something. I'd guess it was Karl, if anything. Can't imagine why he'd have his son and another heavy with him otherwise.'

Karen drums her fingers on the steering wheel as we wait at a red light, and I know she has something she needs to say.

'Spit it out, K. You'll upset me more if I hear it from someone else first.'

'That transparent?' She looks at me briefly before the light changes to green and we're off again – escaping the town. 'Thing is, Con. We've already looked into Peterson's background. He's Tegwin Johns' nephew. Works on the farm sometimes, but mostly on the lobster boats. And here's the thing. He was reported lost at sea a week back.' She glances at me. 'Accident on a boat called *Anwen's Favour*.'

I take a moment to digest this information, or more accurately to process the implications. 'So, you're saying that you don't believe he was pushed off the cliff? K, you saw his injuries. You don't get that from going overboard in rough weather.'

'Just the messenger, Con. I don't know what to believe, if I'm being honest. My gut instinct tells me that what you're saying is true. You're not one for making up elaborate stories. Christ, you don't need to given what's happened to you in the last couple of years. But the more we look for evidence to corroborate what you've told us, the less we find.'

I open my mouth to protest, then let out a long weary sigh. I don't have the energy for this fight right now. Don't know if I ever will.

'Something happened that night,' Karen says, after we've covered a few more silent miles. 'Don't matter what anyone else says, there's no way Con Bloody Fairchild jumped off a cliff or even walked into the sea. But the team's . . . well. We're getting nowhere, you know? And the boss wants to cut our losses.'

That gets my attention. 'They're closing down the investigation?'

'They can't find anything, Con. Not the tunnels, not the hidden cove. Everyone's got solid alibis for the night you went missing, even Peterson back there.' Karen tilts her head to indicate the hospital. 'Local police reckon they've wasted enough man hours already, and you know how hard it is to work without them.'

I stare at the road for a while, try to rub the tiredness from my eyes. Nothing makes sense any more. I think of Lila and the promise I made to get her to safety. Not much chance of me keeping that now, and that realisation brings me more pain than any injury, imagined, miraculously healed or otherwise. I've failed her, and it was my own stupid fault.

'Guess there's not much point my staying here in Wales, then.' The words are out before my brain has processed the idea properly. Karen's quick glance at me suggests they've struck a chord though.

'That was the other thing Diane wanted me to talk to you about. Nice of her to leave me all the easy assignments, right?'

'Are you really sure it's such a good idea, Con? What with you in your current condition?'

The kitchen at Plas Caernant has become something of a second home these past few days, Gareth and Amy surrogate parents. As if I was some small child rather than a thirty-three-year-old woman. The four of us are sitting around the table, and I can't help getting a Last Supper vibe from the way my hosts are treating me. Gareth, in particular, seems adamant that I should ignore Diane Shepherd's summons back to London and stay here in Wales. It's tempting, but also impossible.

'You make it sound like I'm pregnant,' I say. When Gareth's face reddens I quickly add 'And I can assure you, there's no chance of that.' Which only makes things worse.

'But London? Will you be OK?' Amy makes it sound like the capital is as inhospitable as the moon.

'I'll be fine, really. And I have to go back, at least for a while.' Not least because I've an Operation Cantre'r Gwaelod debriefing scheduled for next week and Shepherd wants the whole team there. I don't think I'm so important they would come to me.

'Should you be going back to work?' Gareth asks, genuine concern on his face. 'What does the doctor say?'

I haven't seen a doctor since I was discharged from the hospital, but the advice then was at least a month of rest.

'I'm not going back to work. Not technically. Just a few meetings, going over my experiences. There's a specialist I'm going to work with to help try and recover my lost memories, too. I can't do that here. Not really.'

'Well, I can't say as I am all that happy about it. You were unconscious for a fortnight, almost died. Can't they give you a little more time? Surely rest is what you need, and your memories will come back on their own.'

I shrug an answer at Gareth; there's not much else I can do. He offers me some wine to go with the plate of stew I've barely been able to make a dent in, but I place my hand over my wine glass. I might not be pregnant, but my current condition doesn't feel like it would be helped much by alcohol.

'Perhaps some water, then.' He doesn't wait for an answer, reaching for a jug. I take a sip, enjoying the clear, refreshing, almost sweet flavour of it. London's chalky, hard water will be an unpleasant reminder of what I've left behind, although I'd never contemplate drinking that without boiling it and steeping a tea bag in it first.

'You'll be keeping an eye on her, Karen?' Amy's accent puts the emphasis on the first syllable, making the name sound much nicer than when spoken by an East Ender. I see Karen's shoulders stiffen at the question, but she recovers her composure swiftly enough.

'I'm sure Con's capable of looking after herself. But of course, I'll be around to help out if she needs it. As will the rest of the team. We look after our own.'

I smile at her uncertainly as she says this, not sure how much of it is true and how much of it is to put Gareth and Amy's minds at ease. They've done so much for me, and taken Karen into their home with as little fuss as they did Lila. True, it's easy enough to be hospitable when you've a mansion and the income from a large estate, but not everyone in their position would be so genuinely kind. It's another thing I'm going to miss about this place. I take a drink to hide the tears that have started to well up. When did you get so sentimental, Con?

The stew has lost all its appeal, even though I know Amy will be offended not to see me clear my plate. At least Gelert won't go hungry tonight.

'I'm very sorry, Amy. I did my best,' I say as I place my knife and fork to the side of the plate. Glancing up at the old grandfather clock by the door, I see that it's almost an acceptable hour to retire. I'm dog tired, but then I've been dog tired all day.

'I think I'll turn in. It's going to be a long day tomorrow, early start.'

Karen has finished her plate, and pushes back her chair.

'I should probably get some kip, too. Con's old Volvo's not the easiest bus to drive.'

It takes a while to say our thank yous and farewells, even though we'll go through the whole rigmarole again in the morning. Perhaps unsurprisingly, Gelert follows me up the stairs and nudges open the door to my bedroom, turning a couple of times before flumping down onto the threadbare rug at the end of the bed.

'He's not coming with us,' Karen says, with just enough of an inflection at the end that it could be taken as a question. I'd laugh if I wasn't so tired.

'You've seen the size of my flat, K. Where would I put him?'

'Good point. Well. Get some sleep, OK? I want to be gone sharp in the morning.'

'Yes boss.' I wave her a weary salute, then step into the room. Most of my belongings are in the car already, only my rucksack on the chair with a change of clothes in it. Gelert thumps his tail on the floor a couple of times, but doesn't move as I sit down on the bed to wait for the click of the bathroom door that means Karen's finished in there. Somehow the sit becomes a lie, and before I know it, I'm away.

24

Having woken at dawn, still fully clothed and lying on top of the covers, I fall asleep in the car somewhere near Carmarthen and miss most of the journey back to London. It's probably for the best; crossing the Severn Bridge, seeing the sign for England after all these months, might be too much for my fragile mental state. Karen lets me sleep, and while my elderly Volvo isn't as comfortable as the bed at Plas Caernant, the rest does me no harm at all. If I dream of anything, it's unmemorable, disappearing the instant I rise into groggy wakefulness somewhere between Reading and Heathrow.

'Back with us, are you?' Karen stifles a yawn with the back of her hand. Has she stopped anywhere en route? Surely the car must have needed filling up, at least. I glance at the dials in front of her and see the tell-tale red warning light that means we're going to stutter to a halt soon.

'Sorry. Must have nodded off.' I flex my shoulders and hips as best as I can in the seat, shuffle my bottom around and then realise I need a wee. 'You want to pull into the next services. We'll need to fill up before chancing London traffic.'

Karen nods, and soon enough we're pulling off the motor-way into a scene far busier than anything I've encountered in a while. Not many masks on the people milling about outside, but then I guess they've been rolling out the vaccine for a few months now and everyone thinks it's not necessary any more. Except me. I cope with the surprisingly hostile looks as I wear mine while filling up the car, and then all the way to the toilet and back, but by the time I slump into the passenger seat again I'm exhausted.

'Everyone seems so . . . unfriendly?' I say as Karen pilots us back into the traffic. She laughs, then stops herself.

'You've been away from the city too long, Con. Forgotten what it's like.' She takes one hand off the steering wheel and points at her face. 'A lot of folk see the mask as a personal attack. Like you saying you're better than them, looking down on 'em. Idiots.'

I hear the bitterness in her voice and not for the first time reckon I caught a very lucky break escaping the city when I did. Even if I'd headed north to Newmore or stayed with my aunt in Harston Magna it would have been easier than life in London during lockdown. I knew it had been hard work for the team; Karen's regular emails and the occasional phone call kept me up to speed on that. But there's a big difference between hearing about something and experiencing it first-hand. Maybe it's not so surprising Billy Latham hates me so much. I'm surprised the rest of them don't too.

We talk about inconsequential things, skirting around the events of the past few weeks as Karen negotiates the busy streets to my flat. It takes a long time to find anywhere to park, yet another little reminder that I'm not in Ceredigion any more. The climb to my front door wears me out far more than it should. Seems living on the third floor of an ex-Council concrete lump wasn't such a good idea after all. Karen dumps my bags in the hall as I do a quick check of the rooms. Nothing has changed since I left – save for a thin layer of dust on everything.

'You want a cup of tea?' I ask, before it occurs to me I probably don't have any teabags, certainly don't have any milk. The fridge stands silent in the kitchen, its door propped open to avoid a repetition of the last disaster. Looks like my first task will be a trip to the corner store for essentials.

'Nah, I'm good.' Karen stretches one arm behind her neck, then the other one. She's been driving for hours while I've slept.

'Probably got a bottle of wine in a cupboard somewhere if you want something stronger? You deserve it after today.'

That gets me a smile. 'Careful, Con. I might get the wrong idea.' She shakes her head. 'But no, thanks. I need to be going. Someone I've arranged to meet.'

'Let me guess. Your ex with the detailed knowledge of the Grail mysteries isn't quite as ex as you made out?'

The normally self-assured demeanour momentarily disappears and she stares down at her hands. I've never seen Karen anything less than completely in control of herself before.

'I said I'd tell her what I saw at the hall. Nothing more. It's not often people like me get to mix it with the toffs. Not that Gareth and Amy acted much like toffs.'

'Gareth and Amy, is it?' I see that I've laid it on a bit thick with the sarcasm. For a moment, I'd forgotten Karen comes from the East End, that her dad drives buses for a living and her mum cleans offices. Or, at least, she did until most of them closed when everyone started working from home. 'They're good people, K. And you are too. I don't know how to even begin thanking you for everything.'

'Hey. You'd have done the same for me. But I've gotta run, OK?' Karen looks like she's thinking of giving me a hug, and I could really do with one right now. Then she changes her mind. 'I'll check in tomorrow. Let you know what's going on. Rest up, Con.'

And without another word, she's gone.

★ ★ ★

177

The flat doesn't feel like my home any more. I wander between kitchen, living room and bedroom, the walls closing in on me as the noise of the city rumbles all around. I used to love that sound. It meant I'd made it. Escaped the narrow-minded country bumpkin idiocy of my upbringing and reached the place where streets were paved with gold. Only they weren't, really. Mostly, they were paved with misery and discarded chewing gum. A rush of people too busy trying to make a living, or even just stay alive, to stop and look around them. I threw myself into that life with all the gusto of a true believer. I could make a difference. I could make it better.

Well, that didn't exactly pan out now, did it?

I've switched the fridge back on and closed the door, but there's still nothing in it to chill except the ancient bottle of white wine I find in a cupboard. It's not been opened, so it should taste fine once it's cold enough, although since my little brush with death I've found one glass does as much damage as a whole bottle used to. If I'm going to drink anything tonight, I'll need coffee in the morning, and probably toast. That means three flights of stairs and a couple of hundred metres walk to the corner shop, then the whole route done in reverse. A month ago, I wouldn't have thought twice about it. Wouldn't have thought at all. Now, it takes me half an hour to gather my strength before I head for the front door. How long will I be this weak? When will I recover enough to even contemplate going back to work? And do I want to go back to that work at all?

Nobody accosts me on the epic journey to the corner shop, not even to say hello. I'm torn between buying all the stuff I might need come the morning and exactly how much I can contemplate carrying up the stairs to my flat. The best compromise I can manage is some teabags, a pint of milk, a plastic loaf and some butter. Mr Patel takes a long time to recognise me when I present my goods at the till, which is hardly surprising given the mask covering the bottom half of my face and the long hair obscuring the rest. Karen and Amy have both mentioned how thin I look, too.

'Detective Constable. You are back with us?' It's a statement and a question both, as is often Mr Patel's way. I shrug, not sure I've got the energy to enter into much of a conversation, particularly with a Perspex screen in between us.

'Just got in this afternoon,' is about all I can manage. Mr Patel takes the hint, packaging up my purchases in a bag for me even though I don't ask for one. I thank him, then shuffle out of the shop. It's a relief to slip the mask off, my breathing is so ragged, and as I stare up into the night sky towards the third floor of the concrete housing block, I can't help wondering if coming back to London hasn't been a big mistake.

I'm almost at the bottom of the steps when a voice sounds out behind me.

'And did you think you could sneak back home without coming to see me? It's been months, and not even a postcard.'

That last quip is a lie. I sent several, and tired though I am, there's no way I can't go and speak to my neighbour. Mrs Feltham has been a friend, an ally, a guardian angel even. She makes a mean goat curry, and the best coffee I have ever tasted.

'Hey, Mrs F. I've hardly been back an hour. I was going to pop in later, honest.' As I speak, I watch something like horror creep across her face. She was standing in her open front doorway, but before I've even finished she's crossed the distance between us, grabbed both my forearms in her massive hands. The shopping bag swings uselessly from where I looped its handle round my wrist to avoid dropping it.

'Con, child. What you been doing to yourself?' Her gaze darts back and forth, taking in my face, my hair. She steps back without letting go, the better to see how frail I have become, I guess.

'It's a long story. I wouldn't want to bore you with it.'

'Nonsense, child.' Mrs Feltham finally lets go of my arms. The weight of the bag takes me by surprise and I almost drop it to the ground. The effort of catching it before the milk bottle bursts against the concrete drives an impolite 'oof' out of my mouth that makes me sound like a pensioner.

'I'm sorry, Mrs F. I'm really tired. I was hoping to get an early night, maybe feel a bit more human in the morning. I'm off work at the moment, so I could drop in tomorrow?'

She looks at me with that suspicious narrowing of the eyes I've not seen in far too long, then reaches out and slips the bag off my wrist, taking my hand in her massive paw. 'You can drop in now, sure. You need feeding up, girl. And a cup of my special brew will help you with those stairs later.'

There's no point in arguing with Mrs Feltham, I know that better than most. And the three flights of stairs to my flat might as well be a mountain. I allow myself to be led into the ground floor flat and through into the kitchen. The warmth is like sinking into a bath, only one that smells of Jamaican spices. Something is bubbling away on the stove in a pot large enough to feed an army.

'Sit down before you fall down, girl.' Mrs F places my shopping carefully on the kitchen table, pulls out a chair and guides me into it. I'm reminded of the last time she nursed me, after I'd escaped the clutches of the mad pastor, Reverend Masters. I was exhausted and injured then, but that was nothing compared to how I feel now.

'Here you go. Drink this. It'll give you a bit of strength for now.' A mug has appeared on the table in front of me, and Mrs F pours thick black coffee into it from an ancient metal pot. I know I should steer well clear of caffeine this late in the day, especially something as potent as this. But the smell wafting up to my nose is so delicious I can't help myself from lifting the mug closer for a better sniff, and then I can't help myself from drinking.

It's not quite like somebody switching on a light in a darkened room, but it's not far off. The taste makes me realise how badly I've been abusing myself these past months, drinking what passes for coffee in Aberystwyth. But more than that, the warmth flows through me in slow waves, lifting the weight of tiredness and the fog in my head. Another sip, and I can feel the tightness across my chest ease. I'd not thought my breathing particularly laboured until now, but it must have been.

'Better?'

I look up and see Mrs Feltham standing at the corner of the table. She still has the coffee pot in her hands and is watching me carefully. She reminds me of Rose, up in Edinburgh. Another strange guardian angel.

'I don't know what you put in this, Mrs F, but it certainly hits the spot.' I raise my mug in salute, and before I can tell her not to, she's topped it up. Mrs Feltham's boys, who I suspect may well be her grandchildren rather than children, are well known in local circles for their weed. I've tended to turn a blind eye, mostly because they keep the nastier gang activities away. Their insatiable appetite for Mrs F's curries means I get fed far better than if I was doing the cooking myself, too. It occurs to me, as I sip more of the incredible coffee, that there might be a little bit more than a proprietary blend of robusta and arabica beans in this cup. But if it makes me feel this good, I'm not going to complain.

'That's a better colour I'm seeing in your cheeks now, child.' Mrs F puts the pot on the back of the cooker, stirs the big saucepan, then comes to sit at the table with me. She takes my hand, rolls up my sleeve gently and inspects the arm I can't help imagining broken. No, it's not imagination, dammit. It was broken. I felt it break. But as she runs those massive fingers over my skin more expertly than any doctor, I can see no evidence whatsoever. Feel only the ghost of an ache almost lost behind my total exhaustion.

'That's a powerful healing,' she says as she rolls my sleeve back down again and gives me back my arm. 'You don't have to tell me what happened to you. I can see it clear enough. You've been on a long journey, child. And one not many people ever come back from.'

'It's only Wales, Mrs F. Not the far side of the moon.'

Mrs Feltham smiles at my joke. I smile at it too; it's the first time I've felt like making one in weeks.

25

They've organised a ride across town to meet with the team for my debriefing, which is just as well since I really couldn't face public transport at the moment. I sit in the back of the squad car like royalty, or maybe a recently nicked thief, and I can't think of anything to say to the driver as we pass slowly through London's usual traffic snarl. It's not until we cross Vauxhall Bridge that I realise we're heading towards NCA headquarters, rather than my old police station. I'm relieved more than concerned, in no rush at all to return to my place of work.

I'm given a temporary pass, like any other civilian, and escorted through to a small conference room with a clear view of the building across the narrow street and not much else. Two men are seated at the table when I enter, but only one of them gets up. Detective Chief Inspector Bain has aged in the months since I last saw him, what's left of his hair leans more heavily into the salt now, much less pepper. His eyes widen in surprise when he sees me.

'Good god, Fairchild. They told me you'd been in the wars, but I'd no idea.'

Given that the last time I spoke at any length with the DCI he was tearing me off a strip for getting involved in something that was none of my business, his concern is touching. He quickly pulls out a chair and makes a big show of helping me sit, as though I'm his prom date. Which, you know, is awkward.

'It's nothing, really,' I say. I can hear the weakness in my voice though, so he will too. Across the other side of the table, DS Latham looks up only briefly, but it's long enough for me to see the sneer on his face. I'm not sure he's capable of any other expression any more. Maybe he sneered as a child and the wind changed, making it permanent. Whatever his reasons, it's more tiresome than annoying now.

'Oh, hey Con. You're here already.' Karen enters the room, all business-like in a dark suit. I notice that Latham doesn't even bother raising his head this time. I start to stand, but DCI Bain puts a hand on my shoulder, gently but firmly keeping me in place. Time was I'd have broken at least two of his fingers for that.

'You stay there. Diane will be here any moment. Let's get you a coffee, and then we can make a start, eh?'

Bain draws the line at fetching me coffee himself, of course. That job falls to Karen. There's a plate of biscuits too, which is a step up from my old station. The NCA clearly has a better budget.

'Everyone's here? Good.' Diane Shepherd enters the room before I've even had a chance to sneak a biscuit off the plate. Latham immediately springs to his feet and fetches her a coffee.

'How are you feeling, Constance?' Shepherd turns her attention to me first, which must annoy Latham considerably.

'Tired, weak. But on the mend. Thank you.'

'And your memories of that night?'

'Coming back. Slowly, fragments in the main. Sometimes an experience will trigger another image, but it's still a bit of a jumble. I know I didn't accidentally fall off the cliff, and I certainly didn't jump. They threw me off one of the higher points along the path, so you'd all think it was an accident. Or maybe suicide. That way, nobody would look harder into what's been going on there.'

'And what exactly has been going on there?' DS Latham still doesn't look at me when he speaks. The effort he puts into disliking me is exhausting.

'Everything that Operation Cantre'r Gwaelod was looking for. They're using the old smugglers tunnels and caves to bring in hard drugs and people. At a guess, I'd say sex trafficking and slavery, not illegal immigrants. But it could be both. Easy enough to take a desperate immigrant's money on the promise of getting them across the water, then trap them into indentured service once they're here, right?'

Latham's sneer hitches up a notch. 'Nice little story. Only problem is, we've had teams walk that whole stretch of coastline. There's nothing to indicate any of what you suggest. No tunnels, just a lot of shallow caves and a few long-abandoned stone jetties. Face it, Fairchild. You've made the whole thing up to try and save face. Just like you always do.'

'I . . . What?'

'What Billy's trying to say . . .' Bain interrupts, 'is that we can't find any evidence to corroborate your story.' He keeps his tone level, but I can hear the accusation in his voice.

'Why would I make it up?' I can see the answer forming on Latham's lips, but I cut him off. 'And what about Peterson? You think he was just a figment of my imagination, too?'

'Karl Peterson was reported lost at sea two days before he was washed up on Aberystwyth beach. Tragic accident involving a lobster boat, apparently.' Bain doesn't even have to look it up, which puts me on my guard even more than Latham's expected hostility. What's going on here?

'So I was told. The *Anwen's Favour*, sailing out of Fishguard.' I try to gather my thoughts, knocked off balance by the way this meeting seems to have turned into some kind of inquisition.

'Convenient, isn't it? A boat belonging to Erinka Fisheries. Weren't they on your radar for Operation Cantre'r Gwaelod?'

'The *Anwen's Favour* is privately owned. Sells to whatever buyer it can find.' Bain pauses a moment, considering his words. 'We spoke to the captain about the incident. Poor bugger got his leg caught on a rope, went over and down with the lobster pots. They hauled it up soon as they saw what had happened, but Peterson was gone.'

'You saw his body, right?' With a look of disbelief, I glance from Bain to Latham, and finally at Karen. Her expression is one of quiet horror, which makes me think she didn't know what was going to happen here. She doesn't say anything, and while I can't blame her it's not exactly helpful.

'I read the post mortem report.' Latham opens up a folder that's been sitting on the table in front of him since I arrived. '"Death by drowning, injuries consistent with being thrown against rocks by the rough seas we had prior to his body being washed up on the shore."' He slaps the folder closed again with more force than necessary.

'That's . . . Who carried out the examination?'

'Not relevant, Fairchild. We've all seen the wild fantasies you come up with to justify your actions. It happened with DI Copperthwaite's death, and again with the Reverend Masters. You'll do anything to stay in the limelight. Don't care who gets hurt. Not Detective Sergeant Dan Penny. Not even your own mother.'

My heart's hammering like it's trying to break out of my ribcage, anger mixed with confusion as I try to stand. I'm ready to go around the table and rip Latham a new one, but I get my arse maybe six inches off the seat before my head starts to spin. My legs give up, dropping me back into the chair.

'I think that was uncalled for, William,' Bain says. Through my dimmed vision, I can see Shepherd watching the scene unfold with narrowed eyes. She hasn't said anything since asking me how I was. If she really cared, wouldn't she have intervened by now?

'Just laying it out how I see it, boss.' Latham is all smiles for the DCI. 'DC Fairchild has been on extended paid convalescent leave for months now while we've had to carry the can. Soon as she gets a sniff of an interesting case, she charges in like a bull in a china shop and fucks everything up. Again.'

My head's cleared enough now to see what Latham's doing. What bothers me is that Shepherd and Bain seem happy for him to do it, and he's well prepared too. Time to go off script, I guess. It's not as if I'm in any fit state to come back to work, anyway.

'It's quite clear I'm not needed here, since DS Latham knows everything already.' I stand more slowly this time, giving my traitorous legs time to work properly. Nobody stops me, although I can see by the panic in Karen's eyes that she wants to help. I'd like to think my exit is sufficiently melodramatic, but in truth I probably look like an old woman as I don't so much stride as shuffle to the door. Before I leave, I turn back into the room.

'I'll write up a report for you by the end of the day, Ma'am.' I look at Shepherd. 'You can do with it as you please. My suggestion would be to roll it up into a tube and shove it up Billy Latham's arse.'

I stumble down to reception and hand in my visitor's badge. If I had my warrant card with me, I'd probably turn that in, too. I know Billy Latham hates me, and I've accepted that he'll never change. But I'd not expected that level of scrutiny from DCI Bain, or the way Diane Shepherd sat back and watched it all unfold. Only Karen seemed to have any sympathy. And since she's the newest member of the team, it's not like she could say anything.

On the plus side, it appears that anger restores my strength.

I'm raging so much that when I leave the NCA headquarters I almost contemplate walking the whole way home. Fury gets me halfway down the road before a black Mercedes slows beside me and winds down its rear passenger window.

'Get in, Constance. Before you give yourself a heart attack.'

Diane Shepherd's face is as inscrutable as ever, but I'm more concerned with who might be her chauffeur. A quick crouch and I can just make out the back of a man's head. He's wearing a uniform though, so not DS Latham. Reluctantly, I climb in.

'You did well back there,' Shepherd says as the car pulls smoothly into the traffic and heads towards the bridge.

'I wasn't expecting the Spanish Inquisition.'

'Nobody . . . Oh, never mind.' Shepherd allows a little smile to crease around her eyes as she almost falls into the trap I set for her. 'I'm sorry. That was brutal, but it was necessary.'

'Necessary? They think I'm suicidal. Surprised you haven't had me sectioned and thrown in a loony bin.'

'Believe me, it crossed my mind when I had a team searching through the barns at Penparc Uchaf Farm.'

In my surprise, I almost don't notice Shepherd's near flawless pronunciation of the Welsh. 'I heard you sent a team in. Why did nobody tell me?'

'You're on medical leave, Constance. Why would we? You're not involved. More than that, there's all manner of complicated reasons why you can't be involved.'

That doesn't ring true at all, but there are more important things to consider than Shepherd's games right now. 'So, you really didn't find anything at the farm, then?'

'Oh, we found lots of things. A thousand or so cows, state of the art milking parlour, tractors and other machinery worth the best part of a million quid. A couple of lagoons filled with slurry, ongoing construction of an anaerobic digester that'll supply gas to Aberystwyth once it's finished. All the signs of a thriving business that's been in the same family for so many generations there's probably a mention of them in the Mabinogion.'

'But no signs of drug smuggling or people trafficking.'

'None whatsoever. And as Billy said back there, we've walked the coastline between your cottage and the farm and nobody's found any evidence of anything more suspicious than a couple of shallow caves, a few washed up fish boxes and the odd dead seal. There are local legends about smugglers' tunnels and the like, but they're just that. Legends.' Shepherd turns to face me. 'So, you can understand how we're beginning to wonder if our main witness might be a little unreliable. That's why Billy got to play bad cop, so I could see how you reacted. Can't say he didn't enjoy it maybe a little too much. Until your suggestion at the end.'

I lean back and stare at the roof of the car, all the tiredness dragging me down under the waves. 'I'm not making any of it up. It's not some cry for attention. I didn't even know about your precious Operation Cantre'r Gwaelod until you turned up at the cottage unannounced that day.'

'The attention-seeking? That's Billy's take on it, not mine. I know you don't crave the limelight. But I also know you're battling demons, Con. I've seen more than my fair share of good soldiers laid low. What they've had to do to survive.'

'I'm not a soldier.' Even I can hear the petulance in my voice, the thinness of the excuse.

'You'd have made a good one.' Shepherd tilts her head, silent for a few seconds. 'Apart from the whole not following orders thing.'

'It's not PTSD. I'm fine. Was fine until . . .' I can't bring myself to have this conversation right now.

'I've a doctor friend who'd tell you the worst person to make that kind of diagnosis is the patient. You might talk to your old friend, Captain Fortescue, too. He's been through the wars, after all. Quite literally.'

'Charlie?' My mind goes back to my brother's wedding, the best man turning out to be not the annoying teenage public school boy I remembered, but a much more interesting prospect altogether. We'd even met up for a drink a few days later, but that was as far as it had gone. A missed opportunity, perhaps.

'He's back in the UK for the foreseeable future. You should give him a call. Or I could ask him to get in touch with you himself. Can't imagine he'd need much prompting.'

Tempting though it is, I shake my head. 'I don't—'

'Need any help? Yes, I know. I've heard it far too many times before. Usually, the next I hear is that the individual has been found dead on a park bench under a sheet of cardboard, or that they've driven the family car into a wall at speed. Or they've taken off all their clothes and walked into the sea.'

I can't think of anything to say to that. It's all too obvious where this is going, and I really don't like the direction.

'You're a good detective, Constance. Despite your lack of respect for the rules, maybe because of it. You see the world differently to the way most people do, and that's a valuable talent. That, and your pig-headed stubbornness are why I wanted you on my team.'

Wanted. Past tense. Here we go.

'You've been away for a long time now. I know the pandemic played havoc with everything, but you were supposed to be getting help, remember? That was part of the deal.'

I want to ask what deal she means, but I can't. I've been lying to myself about it for so long, I don't really know what's the truth anymore. But I do know that Shepherd only agreed to my extended leave if I agreed to seeing someone about my panic attacks. And I did, too. Three sessions of asking me how I felt, and then an email from my therapist telling me he'd given up doing that work. And of course he'd recommended another therapist, but I'd taken it as a sign, hadn't I. Christ I can be a stubborn idiot sometimes.

'So, that's it. Therapy or I lose my job?'

Shepherd shakes her head. 'No. Therapy and when the therapist gives you the OK, we'll consider what part you might be able to play within the team.'

I guess that was to be expected. In truth, I'm lucky to have stayed on the payroll as long as I have. I might have single-handedly taken down a group of corrupt detectives in the Met, unmasked one of the country's wealthiest men as a paedophile and uncovered a religious cult that mutilated and killed with impunity for a decade or more, but I've also been off sick for the best part of a year now. And if I'm being honest with myself, I know I need help. I just don't like asking for it.

'This doctor friend of yours. Will he be able to get me back to my old self?'

A wry smile spreads across Shepherd's face as she leans back in her seat. 'She'll do her best. The rest is up to you.'

26

The doorbell wakes me with a start, and it takes me a moment to work out where I am. I must have fallen asleep in my armchair, and judging by the untouched mug of cold tea on the occasional table beside me, almost as soon as I sat down.

'Coming,' I yell as I haul my weary body out of the chair and shuffle to the hall. This time, I remember to check the spy hole before opening the door. Outside, lit by streetlamps and rain, is Karen. Standing a little behind her, another young woman looks at the other flats around us, and then finally back to me. She's a head taller than Karen, pale as a vampire, and with long black hair that tumbles down over her shoulders from under a purple woollen hat. She peers at me through thick-rimmed spectacles, her expression as inscrutable as any I've seen in a police station interview room.

'Hi, Con. Peace offering?' Karen holds out the boxes she's carrying and I catch the scent of freshly baked pizza. I could hug her, but instead I step aside to let her in.

'Hope you don't mind us dropping round. I tried to phone but it just kept going to voicemail.' Karen moves past me, the young woman taking a moment to realise she's meant to follow. I've seen my little sister Izzy behave the same way, and it usually means she's utterly absorbed by whatever it is she's thinking about.

'Phone might have rung. I fell asleep as soon as I got in. This morning's meeting was a bit intense.'

'Yeah . . . about that.' Karen looks at her feet.

'Don't sweat it, K. There wasn't anything you could do, and we all know how Billy feels about me. Come on in, and introduce me to your friend, eh?'

'Oh, right. Yeah. This is Aisha.' Karen elbows the young woman, who's been staring at my bent umbrella by the door. She immediately switches her entire focus to me.

'Hey,' she says, but makes no move to offer a hand.

'Would I be right in thinking you're the one who knows all about the Caernant grail?'

That gets me a shy smile. 'You saw it, didn't you?'

'Yes, I did. Look, why don't we all go through to the kitchen?' I lead the two of them, heading straight to the fridge while they pull off their coats and sit down. It occurs to me that I've no idea what time it is, and glance at the microwave's clock. Diane Shepherd dropped me off at a little after midday, and yet somehow it's now almost eight. I guess I must have needed the rest. Opening the fridge, I pull out three bottles of beer.

'You know it's a fake, right? The grail?' Aisha says as she takes her bottle. 'Thanks.'

I'm beginning to see both why Karen likes her and why she's her ex.

'K said. Something about the Victorians making up all the Arthurian myths.'

That gets me a look I've not had since I was studying history at St Berts, a very long time ago.

'Scrape that from Wikipedia, did you?'

'Play nice, Ai. Con's a friend, you know?' Karen reaches across the table and takes the young woman's free hand. From the reaction, maybe I'm being hasty about the ex part of their relationship.

'I'll admit, I'm completely ignorant about the whole thing,' I
say. 'I'd never heard of the Grail until Lord Caernant showed me
his underground chapel. Did K tell you about that?'

'Yeah, she did. Sounds wicked.'

'So, what is the story, then? I assume that's why you asked
Karen to bring you over, right? To tell me what you know and
ask me what I saw?'

Aisha stares at me through her bottle-end spectacles. I've had
two sips of my weak lager and I can already feel it going to my
head. That might have something to do with not eating since
breakfast, but I'm not half the person I was before I went over
the cliff.

'You know that monastery inland a bit from the mansion,
right? Ystrad Ffleur?'

'Strata Florida, yeah. I went there in the summer last. Nice,
if you like ruins. There's some good hill walking around there
too.'

Aisha nods approvingly. 'It's where the last true princes of
Wales are buried. And Dafydd ap Gwilym, the poet. Cistercians
built it in the twelfth century and then Henry the Eighth did for
it a few hundred years later. Your Lord Caernant's grail is
supposed to have been found there, in a cache of relics hidden
away when the place was first ransacked.'

'But it's a fake, you said.'

'Yeah. Shame, really. Dates don't add up for the story. Best
guess is what you saw's just some old cup, belonged to a monk
or something. The earliest stories about it are only from the mid
1800s, so it might not even be that. Just a trinket someone made
to con Victorian tourists.'

'That's . . . disappointing. I mean, I know it couldn't have
been the real Holy Grail or anything, but it would be nice if it
had been something a bit less commercial. The chapel it's kept in
was pretty impressive, even if the goblet is a fake.'

Aisha's entire posture changes as I mention the chapel. She straightens her back, pushes her spectacles up her nose and focuses on me with the intensity of a Labrador when you have a dog biscuit in your hand.

'That's what got me interested. When K told me about the place. I've read everything there is to know about the Grail, and about Plas Caernant too. But there's no mention of this chapel anywhere. It's the first I've ever heard of it.'

'Well, I'd never even heard of the Grail, so you've got one on me there.' I take another swig from my bottle. I need to eat something before I fall over. The pizza boxes are lying on the table unopened, which is just wrong. 'Let's eat. Then I'll try and tell you everything I saw.'

We move to the living room, where the chairs are more comfortable. Karen and Aisha take the sofa, which is so small they've no choice but to sit close together. They're comfortable in each other's company in a way I've not seen for a while. For a moment, I can't think when at all, but then I remember Charlotte and my brother Ben, before they got married, cuddling on a much larger and more expensive sofa and carrying on as if I wasn't there. My afternoon's sleep has done me a power of good. Otherwise, I'd be out for the count by now.

'K told me you had a nasty accident. Fell off the cliffs and nearly drowned.'

I can tell by the way Karen flinches at Aisha's words that she thinks them insensitive. Aisha strikes me as the sort of person who is always unwittingly insensitive. She has an intensity about her, a single-mindedness that doesn't really care what other people think. Once again I'm reminded of Izzy. Should really give my half-sister a call. Perhaps it's that similarity between the two of them that makes it easy for me to talk to Aisha, or maybe I just need to talk. Either way, I find myself telling the whole story as I currently remember it, even though I've only known her a couple of hours.

'Jury's out over the accident part,' I say, and do my best to fill in the details. There are fewer gaps in my memory now, but still the whole thing has a jumbled, second-hand feel to it. As if it's someone else's experience, not my own. If I hoped that speaking it out loud yet again might cement it more firmly in my mind, I'm disappointed. Aisha's eyes grow ever wider in the telling, though.

'And they found you on the beach, almost dead?'

'Apparently, so.' I frown at the thought that I never sought out the couple who rescued me and called the ambulance. I owe them a great deal more than thanks, but that would have been a start. 'And all things considered, I came out of it pretty much unscathed, too. Some nasty aches and bruises, scrapes on my arms and legs. I can't quite understand how I never broke anything.' I hold up my arm, flex my fingers slightly. 'Sometimes I think I did.'

Aisha says nothing to that for a while, although she stares at me with an intensity that's deeply uncomfortable until I realise that she's gone off on a train of thought and forgotten where her gaze is pointing. How on earth did she and Karen meet? They're much the same age, and they both have that East End edge to their accents, so maybe they were at school together. I'm about to ask, but I don't get the chance.

'What if you actually did?' Aisha asks. 'What if you broke bones, got all smashed up on the rocks. What if you actually died?'

'Erm, Ai? Con's here. Alive. She gave you that beer you've probably had too much of, remember?' Karen reaches for Aisha's empty hand.

'I know that, K.' Aisha tugs her hand away. 'But she drank water from the grail just a few days before.'

'I thought you said it was a fake,' I say.

'Oh, it is a fake. But the Grail myths are just a branch of a much older tree. You've read the Mabinogion, right?'

'I know what it is, but I can't say I've actually read any of it.'

Aisha raises her eyebrows in an expression that speaks volumes. Might as well call me an amateur to my face.

'According to who you ask, the grail's the cup Jesus drank from at the last supper, or it's the cup Mary Magdalene used to collect his blood in when he was dead on the cross. Or it's a cup carved from the cross itself.'

'Or it's not a Grail at all but a bloodline. Yeah, we all saw the movie, Ai.' Karen's tone suggests this is a conversation they've had before. Perhaps more than once.

'Nah, that's all made-up stuff for conspiracy theory nutters and comic book geeks. It's fun, but it's not real.'

'Umm . . . Is any of it real?' I ask.

'Well, that depends on what you mean by real, right? But before the Grail there were other magical objects. Stuff given to us mere mortals by the gods, right? The Greek myths are full of it, but the Celts have some interesting ideas too, and they're much closer to home.'

'Hence the Mabinogion?'

'Bingo. I'm thinking about Bran the Blessed and his sister Branwen. Long story short, there's a cauldron in that myth. The Pair Dadeni or cauldron of rebirth. If someone dies and they're chucked in the cauldron, they come out the next day alive.' Aisha pauses, looks at her bottle as if there might be inspiration there, then shakes her head slowly. 'But that wouldn't work, would it? According to the legend, anyone revived by the cauldron loses the power of speech. And far as I can tell, your voice is working just fine.'

Karen looks at me with an expression almost as uncomfortable as the one she gave me in the debrief this morning. I don't really mind, though. Aisha's theories might be batshit, but her intensity is quite refreshing. 'That's just a myth though, isn't it?' I ask. 'Same as the Grail stories and everything else. Handed down over the generations, told around the fireside in the depths of winter. Maybe morality tales, maybe just entertainment. I don't know.'

'Yeah. Guess you're right.' Aisha's expression drops. She takes a swig from the bottle, then stares at me with suddenly renewed excitement. 'It'd be cool though, wouldn't it? Smashed to bits on the rocks, your body washed up on a beach somewhere, hidden by the rising tide. Found by the last descendent of a long line of guardians, tasked with keeping the cauldron safe. He places you in it, not hoping for anything to happen maybe. But it works! You come out healed, the forces of evil defeated.'

I can't think of anything to say to that. Fortunately Karen comes to my rescue. 'Sounds like a great storyline for your next D&D campaign, Ai. You always did have the wildest imagination.'

'Aw, you say the nicest things, K.' Aisha wraps her free arm around Karen's shoulders and pulls her into a tight hug, plants a wet kiss on her cheek.

'We should probably get going.' Karen extracts herself from Aisha's embrace, puts her empty beer bottle on the table as she stands up. 'You're looking better, Con, but I can see you're still flagging after an hour or two of being sociable.'

It isn't until I go to stand up myself that I realise she's telling the truth. The weariness that drags at me like I'm underwater still has nothing to do with beer, although I suspect to my two guests the way I collapse back into the chair looks like it does. I am so tired of being tired all the time.

'See what I mean?' Karen picks up the empty bottles and tidies the pizza boxes. I'm glad to see there's a few slices left, and even more pleased when she leaves them on the table. That's breakfast sorted. Maybe lunch, too.

'I feel pathetic. You have no idea how frustrating it is to be this exhausted after the tiniest of things.' I manage to stand by the time the two of them have gathered their coats.

'I'll keep you up to speed with what's going on at work, OK?' Karen says as she pulls open the front door. Outside, it's raining hard now. A little bit of Wales comes to London.

'Thanks, K. And for the pizza.' I almost give her a hug, but decide against it. Even having the two of them in the flat is probably against all the social distancing guidelines, and the last thing I need in my current state is to get even sicker. 'Lovely to meet you, Aisha.'

'You should read up about Bran the Blessed. And the stories about Llasar Llaes Gyfnewid and his wife. Think you'll find them interesting.'

'Come on you. Leave her alone.' Karen grabs her not-so-ex and pushes her out the door, giving me a cheery wave as they leave. I watch them hurry to the stairs, arm-in-arm and chattering to each other without a care in the world.

27

'I want you to go back to last year, if you can. Tell me, Con. Why did you run away to Wales in the first place?'

I can't make up my mind whether I'm going to like Dr Helen McCullough or not.

I didn't really know what to expect when I agreed to contact Diane Shepherd's recommended therapist, but Dr McCullough is friendly enough. She's young, too. Not much older than me unless she has a portrait of an old crone hidden away in her attic. Her surgery – if that's the right word – is in an old apartment block in Bloomsbury that must have been converted into offices a long time ago, judging by the dividing walls that cut through the delicate ceiling cornices.

I arrived fifteen minutes early for my appointment, having badly overestimated how long it would take a taxi to fight its way across the city, but a smiling and efficient receptionist ushered me straight in. Now, I'm sitting in a comfortable leather chair, cup of coffee in my hands and wondering whether I haven't made a big mistake. At least we're sitting a good distance apart, and the gentle whoosh of air from a ventilation unit by the window suggests she's taking biosecurity seriously. I don't think I'd find it so easy to talk if we were wearing masks, although it might have hidden my defensiveness at the question.

'Run away?'

'Well, that's what you did, isn't it?' Dr McCullough has a notepad balanced on one knee, held in place by the heel of her right hand, expensive pen poised.

'I guess, in a manner of speaking. On the other hand, a place became available at a price I could afford. I only meant to take a month off, but . . .' I wave a hand as though that might explain it all, then remember why I'm here.

'The pandemic upended all of our lives, it's true. But you were still at work when it started. Only took time off when it was in full swing. I believe it was your aunt who persuaded you – found you the cottage. Is that right?'

I don't have a problem with Dr McCullough's directness, but the fact she's been speaking to people about me, when I only agreed to this first therapy session twenty-four hours ago, seems a little unethical. On the other hand, work is paying for it, and given the location I doubt it's coming cheap. Work is the reason I'm in this mess too, so I guess it's only reasonable that she's spoken to my boss. And Diane Shepherd found out about my panic attacks from Aunt Flick. Such is the way the gossip mill works.

'I was having trouble sleeping. Nightmares, you know? I'd wake up in a cold sweat, which is a rubbish description, if you ask me. It's always a warm sweat and it's always horrible. I was tired all the time, irritable. It was affecting my work.'

'So, Diane agreed to letting you have some time off. Compassionate leave, even though it was a few months since your mother's death.'

'Pretty much.'

'And she didn't suggest you see me back then?' Dr McCullough taps her pen a couple of times on the blank page, then seems to notice what she's doing and stops herself. 'Or anyone else?'

'I saw a therapist, but . . .' I pause, trying to find an explanation that doesn't sound pathetic. Failing badly. 'Let's just say it didn't really work out? I thought all I needed was a break. Change of scenery, some time off to rest and recharge the batteries, away from the prying eyes of the press. Only . . .' I shrug.

'Yes, you already said. Covid 19 got in the way. It upended everyone's lives. But was that all that kept you away from London, from your work? The press had pretty much moved on from Posh Cop, hadn't they?'

Five minutes and she's already got the measure of me. I could hate her for it, but that's such a cliche. I've only myself to blame for the mess I'm in. Can't keep on taking it out on everyone who tries to help. I sip my coffee, think, breathe. Where to even start?

'You're right. That wasn't what was keeping me away. Like I said, I was only meant to be there a month. Lockdown stretched that out a bit, but I'd already discovered that I wasn't so much recovering as coping. Have you ever been to Wales, Dr McCullough?'

'Helen, please. And no, not really. Unless you count a mid-week conference at a horrible hotel on the outskirts of Cardiff, which I don't. I did get to see the Senedd though.'

'You're one up on me then. I only ever went past Cardiff on my way in and out.' I lean forward in my seat, committing myself more to the conversation. 'The thing you have to remember about Wales is that it rains there. A lot. Especially on the west coast. I could be stuck in my little cottage for days on end, and it wasn't a problem. I had access to the world through the Internet, plenty of books to read. Even started writing some things down myself, but I don't imagine they'll amount to much. When it wasn't raining, I'd go for long walks, along the clifftop path, over the beach at Llantwmp where they found me, up into the hills. You can wander for miles there, hour after hour without seeing another soul. And all the time I slept well, woke up refreshed. Until the night before I was due to pack up and come home. Back to London.'

'The nightmares returned?'

'Is it a nightmare if you're awake when it happens?'

Finally, Dr McCullough writes something down, although I can't see what it is. 'Sounds a bit like a panic attack to me. Can you describe the symptoms?'

I think back to that first time, standing in my bedroom at the cottage, bag almost packed, a few clothes strewn over the bed. It felt like someone had crept up behind me and wrapped a hand around my neck, squeezing so tight I couldn't breathe, feared my head would burst. All the dead people paraded in front of me, their eyes accusing, wounds horrific mutilations. And then finally my mother, standing silent, eyes closed, head bowed, radiating her condemnation in death as loudly as she ever did in life. As I describe it all to Helen, and I think after revealing my innermost secrets to her, I can call her Helen now, I feel a horrible sense of deja vu. Another chunk of memory falls into the mess of disjointed images and half-remembered details. I don't have time to process it now. Something to enjoy later.

'That sounds very much like a panic attack, yes.' Helen underlines whatever it was she has written. 'Good.'

'Good?' I almost spill the last of my coffee. 'How is that good?'

'The first step towards recovery is acknowledging that you have an illness from which you need to recover.' Helen uncrosses her legs, puts her pen away and closes her notebook, all in one fluid set of motions that is so well practised she must have done it hundreds of times before. 'It's taken you a while to get to that stage, but I think we're there now. Even if it did take a life-threatening trauma to bring it all out.'

'You think I tried to kill myself, don't you.' I'd been starting to like this woman, but now I'm not so sure.

'At this point, Con, I genuinely have no idea. From what I've learned about you, it seems unlikely, but then the mind is a strange and ill-understood thing. My strategy, if you'll agree to further therapy sessions, will be to try and find out what happened. To reawaken the memories you have suppressed, so that you can acknowledge them. Either accept them, or find ways to cope with them. Does that sound fair?'

It's not really as if I have a choice in the matter, if I want to stay employed. And sane. Even so, I can feel the tears threatening to well up, and all I can do is wonder why I never asked for help before. Worse, why I actively pushed it away. Pride is a stupid thing to die for.

'Yes. Thank you, Helen. I think that sounds more than fair.'

I'm feeling so relieved when I step out of Dr McCullough's front door, details of my next appointment neatly written on a small slip of paper, that I set out along the road at my Welsh hills walking pace. Reality comes crushing down before I've reached the end of the street, and by the time I get to the taxi rank at the corner of Bedford Square I'm breathing harder than a marathon runner at the finish line.

'You alright, love?' the driver asks, as I collapse into the seat, my mask not helping things at all. It takes me three attempts to convince him I'm fine, just winded, and to give him the address. I fight the urge to fall asleep as the taxi makes its slow progress through the traffic. The driver, mercifully, doesn't try to engage me in conversation after I've told him where to take me. Either he's worried I might collapse from the effort or he's not the chatty type. There are one or two introverts driving black cabs, I've discovered over the years, but they're few and far between.

It takes me a mile or so, and fifteen minutes, to get my breath back, and even then I can feel my muscles trembling. So much for thinking I was getting better. At least the taxi is new, warm and clean, the seat reasonably comfortable. It's silent, too, and after a while I realise it's one of the new electric ones. The quiet helps me get my thoughts back together.

I'm cautiously optimistic about Dr Helen McCullough. She came highly recommended, for one thing, but she also managed to tread that fine line between being too clinical and overly chummy. Outside of a patient-doctor relationship, I could see us being friends. That puts me a little on edge, of course. A lifetime's conditioning in reserve and being aloof can't be undone so easily. Our next session, the day after tomorrow, should be interesting. Part of me wants all my memories back along with my old life, but another part of me wonders whether I've not shoved them all out of sight for a reason.

In the meantime, there's that nugget of memory to dissect. Another piece of the puzzle, or my brain getting ever more creative? It's hard to tell any more, but talking to Helen about seeing the dead opened something in my mind. I still have a sense of being on a beach somewhere, arm broken, no feeling below my waist and Gelert the deerhound licking my face, lying beside me, howling like a wolf at the moon. Then I'm moving down tunnels hewn in the rock.

My vision is blurred, hard to make out details, but these aren't the same tunnels Tegwin Johns led me down before throwing me to my doom. My sense is that they are older, far older, than that. And I'm not walking, either. I'm being carried.

And then I'm in a cavern, white light refracting and sparkling high overhead like some immense crystal chandelier, so bright it should hurt and yet somehow doesn't. I sense gentle hands ease away my clothes, hear what might be scissors slicing through sea-soaked fabric, but I can feel very little. At least the pain is a dull, second-hand thing. Far away, even as part of me screams in agony, the sound of it echoing off distant stone walls like a long-forgotten memory.

Something is pressed to my lips, cool liquid like the sweetest of nectars dribbling into my mouth. I lack the strength even to swallow, but somehow a little makes its way down my throat. Then I'm lifted once more, and I can feel the wrongness of the way my body hangs from the arms of whoever is carrying me. I am broken utterly, barely alive. Maybe not even that.

The water is warm when I'm lowered into it, like a perfectly drawn bath. Its touch soothes away aches I didn't know I had, and it supports my body so softly, so completely, I feel weightless. Only when I sink below the surface, the liquid oozing over my face and covering my eyes, do I realise what has been bothering me all this while.

I'm not breathing.

With a gasp that is almost a scream, I am back in the here and now. Startled from my dream, I find myself still in the back of the cab, crawling through London's nightmare traffic at a pace even I could manage on foot.

'You OK, love?' The driver looks at me through the rear-view mirror.

'Sorry. Just remembered something. Not important.' I look out through the window, pleased to see that we're almost home now. I'm trying to dredge up more memories, but it's all piecemeal, out of place. Sometimes I'm looking out over the sea on a still, clear night, just barely making out the shape of a boat slipping through the waves. And then the sky is blanketed with cloud, the waves choppy with a stiffening breeze, the chill cutting through my coat. I lost that coat, and my favourite boots. Did someone really cut them from me? How could the sea undress me so completely when it left Greasy Rat with pretty much everything on? Unless I stripped off on the beach and walked into the water like everyone thinks. But then what happened to my clothes? And what happened to the missing day?

'Twenty quid, love.' The taxi driver's words cut through me. We've arrived outside my block of flats. I was so distracted, I never even noticed. With a weary sigh, I tap my card on the reader built into the partition, decline the offer of a receipt, mouth a quiet thanks and climb out. My legs are still shaky as I watch the cab perform a U-turn that would make a Tory politician blush, and head back to the city. Once it's disappeared around the corner, I turn and look up to the walkways stacked one atop the other, rising into the impossible sky. Three flights of concrete stairs. You can do this, Con. At least it's not raining.

By the time I reach the top, I'm ready to pass out. Never mind being bruised and battered by the sea, my legs feel like someone's taken out all my muscles and replaced them with burning rope. I pause a moment, both to catch my breath and to fish out my keys. And that's when I notice a figure lurking by my front door. Well, lurking is maybe overstating it a bit. They're bent over, one hand to my letterbox, pushing the flap open so they can peer inside. Normally, I wouldn't think twice about rushing them, putting them in an arm lock and then asking them exactly what they think they're doing. But these aren't normal circumstances, and I'd struggle to put an infant in an arm lock right now, let alone hold it.

'Can I help you?' I ask from a considerable distance, in case my visitor startles. I'm quite prepared to let them go if it means I can get inside and sit down. The figure stands up, hands tucking into their sides. Then I see who it is, and relax a little, although my confusion still remains.

'Aisha?'

Karen's ex shrugs, then waits as I walk slowly towards her.

'Sorry about just dropping by. I'd have called but . . . I don't have your number.'

'Could you not have asked Karen? Sure she'd have passed it on. Or asked me to call?'

Still, I unlock the door and step inside. 'Come in anyway. I need to sit down. Seems like a trip across town and back is more than I can cope with these days.'

Aisha follows me inside, closing the door for me. 'That's what I was coming to see you about, actually.'

She shoves her hand inside her shapeless black coat and pulls out a surprisingly large old book. 'Been doing a bit of reading. Think I might know what the problem is.'

28

The book turns out to be a late-nineteenth-century scholarly work on the early Celtic myths and legends, written by a man with the splendidly Victorian name of Fitzhenry Cuthbertson. I don't ask Aisha where she got it from, but its battered leather exterior suggests a dusty old antiquarian book shop, rather than library. Without Karen giving her moral support, she is much more shy, but also quite excited about something and desperate to share it. All the same, I'm utterly exhausted, so there's no way I'm doing anything until I've had a mug of tea.

'What is it with you coppers and your tea?' Aisha asks as she turns down the offer of a mug for herself.

'You ever spent hours outdoors in the foulest weather? Anything that warms you up quick's good, but too much coffee leaves you all jittery. Needing a piss more likely than not, too.' I carry my brew over to the kitchen table with shaky arms, lucky not to spill any as I put it down and then sit rather more heavily than I intended.

'Not getting any better, I see.' Aisha nods at me, before turning her attention to the book. There's a couple of sweet wrappers used as bookmarks, which I guess is marginally better than turning down the corners of pages, but only just. She carefully opens the book at the first wrapper, then turns it around for me to see. It's chapter fifteen, the type close-set and difficult to see. I can read the title well enough.

'The Legend of the Cauldron of Life?' I have a feeling I know where this is going, and wonder if I can make my excuses, go through to the bathroom and text Karen to send reinforcements. I'm still struggling with the half dream half memory I had in the taxi. Not sure I've got the strength for this right now.

'It's just a story, I know. But some of the details are interesting, see?'

Not without reading it, I don't. And the tiny print makes my head ache even without trying to focus. 'I don't suppose you could summarise it for me?'

Aisha spins the book back to face her. 'This chapter tells the various tales of the cauldron, from several different sources. Most of them are the same as you see in the Mabinogion, where the cauldron is made of iron and is so large only a team of giants can move it around. But there's one reference where the translation is disputed, and the cauldron isn't like that at all.'

'Smaller? Easier to transport?'

She frowns. 'The opposite. It's not a cauldron at all. It's a lake in a cavern, deep underground. Its waters are warm, sometimes even boiling. And bathing in them doesn't bring the dead back to life, but it does heal those whose injuries are beyond healing.'

I'm getting used to the slow emergence of forgotten memories now, random images popping into my mind, experiences that feel more solid than a dream but still remain slippery and ethereal. As Aisha talks of an underground lake filled with warm water, I remember my taxi ride home, and now I can smell the place even more strongly than the mug of tea in my hands. A slightly sulphurous, mineral tang that reminds me of showering in a Reykjavik hotel. I can hear the echoing drips as they slide off stalactites far overhead and splash onto the still surface. And then the water is sliding over my face again, covering my eyes.

'You OK, Con?'

Aisha's voice snaps me out of my waking dream. Disoriented by the vision, it takes a while for the kitchen to come back into focus.

'Yeah. Fine.' Even I can hear the uncertainty in my voice. 'Just sparked a memory, I guess.'

'Cool.' Aisha flicks through the pages until she finds the next sweetie wrapper. Again, she opens the book up wide and swivels it around so that I can see. Chapter twenty-seven this time. The Tale of Caradoc the Brave.

'Not to be confused with the other Caradoc. Short arm. The one who was a knight of the round table.'

'I'll take your word for it, Ai. So what's his story?'

Aisha takes back her book with another withering stare. I'm so tired I can't summon the energy to react. I can barely summon the energy to drink my tea, and the kitchen floor's looking more and more comfortable by the minute. Almost in mockery of my exhaustion, Aisha is effervescent, her face a picture of excitement behind her thick spectacles.

'Caradoc the Brave was, well, brave. A bit stupid too, if I'm being honest. He fought and killed the giant Felindre, who'd been raiding farms and stealing cattle all over Deheubarth.' She checks my face, to make sure that I'm keeping up. 'That's west Wales, in case you were wondering.'

I wasn't, but I don't say anything. Hopefully, Aisha will get to the point soon.

'He was pretty badly beaten up in the fight. Legs broken, ribs caved in, one eye gone. Nobody thought he could possibly survive. They were building a pyre for his funeral. But, it so happened the area where he battled Felindre was close by the hidden location of the cauldron. The guardian took him there and placed him in the waters. He stayed there for a night and a day, and when he emerged he was healed.' She pauses and leans back in her chair, as though pleased with herself. 'Sound familiar?'

Again, I say nothing. Aisha doesn't seem to mind. This is clearly her thing, going through ancient stories and imagining what might happen if they were real. I can at least bask in her energetic enthusiasm and hope that some of it rubs off on me.

'Thing is.' She leans back in her chair and looks directly at me. 'Caradoc was fine, and the locals were all happy. They prepared a great feast for him, celebrated and got drunk. The next day, he packed up his sword and shield and set off for home. Somewhere in Gwent, if I'm getting the names right.' Aisha flicks through a few pages, then gives up. I'd not be surprised if she could recite most of it from memory, anyway.

'That's when the problems started. When he crossed the mountains and neared home. A terrible weakness came over him, "such that he could barely walk" I think is how the book describes it.' She reaches a hand toward the page again, then stops herself. 'He fell off his horse at the gates to his castle, and his servants had to carry him to his bed. He slept there for a month, or so the story tells it. The wisest healers in the land were summoned, but none could find a cure. In desperation, they loaded Caradoc onto a cart and took him back to the place where he battled the giant. And a miraculous thing happened. The closer he came to the cavern where the cauldron lake lay hidden, the more he improved. By the time he arrived at the village where he had feasted before leaving for home, he was almost his old self again.'

It's a great story, I have to admit. Even told in Aisha's breathless mix of Estuary twang and archaic English. I'm not so stupid, or tired, as to miss the parallels with my own situation, either. And the fact my jumbled half memories and dreamlike vision of a cavern and lake came to me before I'd ever heard of Caradoc the Brave is a little unsettling. But like most folk tales this one's allegorical, I'm sure. What might have made sense to a tenth-century audience is pretty much meaningless to modern ears. On the other hand, if you're going to take it at face value, then the conclusion is obvious.

'You're suggesting I need to go back to Wales and I'll get better?' I can't say that it's not an enticing idea.

'Not proper better, no. But you'd be less tired all the time. Maybe manage to climb three flights of stairs without stopping for breath after each one, eh?'

But I can't. I can't go back to Wales. Not if I want to keep my job. Got to be here, get through the therapy, slowly piece my life back together. There's no magic remedy, same as I wasn't healed by being floated in some mythological lake in a cavern deep underground, even if my damaged brain is trying to convince me otherwise. It's a good story, though. I appreciate the effort Aisha's put in on my behalf. And I'm so broken now, I'll cling to even the most ridiculous hope for a recovery.

'How did he get better then? I'm assuming he did.'

Aisha beams at me for asking. 'Oh, yes. But he had to find the cauldron again, which is a quest all in itself. See, he'd come out of the lake too soon. Before it was properly done healing him. He was still tied to the place, so the further he went from it the worse he felt. Doesn't that sound a bit like what's happening to you, Con?'

I shrug, and the effort of it dims my vision for a moment. I'm not sure what to say, and Aisha seems to understand. She closes the book, shoves it back in her coat and stands, her earlier almost manic enthusiasm gone. No, not gone. When I look at her, I can see that it's still there. Just guarded, locked away.

'I really do appreciate you telling me all this, Ai. Thinking about me and what's wrong with me. Thank you.' I stifle a yawn, then feel terrible for appearing bored by her presence. She seems to take it all in her stride.

'It's just a story, right. Still, thought you'd like to hear it. K doesn't really believe in all this mystic shit.' She smiles at me, just briefly. 'Her words, not mine.'

'I've seen weirder shit than that, Ai.' I try to smile as I say it, reassure her that I don't think she's mad. But all I can see is a young man with his heart cut out, the ghost of my murdered DI, and my mother's cold dead body lying in an ancient stone sarcophagus beneath a derelict North London church.

It's a couple of days later before Karen calls round. I don't tell her about my visit from Aisha. I'd say I was being kind, not wanting to be the source of any argument between the two of them. Assuming their relationship is rekindling, of course. The truth is, by the time I've had my first proper therapy session with Dr McCullough, I'm so wrung out I can barely string a sentence together, let alone think about what happened two days ago. It's only after she's gone that I remember the visit and the tale of Caradoc the Brave at all.

I'm starting to develop a coping strategy for whatever it is that's causing me this utter exhaustion. If I can manage it, I'll go out only once a day, braving the three flights of steps from my apartment. The corner shop's more expensive than going to the nearest supermarket, but I've certainly not got the energy for that. Nor do I have much of an appetite any more, although I'm sure tea and biscuits cover most of the essential food groups, especially when the biscuits have chocolate on them. The face that stares back at me from the bathroom mirror looks more like a stranger, day by day. Gaunt and thin, with black bags under her eyes and unkempt straggly red hair tumbling to her shoulders. She's not me, I can kid myself.

When I'm not asleep, I search the Internet for more

information about Fitzhenry Cuthbertson, and the ancient Welsh myths and legends he so meticulously catalogued. I come across the story of Prince Llewellyn and Gelert, remembering Gareth's faithful if slightly smelly hound. That story leads me down a rabbit hole that pops up in Ireland and another mention of the cauldron. It's hard to keep a hold of all the contradictory tales, but in this one it seems the cauldron ends up being destroyed. So much for that theory then.

I can only manage short bursts of work, followed by snoozing in my armchair. It's as well the weather's getting warmer now or I'd bankrupt myself running the heating. I'm in that dream place, halfway between awake and asleep, thinking not of Prince Llewellyn's slain hound, but of Gareth Caernant's elderly dog. That first time I saw him after leaving hospital, I had a flashback to something that couldn't have happened. And yet, here I am again, lying on a beach somewhere, sand under my cheek. It's hard to breathe, and all I can feel is the rhythmic pulse of light waves as they break around me, gently rocking me back and forth. One of my arms doesn't seem to work and I can't feel my legs at all. Nothing but cold and wet. At least there's no pain, although it feels like there should be.

I try to move, in that odd way of dreams. Lift my one working hand and dig it into the beach, heave my body up out of the water. There's a reason why this is important, even if I can't think of what it is. No matter how hard I try though, I can't seem to move. And as the dream progresses, so the panic becomes more urgent.

And then I hear something, besides the echoes of the waves. At first, I can't make it out, but it grows louder – a snuffling, breathy sound. It comes closer and closer, until it's right on top of me. I can't see, can't move, but I'm not scared. A wet nose presses against my cheek, nudges my head. A long tongue licks the salt from my eyebrows and forehead. With the last of my strength, I manage to reach up – feel the rough fur, the soft, floppy ears, the smooth leather band of a collar. Then my fingers slide off the dog's neck, too heavy to hold any more. Gelert carries on licking my face for a while, then he lies down beside me, his warmth seeping into me like a blanket thrown over a frozen child. He begins to keen, quietly at first, not much more than a whining whimper. It builds slowly, growing louder, more insistent, until all I can hear is his full-throated howl.

I wake with a start, the wail of a siren dopplering away into the distance. But the dream sticks with me, along with the certainty that it is made up of actual memories, not my mind jumbling together random facts. I remember waking on a gravel beach in a tidal cave. I remember the excruciating pain in my left arm when I tried to move it, and the utter lack of any sensation whatsoever from my legs. I remember the panic, knowing that the tide would come in and I would drown. As if being thrown off a cliff weren't bad enough, and surviving that impossibly unlikely. And most of all I remember with perfect clarity the moment Gelert found me, lent me his warmth and stayed by my side until help finally arrived.

But how can any of that be real? And who did the old dog summon with his howls? As I stare at the darkening walls of my living room, surrounded by the sounds of the city, I no longer have any idea where truth ends and mythology begins.

29

I'm almost a month back into London living, and while my memories are beginning to come together, I'm still constantly tired. If it wasn't for regular visits from Karen and less regular visits from my sister in law Charlotte, I'd probably not get up at all some days. Except that my bed isn't half as comfortable as I used to think, and even I have to pee sometimes. I imagine this must be what life's like for some of those poor sods suffering from long Covid or ME. And who knows, maybe that's what I've got. The doctors haven't found anything though, and I tested negative before they jabbed me with the vaccine.

It's late morning by the time I've managed to drag myself out of bed, into the shower and clump through to the kitchen in my bathrobe. I never used to have to bother with my hair before; now it's got so long I've had to wrap it up in a towel. If I owned a hairdryer once, I've no idea where it is now. Some landfill site outside the M25, probably. Not that it matters. I've no pressing engagements today, nothing I need to pretty myself up for, but as I open the fridge and peer inside I remember that I've no milk either. Dammit.

I can drink black coffee, and even black tea at a pinch, but I draw the line at dry corn flakes. Recent experience tells me that if I don't force down something for breakfast, I'll most likely forget to eat for the rest of the day and then pass out about six. Even I know that's not a good way to get better. Time to face the stairs and visit the corner shop again.

It takes me half an hour to get myself together, and another ten minutes to reach the bottom of the third flight of stairs. At this rate I'd be better finding something for lunch.

'You still here, Con? Thought you would have been long gone by now.'

Mrs Feltham stands in her open doorway, drying her hands with a stained dishcloth. Even as I turn to face her, I can smell the enticing scent of curry wafting over, and all of a sudden I'm more hungry than I can remember ever being.

'Gone, Mrs F? Gone where?'

'Back to the west, child. Back to where you can finish healing. Ain't gonna get no better here in the smoke.'

For a moment, I think she's simply telling me to get out of London and rest up, like she did the last time we spoke. But then my sluggish brain catches up with all of what she said.

'West? You mean Wales?'

'Well, I surely don't mean Jamaica, although a bit of sun wouldn't do you no harm.' Mrs Feltham tucks the dishcloth into the cord of her apron where it's tied around her ample middle, then beckons me inside. 'Come on in, why don't you? I've a pot of coffee needs drinking.'

I don't need to be asked twice, and soon we're both sitting in the kitchen that's fast becoming more familiar than my own. There's a large pot simmering away on the stove, the source of the amazing smells. For a moment I imagine a production line, starting with a small herd of goats out in the garden, a killing shed and butchery somewhere at the back of the apartment, and then the kitchen where it all gets turned into endless meals for Mrs Feltham's boys. And me. Only there's no garden out back, no room in these tiny flats for a butchery, and I know better than to spoil the magic by asking where the meat comes from.

'Should never have come back to the city, Con.' Mrs Feltham pours me thick, black coffee as she speaks, then takes up a mug she's already been drinking from and settles into a seat opposite me. The kitchen table is a mess of spices, onion skins and chilli tops ready for the compost bin. A fearsome-looking cleaver rests on a bloodstained chopping board, more the sort of thing I'd imagine you'd use for disposing of a corpse than dicing up some goat meat. I shudder away the thought.

'I didn't have much choice, Mrs F. Not if I want to keep my job.'

'Can't work when you're in this state, can you?' Mrs Feltham makes the obvious point. 'What good is a job if you're always on sick leave? What good if you're dead?'

'No. But the treatment is here. And there's not many employers would pay my wages and for private therapy.'

'Therapy.' I can hear the disdain in that one word. 'Listen to yourself. There's nothing wrong with your mind, child. It's your body needs healing, and you won't get that here.'

I'd complain that there's nothing wrong with my body apart from weakness, that it's my mind that's been broken and needs time to heal. But I've learned from long experience that arguing with Mrs Feltham rarely works. Her advice is usually sound, even if it takes me a while to accept it.

'Why would I heal any faster in Wales than here?' I ask, then immediately think of at least a dozen reasons. 'I mean, apart from the clean air and lack of noise. That's not what you mean, though, is it?'

'Why you think your brain's all messed up, Con? Why you can't think straight? Barely climb those stairs you used to run up three at a time?'

'I fell off a cliff. Nearly died.'

'Are you sure that's what happened?'

For a moment, I think she's siding with my therapist, and the male section of our little team at the NCA. PTSD-driven depression making me suicidal so that I either stripped off and walked into the sea or threw myself off the cliffs. But that's not Mrs Feltham's angle at all, is it?

'No. It wasn't an accident. I didn't fall, I was pushed.' And who knows? Maybe I did die. Or at least got halfway. That would explain why I feel like I'm in some kind of limbo the whole time.

'You need to find your answers if you're ever going to heal. And you're not going to find them here in London now, are you?'

'I guess not.'

'And there's someone needs your help, too. Someone you made a promise to.'

I tilt my head at that, frowning and surprised. Mrs Feltham is right, of course. I made a promise to Lila that I'd get her away from harm, take her north to Burntwoods and sanctuary. I can't rest easy until I've fulfilled that promise, and it's been squatting there at the back of my mind all this time. But how on earth could Mrs Feltham know about that? I don't remember telling her. I open my mouth to ask, but she speaks before I can get the words out.

'Go do what you do best, child. Find all the pieces and put them back together again. Then you can heal properly, come back to us from this half-life you living right now.'

She makes it sound so simple. I can see with great clarity what needs to be done, even if I've no idea how and even less energy to do it with. Maybe it's the coffee clearing my head, or maybe it's whatever strange herbs Mrs Feltham puts in it making me bold. Either way, I drain my mug and stand up without feeling like I'm about to pass out. In that moment I even feel strong enough to consider making the journey.

'You're right, Mrs F. I need to go back and finish what I started.'

I know this is a bad idea as soon as I lock the front door and lug my rucksack onto my shoulder. There's barely anything in it, but it feels like I've packed enough for a whole new life. Having not long since climbed the stairs from Mrs Feltham's, it takes an age to get down them again and round the back of the apartment block to where Karen parked my car. I end up sitting in the driver's seat for fifteen minutes, unable to do anything but stare out of the windscreen at the car parked in front of me as I get my breath back. At least, for once, there's a decent gap so I don't have to reverse to get out.

How I make it out of London without causing an accident I've no idea. Thank god for power steering is all I can say. I only wish the Volvo was an automatic, too. Things get a little easier once I'm on the motorway. The fuel gauge is on the right side of three-quarters full, which should see me most of the way there. I'm not kidding myself I'll do the whole journey in one.

At least I have a flask of Mrs Feltham's finest coffee to keep me going; her parting gift and worth more than its weight in gold. And I have to admit, deep in the back of my mind, Aisha's mad tales of Caradoc the Brave and the Cauldron of Life give me the tiniest flicker of hope. If two differently strange people have come up with reasons why going back to Wales should make me better, then just maybe there's some truth to it. Guess I'll find out soon enough.

My phone is in its cradle on the dashboard, but I've not activated Hands Free. As I travel west it rings three times, first Karen, then Charlotte and finally my aunt. I ignore them all; if I pull into a service station to call them back or listen to voicemails, I'll lose my nerve and ask someone to come rescue me, take me home.

It starts to get dark as I pass the Newbury turning. I've been concentrating so hard on driving and staying awake that I've not even had the radio on – just my thoughts, the rumble of tyres on tarmac and the muted roar of the engine for company. I'm not exactly going fast; enough to keep up with the HGVs in the nearside lane. I don't trust myself to overtake much, and besides, going slowly ekes out the fuel. If I end up getting sacked for this, then who knows how I'm going to pay for the next tankful.

Swindon slides past, a sprawl of industrial units, shopping centres, Christ only knows what else. Something keeps me going. Probably the coffee, since I finally have to give in to the pressure on my bladder and pull in to the service station at Leigh Delamere.

I don't stay long, stocking up on chocolate and a couple of cans of Irn Bru to keep me awake a bit longer. It's only as I slide back into the driver's seat and dump my spoils beside me that I notice I'm not out of breath. Dog tired and in need of at least twenty-four hours sleep, but not panting like I was when I made it to the third floor walkway leading to my apartment. I briefly consider having a quick kip in the car; there's an old sleeping bag in the back still. But I saw the signs dotted around the car park threatening fines for staying longer than a couple of hours. Knowing my luck, I'd be rudely woken by a bizzy, right after he'd ticketed me.

There's a couple of voicemail messages when I check my phone. The first is my aunt, asking if I'd consider going to Harston Magna at the weekend. I make a mental note to call her in the morning when I've had some sleep. The other message is from Karen, and a little more concerning.

'Hey, Con – K here. Just wondering where you are? Ai and me popped round and it's all locked up, no one home. And your car's gone? Hope you're OK and not doing anything stupid, right? Give us a call soon as you get this.'

I pour the last of Mrs Feltham's special coffee into the mug that makes up the lid of the thermos, tear the wrapper off a Mars Bar and stare out the windscreen at the travellers coming and going. I know I should call Karen. I wouldn't put it past her to run my Volvo's plate through the system to see whether it's been logged on any cameras. In which case, she'll know somebody's left London headed west on the M4. I don't imagine it'll take her long to work out it's me rather than some enterprising car thief. The old beast might have been top-of-the-range when it was new, but fifteen years and over two hundred thousand miles have worn off the shine a little. Not to mention the dents and scrapes where two idiots tried to run me off the road.

Finishing the coffee, I slip the phone into its cradle and plug in the Hands Free before starting the engine. Only once I've pulled out of my parking space and am heading back onto the motorway do I tap the call button. It takes a moment to connect, but is answered almost immediately.

'Con. Where are you? Are you OK?'

'Breathe, K. I'm fine. No need to worry.'

'But we came round. You weren't there. And Ai said she'd been to see you before. Told you some stuff about legends and cauldrons and . . .' A pause, which I hope is Karen taking a breath and calming down. 'Are you in a car? Con, are you driving?'

I catch myself about to joke, 'What are you, my mother?' But that's too raw. Instead I tell her again that I'm fine, as though it's not something only people who aren't fine say.

'Jesus, Con. Yesterday you could hardly walk a hundred yards. You know driving tired's as bad as driving drunk. Worse, maybe. What if you fall asleep at the wheel?'

I notice Karen doesn't ask me how I managed to navigate North West London during rush hour. Not that there's an actual rush hour these days. It's more a continuous lack of rush throughout the waking day.

'I'm . . .' Don't say fine again, Con. 'Actually, I'm doing OK. And yeah, you're right about driving tired, but I need to do this, K. Nothing's going to change unless I do.'

'I still don't know what *this* is. Where even are you?'

A sign whizzes past at the perfect moment. 'Getting close to Bristol. Should be over the bridge within the hour.'

'Bristol? Bridge? Jeez, Con.' I can hear Karen begin to say something, then stop herself. Clearly, it's not only me who does that.

'Aren't you supposed to be seeing Dr McCullough tomorrow?' she asks eventually.

'I'll have to call and reschedule in the morning. I'm sure she'll understand.'

'And Diane? You going to tell her what you're up to as well? She'll find out, even if I don't tell her. You know what she's like.'

'She probably knows already, K. I'm sorry. Didn't mean to drop you in it like this.' I slow down as a lorry in front of me brakes for something, and for a moment I imagine Shepherd setting up roadblocks on all the major roads to intercept me before I can reach Wales. It's such an arresting thought I almost laugh.

'Yeah, well. I'll tell her you said that. And don't get yourself sacked, OK. I don't think I—'

'Can cope with being the only junior female officer on the team. I know, you told me already. And you're not the only one anyway. Billy Latham's a big Jessie too.'

A moment's silence while I overtake the lorry as it peels off onto an exit ramp. Then Karen's quizzical voice comes back over the Hands Free speakers, slightly tinny and lacking in bass. 'A big what?'

'If I have to explain the joke it's not funny. Look, K. I need to do this, but I'm not going to get myself into trouble. I promise.'

Even as I say it I know that it's probably a lie. 'I'll give you a call in the morning. I'll speak to Diane too. Don't worry about me, OK? I'm fine.'

Karen doesn't sound convinced as she grudgingly says good-bye, but at least she's not tried to persuade me to come back to London. I tap the screen on my phone to end the call and settle myself deeper into my seat. The car's running well, still plenty of fuel thanks to my leisurely speed. Up ahead, I can see the dull glow of Bristol's street lights turning the night sky orange. It won't be long before I'm past there and back in Wales. I don't know why, but that feels like a great weight lifted off my shoulders, and even though the weariness drags at me, it isn't anything like the soul-crushing exhaustion I felt before.

Maybe Aisha was right all along.

30

Breakfast at Plas Caernant is a moveable feast. Which is just as well because by the time I make it down to the kitchen it's nearly midday. I'd half-suspected Gareth and Amy were only being polite when they told me that I was welcome back any time. But when I phoned them from a petrol station forecourt near Bridgend, wondering if I might beg a room for the night, they'd been genuinely delighted. Amy took one look at me when I arrived and sent me straight up to my old room. I was too tired to even contemplate arguing; didn't even brush my teeth. I fell into bed and have no memory of my head even hitting the pillow.

'You're looking much better this morning, Con,' she says, as I yawn and stretch at the doorway. Gelert the deerhound rises from his place in front of the Aga like some great shaggy beast, and strides across to greet me with almost as much delight as when I stepped out of the car last night.

'Thank you. I don't think I can say that enough. I feel so much better already. Haven't been this well rested since . . . well, I can't really remember. And my brain fog has lifted, too.'

'Well, sit down and I'll fetch you some coffee. Then we can see if Gareth left any of that porridge. I know you like it, so I made plenty. But he's a devil for helping himself to seconds.'

My joints creak a little, and my body still aches as I settle into one of the wooden wheelback chairs arranged around the kitchen table. What I said to Amy is true; my weariness is much reduced. But it's still there, in the background, always threatening to poleaxe me if I'm not careful.

'Karen phoned earlier,' Amy says as she hands me a mug, steam rising gently off the surface. 'I told her you'd arrived safe and sound, but not to expect a call back for a while. She sounded surprised you'd made it here at all. Thought you'd have to rest before you reached Cardiff, even.'

'She worries about me too much. It's not such a long drive, really. And I stopped a couple of times for a short nap.' Well, a leg stretch, a can of Irn Bru and a pee.

'You have that effect on people, Con.' Amy goes back to the Aga and starts moving pots around. 'Maybe it's because you don't seem to care what happens to you, as long as everyone else is OK.'

I begin to complain, then realise it's a compliment and I should accept it in the spirit it was made. 'Thank you. But not everyone else is OK.'

'You mean Lila, don't you.' It's not a question.

'I let her down and now she's disappeared.' Only she hasn't, has she? In among the jumble of memories I can see her, one eye swollen almost shut, the other filled with fear. I can't place where I saw her, but I know it was during my lost twenty-four hours. And she was with Kieran Johns. I can see him even now, pressing the barrel of a gun into my forehead. Instinctively, I reach up and touch the point where the cold metal rested, even though any mark it may have left is long gone.

'Is something wrong?' Amy asks, suddenly at my side. I never saw her move from the cooker. 'You went very pale.'

'Another memory. Not a nice one. It's all slowly starting to come back now.' I drink some coffee and focus on trying to see more of the image in my head. But it's like a dream, fading away now, mixed into a jumble in that way dreams do when you subject them to waking logic. I need to start being a bit more proactive, as the management bollocks has it. I can't spend the rest of my life waiting for all the pieces to fit together.

'I need to go to Aber.' I place my empty mug down on the table, but before I can stand Amy has put a hand gently but firmly on my shoulder. I look up at her, smiling in the exact same way my aunt always does when she's proving she knows what's best for me. Must have been something they were taught when they were at school together, although I don't remember that being on the curriculum at St Bert's when I was there.

'Not until you've had something to eat,' she says in a voice that brooks no argument. 'Porridge first, then you can go be a detective.'

An hour or so later, when I park the Volvo in the street outside the council flats in Aberystwyth, I'm glad I ate something. Climbing out of the car, my head spins, then steadies as I lean heavily on the open door. I'm still weak, and tire far too easily. How much worse would it be if I'd had only coffee on an empty stomach to sustain me?

The curtain in one of the upper windows twitches as I walk to the front entrance, so it comes as no surprise that Mrs Brady is standing in her doorway when I make it, panting, to the top floor. She looks me up and down in much the same way as the elderly lady who tried to teach me how to dance when I was ten.

'Been in the wars, I see. Come in, love. I'll put the kettle on.'

'Thank you. I could do with a cuppa.' I follow her inside, settling gratefully onto the sofa while she busies herself making tea. The room's unchanged from my last visit, which is hardly surprising. I doubt much has changed in this woman's life since her husband died. I'm hoping her routine might help me, though.

'You look like you need feeding up, dear,' she says as she brings a tray in from the kitchen. Alongside the teapot and milk jug, there's a plate of chocolate biscuits. They're a little soft, and the chocolate has that dullness to it that suggests it's both cheap and well past its sell-by date, but I'm grateful for the sugar boost.

'I'm sorry to bother you, Mrs Brady,' I say, after we've both had some tea.

'It's no bother, dear. I don't get many visitors. Especially not since the virus. Nice to see a friendly face, have a little chat.'

It's clear enough that she wants to ask me what happened, but can't think of a polite way to do it. Putting down my cup for a moment, I smooth the few crumbs away from my legs before starting to explain.

'I had a bit of an accident, ended up in the sea – almost drowned. Not long after I'd come to visit you the last time, actually.'

Mrs Brady looks suitably shocked. 'An accident, you say? You sure it wasn't anything to do with those young ruffians across the hall?' She cocks her head in the direction of the front door.

'I'm not sure. I must have knocked my head at some point. Memories are all over the place. But I remember coming here, and your kindness.'

'And you wanted to know if they'd been back too, I suppose.' Her smile is genuine as she makes her point. I relax a little; this will be a lot easier if she's on my side.

'It had crossed my mind.'

'Well, they did. Must be, what? Five weeks ago? Six? Something like that. I could work out the date if it helps. Just need to find last month's *TV Times*. I was watching that dancing programme. You know, with the celebrities? Never know who any of them are, but I like the music and the dances.'

Six weeks. That would be around the time I was found on the beach. It could be a coincidence of course, but in my line of work it's best to assume there's no such thing.

'You said they came back, Mrs Brady. Who exactly was it? Did you see them?'

A little shudder and the ghost of a frown scurries across her face. 'Kept well out of their way. But I had a peep through the spy hole and there were at least six or seven of them. Big strapping lads. They had a van, too. Parked on the double yellow lines out front. They must have emptied the place, the number of times they tramped up and down those stairs. All the furniture, even the carpets. And then someone went in and cleaned with some powerful stuff. Fair stank the whole building out for a while. I guess they've either sold it or the council are moving someone else in. It's been a few weeks mind, and nobody's been back.'

It sounds to me like a professional clean-up crew got sent in after I was chucked off the cliff, just in case. That might explain why there was nothing suspicious at Penparc Uchaf Farm either, although not the lack of caves and tunnels. I still need to see the flat, though. I need to stand in it and get a feel for the place. Close my eyes and imagine how it was, perhaps.

'You've been very helpful, Mrs Brady. Thank you.' I finish my tea and put the cup carefully back on the tray. There's one biscuit still left on the plate, but I reckon I've had enough sugar and fat to keep me going a little longer. When I stand, the world stays pleasantly level and I don't feel like I'm going to pass out.

'Are you sure you wouldn't like another?' The old lady stands more slowly, her swaying far more like I'd expect to feel myself.

'No, I'm fine. Thank you. Think I'll maybe go and have a wee look next door though.'

Another slight frown crosses her face, this time one of confusion rather than concern. 'I'm afraid I don't have a key. Not sure who does.'

'Don't you worry about that, Mrs Brady. I'm sure I can manage.'

31

I'd assumed the lock for the flat would be the same as that on Mrs Brady's front door, a simple latch with a bolt on the inside but no deadlock keyhole. The old lady watches me from her flat as I cross the short landing, but I block her view of what I'm doing as I wiggle a thin, flat credit card shaped sheet of metal into the narrow gap between door and jamb, pushing it against the latch until it slides out of the way. You can get the same result using a credit card, but it's not much use for buying things with afterwards. The metal sheet usually lives in my wallet, and has the added bonus of stopping enterprising thieves from scanning the chips on my cards even whilst they're still tucked away. Tap and Go is great, but it's also an easy way for electronic pickpockets to prosper.

The door swings open onto a cold, empty hall. The layout is the mirror image of Mrs Brady's, but there the similarities end. All the furniture has been removed, and even the light bulbs have gone. I've seen flats in London stripped of electrical fittings, plumbing and even the cables ripped from the walls for the minuscule value of the copper wire in them. This isn't quite so bad, but as I move from room to room I can tell it's been forensically cleaned. That's suspicious enough in itself, of course. There's no way someone would go to all that trouble if they didn't have something very valuable to hide.

I can smell the faintest whiff of bleach as I go through the empty kitchen cupboards, but there's nothing else in the room, not even under the sink where there's always an old plunger and a half-empty bottle of toilet duck. The two bedrooms are similarly bare, although the concrete floor in the larger one has a dark mark in the middle. The bathroom is probably more spotless than it's been since this block of flats was built, and the living room looks huge without any furniture taking up space. All in all, it wouldn't be a bad place to live, provided the downstairs neighbours aren't noisy. I've not heard anything from them yet.

Neither have I found any inspiration in this empty shell. The only thing in the flat that hasn't been taken away is the gas fire. I stare at it for a while, my brain not quite able to tell me why it's important. Then I go back through to the kitchen. There's a power outlet for connecting an electric cooker, and sure enough tucked out of sight behind the built-in cupboards, a gas line and tap. Further along the counter, one of the wall unit doors opens to reveal a compact gas boiler, switched off. Back out in the hall, I find a small cubbyhole where the meters live. Surprisingly, this flat doesn't have a pre-pay card slot or even a box to feed pound coins into. But then, if it was being used by a gang of drug smugglers and people traffickers, they'd likely make sure the utility bills were paid on time to avoid drawing unwanted attention.

I still can't work out why the gas and electricity have set my internal bells ringing. Back in the living room, I peer out the window down to where a couple of kids on bicycles are eyeing up my car. For a moment, I think one of them is going to take a brick to the window, which would be doubly annoying as I'd have to replace it and there's nothing inside worth stealing anyway. Before I've had time to open the window and shout at them, something else has distracted their attention and they speed off.

Turning away, I find myself staring blindly at the gas fire again. Lila gave this flat as her address when the police picked her up, and I'm still not sure why. I suppose she couldn't give Penparc Uchaf Farm; nobody would have believed her. She could have claimed to be homeless though. That might even have got her some sympathy rather than a cell. But she chose to name this place. Why?

Still pondering, I notice that the gas fire doesn't sit quite square in its surround. There's nothing so unusual about that, really; the world's awash with bad workmen who can't be bothered to do the job properly. It's grabbed my attention, though. I tilt my head, as if that might make it clear why it's interesting, but it doesn't. I stare at it a little longer, then cross the room and hunker down in front of the fire to investigate further.

It's the type of model I've often seen in people's flats and houses over a decade of police work. Nothing special. Three ceramic burners behind a steel mesh guard, surrounded by a shiny metal and polished wood box whose design has probably fallen out of fashion and come back round again at least twice. It's fitted into a space made to look like a fireplace, although there would never have been an open fire in these council flats. Like everything else in the place, it's spotlessly clean, but whoever has scrubbed any incriminating fingerprints or DNA off it has also knocked loose a panel in the surround, and that's what caught my attention.

Crouching is far harder than it should be, forcing a tired 'oof' out of my lungs as if I'm older than Mrs Brady across the way. Without thinking, I shove a hand in my coat pocket, but there's no latex gloves in there. I lost that habit a long time ago, although there's probably a box of them in the car. Ah well, I've already left my prints on the front door, and probably a few other places besides. We'll cross that bridge if it becomes necessary.

When I press at the loose fire surround, it wobbles slightly but doesn't give way. I study it a bit closer, running my fingers around the edge of it, and as I do so it slides slightly to the left. Behind it, there's a narrow gap where the exhaust vent for the fire runs. I pull the panel some more, and it pops out completely, revealing the shiny metal flue as it disappears up towards the roof. I can't see anything that shouldn't be there, but I gently work my fingers up alongside the metal, just in case. As the flue flexes out of the way, something slides down into my hand, surprisingly large and weighty.

Bingo.

I pull whatever it is out, along with a small mound of dust, cobwebs and other detritus, and discover a padded envelope, somewhere between A4 and A3 in size. The name and address on the label have been scored out with black marker pen, but not so well that I can't make out 'Johns' and 'Penparc Uchaf Farm'. That's evidence enough as far as I'm concerned, but it's what's inside the envelope that really catches my attention. Bundled in small groups, held together with elastic bands, are perhaps twenty or thirty passports.

I pull out the first bundle, slip off the rubber band. There's three little books, all bearing the same gold-stamped Eagle sigil, the arabic lettering and then Syrian Arab Republic underneath. Flicking them open reveals a man, a woman and a teenage boy, all bearing the same surname, Mohamed. I've no idea if they're fake; they certainly don't have the battered around the edges feel of a regular traveller. But I can think of only one reason why they would be hidden away here.

The next bundle don't appear to be related, but all are Libyan. I'm about to take out a third set to look through when I remember where I am. I need to get this evidence out of here and back to the team as soon as possible. I drop the bundles back into the envelope, stand up again with only a minimum of swaying, and head for the door.

The two kids on their bicycles are back when I unlock the car and climb in. As I sit in the driver's seat, contemplating what to do next, the older boy stares at me in that angry, arrogant manner of all teenagers kicked out of the house to get some fresh air when they'd rather be sitting in a darkened bedroom playing with their Xbox. I'm half-tempted to stick my tongue out at him, but my poor old Volvo's beaten up enough as it is. No need to risk having a brick chucked at it. I watch them in the rear view mirror as I drive away, something about them bothering me in the same way the fire surround did back in the flat.

The niggling worry is soon swamped as I try to negotiate Aberystwyth's unique one-way system, and get it wrong yet again. Whatever sugar rush energy I'd taken from Mrs Brady's tea and biscuits has worn off now, leaving me with an all too familiar numbing weariness, and none of Mrs Feltham's magic coffee to help me overcome it. There is a chain coffee shop on the way out of town though, so I pull in to the car park and head inside for a wake-me-up.

Double cappuccino with an extra shot of espresso and a chocolate chip muffin secured, I take myself off to an empty table in the corner, pull out my phone and do what I should have done the best part of an hour ago. Karen's number goes instantly to voicemail, so she must either be in a meeting with her phone switched off or talking to someone else. I wash down some muffin with too-bitter coffee, and look around the almost empty cafe. Time to get to work, and this is as good an office as any.

I've brought the padded envelope in with me; there's no way I'm letting it out of my sight. I use my phone to take a photo of the front, with its damning name and address. Then I pull out the top bundle of passports and snap a picture of the details page of each one. Karen probably won't appreciate the multiple texts, but sending them one-by-one is easier than trying to lump them all together. I figure that by the time I'm done, she'll either have finished talking or the buzz of multiple incoming texts will have alerted her to something more important than some boring team meeting.

By the time I'm finished texting, the coffee and muffin are nothing but a memory. I'm slightly irritated to find Karen hasn't texted me back yet, and when I call it goes to voicemail instantly again. Well, I did my best. I check my watch, glance up at the cafe window. It's later than I thought, dusk painting the underside of the clouds orange and pink. Time to head back to Plas Caernant; I can try Karen's number again when I get there.

In my defence, my brain's not been working properly since I woke up in the hospital, and I've got chronic fatigue on top of PTSD. So I can probably forgive myself for spotting the flat tyre on the car, but not noticing the white panel van parked a few empty spaces away. Seeing the tyre fills me with a kind of existential dread. Normally, I wouldn't think twice about hauling out the jack and the spare. Normally, I could have the thing changed almost as quickly as an F1 pit stop crew. But now, even with a triple shot of espresso and all the sugar of a chocolate chip muffin in my system, I doubt I'd have the strength to lift the spare wheel out of the boot. Why do these things keep happening to me?

I've got my phone in my hand and I'm contemplating calling the AA when I sense more than hear a presence behind me. Perhaps part of the old me is still in there, hidden deep under all the other shit. I shift my balance as I turn to see who it is, which means the cosh meant for the back of my head merely grazes my cheek and collides with my shoulder. It's still enough to send me crashing to the ground.

'Grab her. Quick. Before anyone sees.' The voice is vaguely familiar, and I'm so shocked that it takes me a moment to realise I've dropped my phone. Fuck, I hope the screen's not cracked. I only just got that to replace my old one.

As rough hands grab my arms, I spot it lying under the car, try to reach and grab it. This time the cosh doesn't miss. I feel a sharp pain as if something inside my head has exploded. There's a flash of brilliant bright light, and then everything goes dark.

32

I snap awake as an ocean smashes into my face, water flooding my nose and mouth. For a moment, I think I'm back in the sea again, drowning. Then I realise I'm sitting in a chair, hands tied behind my back. Someone's thrown a bucket of water over me. I can't believe they'd actually do that in real life. I shake my head to get rid of the water from my eyes, then regret it as a brutal pain blossoms at the back of my skull.

'So you're awake now. Good.'

Blinking and spitting, I move more slowly as I raise my head to see who's talking. There are three men in the room facing me, but it's the one in the middle who is clearly in charge. His face isn't easy to make out, silhouetted by a bare lightbulb hanging from the ceiling so that it appears to be right behind his head. I don't need to see him, anyway. The voice alone is enough to bring more memories crashing into my bruised brain. And the halo's fooling nobody.

'Tegwin.' The croakiness of my voice surprises me. 'Tegwin Kieran Johns. We meet again.'

If he's surprised I know his name, he doesn't show it. I look around the rest of the room, trying to work out where I am. The walls are slate stone, lime-mortared and slick with condensation. Bare wooden rafters make up the ceiling. To one side, I can see a small window, shuttered, its frame half rot and half peeling green paint. My legs are tied to the chair, my boots resting on a smooth cobbled floor. So, I must be in an old farm building then. Most likely one of the range that make up the courtyard around Penparc Uchaf Farm at a guess.

'You're a hard woman to kill,' Tegwin says. I take my time turning my attention back his way, pleased to see how much it annoys him.

'Shame you can't say the same about poor old Karl.'

Tegwin hardly reacts, but the man to his right tenses. The light's cast his face in shadow, which is probably why I didn't recognise Slaphead at first. I certainly recognise him now. I make sure he's staring right at me and then smile. 'Did you not know? The old man pushed your boyfriend off the cliff with me.'

The slap comes out of nowhere, and I realise I've been concentrating so hard on Billy Kendall that I've completely forgotten the other man.

'Shut your fucking mouth, bitch. I was there. Saw you grab him and take him with you.'

As the stars in my eyes dissipate, I switch my focus. I recognise this one now I'm concentrating on him. And the smack to the head has loosened up a few more memories too. 'You kiss your mother with that mouth, Hefin?'

He raises his hand again, this time clenched into a fist. But the old man grabs him by the wrist and spins him around with more strength than I'd have given him credit for.

'Enough. She's winding you up on purpose. Go check on those idiots loading the van. We need this place cleaned out by dawn.'

Hefin pauses a moment, his eyes still full of hatred, but he's no match for Tegwin and he knows it. A stiff, minimal nod and then he turns and leaves.

'Lady Constance Fairchild.' The old man brings his focus back on to me. 'Or perhaps I should say Detective Constable

Constance Fairchild, formerly of London's metropolitan police, now working in counter-narcotics at the National Crime Agency.' He's been leaning against a table until now, but he stands, moves aside to reveal a pile of folders and other paperwork.

'Operation Cantre'r Gwaelod.' He smiles like a lunatic. 'You police and your operation code names. Such a flair for the dramatic. Do you know the legend of Cantre'r Gwaelod? No? I'm surprised your friend Gareth Caernant hasn't told you. He loves all that mystic bullshit.'

A cold shiver runs through me at hearing Gareth's name. I know a threat when I hear one. I'm not about to give this piece of shit the satisfaction of seeing he's hit a nerve, though. I stare at him, as if simply thinking it could make him drop down dead, but I say nothing.

'I'm impressed that you managed to keep your cover for so long, you know. My sources have been very reliable up until now, but it seems you were in place almost a year before we learned of you. That's . . . unprecedented.'

'What can I say? I'm good at my job.' He doesn't need to know I was only here for my health, on sabbatical from work.

'Very good indeed, I see.' He turns away, picks up the padded envelope from the table and pulls out a bundle of passports. 'We've been looking for these for quite a while, now. Seems you found them in just a few minutes.'

'I don't suppose you want to tell me how you got those?' I nod my head towards the envelope, then wish I hadn't as a jolt of pain sears behind my eyes.

'I don't suppose I do, no. It's no matter, I have them back now. Although I expect at least half of them have no value any more.' Tegwin taps one of the passports idly against his chin for a moment. 'But what to do with you, now. Since throwing you off a cliff clearly didn't work.'

240

'You could always let me go. Pretend none of this ever happened.'

The old man smiles that lunatic grin again. 'Shame, really. I like a woman with a bit of spark.' He turns to Slaphead. 'You searched her? Took her phone off her?'

'Searched her and her car, boss. She didn't have no phone on her.'

I can see it now, from before the blow to the head knocked me senseless. My dropped phone lying underneath the car. No reason they need to know that.

'It went in the sea. When you threw me and poor old Karl over the cliff. Haven't had time to get a new one yet.'

Tegwin's not so easily fooled, which I guess would explain why he's in charge. And why this little operation of his hasn't been uncovered yet.

'Snooping around without a phone? Don't take me for an idiot.' He turns to Slaphead again. 'Get back to town. Bring the car here and search it properly. Have someone go into the cafe too, just in case she left it in there. And hurry. I want you back within the hour.'

Slaphead pauses for only the briefest of moments before hurrying off, which leaves me and Johns alone. I don't know why, but I felt safer when there were more people here.

'You know it's over, right? Your little criminal empire? No more bringing drugs in on the lobster boats. No more trafficking people. We know all about it.'

Tegwin scowls at me. 'I doubt that very much indeed. And anyway. It doesn't matter. They'll not find anything here, not even your dead body.'

He reaches into his pocket and pulls out a faded red penknife, not unlike the one my brother Ben pestered my father into giving him when he was still at school. I almost laugh at the incongruity of it, but old man's evil stare stops me. He flicks open the blade

241

with a practised ease that would have made teenage Ben green-eyed with jealousy, then before I can even react, he bends down and cuts the ties holding my legs to the chair.

If I was a character in a movie, I'd lash out and kick him over before springing up and pinning him to the ground. In reality, when I flex my legs the pins and needles almost kill me. He knew it would be like that, I can tell by the nasty smile on his face as he carefully folds away the blade and puts the knife back in his pocket. By the time I've eased a little bit of life back into my stiff muscles and the agony is seeping away, he's produced a gun. Unlike his son, he doesn't press it to my forehead.

'Up. We're going for a little walk.'

I'm about to complain that my hands are still tied to the chair, but when I move them, I find that they're only tied together, pulled behind me so that the chair back pokes uncomfortably into my armpits. It's a bit of a struggle, but I manage to stand up, swaying slightly at the effort. Johns watches me for any sign I might do something stupid, satisfies himself I'm no threat, then waves the gun towards the door.

The first few steps are agony. And the next few, too. Outside the room, there's a narrow corridor leading to the courtyard, where I can see lights and vehicles parked. The old man prods me in the back with his gun, directing me the other way.

No chance of escape here.

The ancient buildings remind me of the stable block at Plas Caernant, made from the same slate stone and lime mortar. As we progress to the end furthest from the house, I begin to see signs of more modern construction, shiny steel pipes bolted to the walls and snaking into the ground. I can't quite work out what it's all about until we step from the end of the steadings and into a brightly lit building site.

Diane Shepherd's words come back to me. When she told me they were building an anaerobic digester to produce gas for

Aberystwyth, I'd imagined something the size of a small barn, maybe a house. The dome of the main digester tank is so big it should be visible from the moon. There are more pipes than an oil refinery, and a chemical tang to the air that suggests it is at least partly functional.

'Enough gawping. Keep moving.' Tegwin prods me with the gun again, pushing me towards another entrance back into the old steadings. He directs me past more pipework, through a stone arch and then makes me wait while he opens a thick wooden door. Beyond it, steps lead down into darkness. More basements and underground tunnels. Brilliant.

A faint breeze whispers up the stairs, rippling my hair. It takes away the gaseous odour, replaces it with a smell of damp earth, cold stone and something else I can't readily identify. And then I have it.

The sea.

A none too gentle shove in the back forces me down the steps. I move carefully, one shoulder grazing the rough stone wall for support. Tumbling headlong into the darkness would be an undignified way to go.

I jar my feet when I reach the bottom unexpectedly; there's precious little light coming from the open doorway above. We're plunged into darkness when Tegwin pulls a lever that swings closed something much heavier than the wooden door. Under-ground tunnels with cunningly hidden entrances. Even more brilliant.

'Is this not all a bit James Bond villain?' I ask the darkness, then wish I hadn't as I hear the metallic clunk of a heavy-duty switch. Low-illumination wall lights flicker on, showing a tunnel that arcs away into a fuzzy distance.

'Move.' Tegwin jabs me with the gun, which is also a bit James Bond villain, or at least James Bond villain's henchman. Still, I do as I'm told. We walk through a seemingly endless network of tunnels, steps and wider caverns, quite breathtaking in its complexity. Sometimes the walls show the marks of careful construction, where industrious miners have carved them from the rock. Sometimes they're rough, jagged and clearly part of the natural rock formations. The further we go, the more impressed I am by the sheer improbability of it all. It must have taken lifetimes . . . centuries. How on earth has it been kept secret all this time?

The salty scent of the sea is growing stronger now. I've been counting under my breath, but I don't imagine I'd be able to retrace my steps should the opportunity present itself. Mostly, it gives me something to focus on other than the weariness and the deep ache in my muscles and bones. How long since I came to? It's hard to gauge time in this subterranean world, especially with the throb in my head from repeated blows.

'Stop.'

The command comes out of the blue, so unexpected I take two more paces before the word registers in my exhausted brain. I must be knackered as I've both forgotten where I'd got to with my counting, and not noticed the door I've just walked past. Tegwin unlocks it and swings it open with no creak of hinges. Well-maintained, then. Somewhere used regularly.

'In there.' He waggles the gun. I stare into utter darkness, save for the triangle of light splaying across a flagstone floor. I can see a few strands of what could be straw – but there's nothing else. The room is bare.

'Scream and shout if you want. Nobody will hear you.' Tegwin grabs my arm with his free hand, starts shoving me towards the opening. I'm not in any state to put up much of a fight, and soon enough I'm inside, teetering on the edge of collapse. When it clangs shut behind me, I see that the door has a tiny, barred window at the top, the light from beyond it doing nothing to illuminate my cell.

'I'll come back and deal with you later,' the old man says. Then he chuckles. 'Unless your friends in the NCA arrest me first, of course. Then you'll starve to death.'

33

As parting lines go, I have to admit Tegwin's is a good one. If I wasn't so completely washed out from being smashed over the head and all that walking, I might even have applauded. Instead, it's all I can do to sink slowly to the floor rather than collapsing in an untidy heap. Hands still stuck behind my back, I somehow manage to roll onto my side, let my head rest against the cold flagstones in an attempt to ease the pain.

Something changes as I lie there, although I can't say what. I still ache all over, but it feels as if the air has changed. Did I fall asleep? I don't get the sense of time having passed, but there aren't any cues to help me. I can't even say the stiffness in my neck is any indication, since all of me hurts anyway, particularly my shoulders where they're pulled back by my hands tied behind me. I really need to do something about that.

When I was at St Bert's, there was a game we used to play where we would clasp our hands together behind our backs and try to bring them round to the front without letting go. I'm not as athletic or supple as I was when I was thirteen, but I know I can't stay like this for much longer without doing serious damage to my neck and shoulders. The cold seeps up through the stone floor, leaching away my limited body warmth as I roll slowly onto my back and try to wriggle my hands down beneath my bum. Eventually, I get there. The effort leaves me breathless and I just lie still for a while before attempting the next bit, knowing my stiff joints are going to make it almost impossible.

I'm about to pull my knees up to my chin and try to get my hands down under my feet, when I sense more than hear something move in the room. Did I imagine it? I've been so preoccupied with recovering my strength and trying to stay awake, I've not really paid much attention to my darkened surroundings. But the space feels large, I'm tempted to say cavernous.

That noise again. And this time I'm fairly certain it's something moving. The sound isn't quite right for scraping over stone, but then I remember the straw I saw in the light of the open doorway. I can feel it prickling into my neck, which makes me think there must be more of it strewn around. As if this were a stable rather than a dungeon. It doesn't smell particularly mouldy, although now I'm concentrating more, there is a scent. Dirt and sweat and something else. Is it fear?

With a spasm that makes me gasp, I jerk my feet upwards and thrust my shoulders down at the same time. Blessed relief floods down my arms as my hands swing forward, but the effort has left me breathless and weak as a kitten. All I can do is lie there as the rustling sound of something moving through straw comes ever closer. Is it a rat? I don't mind rats, at least not the fancy ones, but a ravenous, wild rat that's been trapped in a deep cellar for any length of time likely won't be as friendly.

I have to sit up, I know, but I hardly have the strength to even roll over and try to see what's coming towards me. Judging by its slow progress and the noise it's making, it's not a rat. Much bigger than a rat. And as it comes closer, I can hear ragged, hitching breaths. Sobbing. Crying. My god, human.

'Hello?' My words echo, adding to the sense of space all around me. The movement stops, but I fancy I can see the faintest of shapes in the near total darkness.

'Hello?' I try again, using up the last of my strength to roll and shuffle until I'm on my knees. My hands are still tied together, but at least they're in front of me now and I can try to fend off an attack.

'C . . . Con? Is really you?'

I know that voice, its stilted, foreign accent. A thousand different thoughts rattle through my brain, the shock of recognition so strong it almost floors me.

'Lila?'

The dark shape shuffles towards me with greater speed now, and before I can even react, I'm enveloped in an awkward, desperate embrace. Close up, she stinks as if she's been here since that night on the cliffs, but I don't mind. It's all I can do to stop myself from bursting into fits of hysterical laughter as I realise we've once again been thrown into the same cell. Fate has a bastard sense of humour that way.

I don't know how long we sit, clinging to each other as if that's the only way to stay alive. Well, I say clinging to each other, but my hands are tied together so it's more Lila clinging to me, sobbing. I do my best to comfort her, even though I can barely see anything, only shadows in the greater darkness and that one tiny square of light at the top of the door. Certainly not her face, although when I finally lift both hands towards her head, she flinches as if expecting pain.

'It's OK.' My disjointed memory of her returns – one eye swollen shut, lip split. I can see more of that scene now, the narrow gap in the cliffs. How had I ended up down there? It's hard to unreel the memories. Like digging up a long-buried corpse, the images come in chunks. I'm on the clifftops, gazing out across a moonless sea. I'm hiding behind a bench as two men, Hefin and Karl, walk along the path. I'm following them, then looking down at the choppy waters far below, the pinprick lights of head torches. I'm discovered. The press of a gun barrel into the back of my neck, and with that memory comes a flurry of emotions. Embarrassment, anger at my own stupidity, fear.

I see it all now, as my captors force me down a treacherous narrow path that zigzags to the bottom of the cliffs. There's no way I'd have been able to do it in daylight, only darkness lessening the vertigo. On the other side of the gully, a line of people is being led along a narrow rock ledge and in through a cleft in the cliffside. You'd never spot it, if you didn't know it was there. The memories come in jumps, and now I'm facing Kieran Johns. Alwyn Kieran Johns, I should say. He takes the gun that was pressed into my neck and holds it to my forehead. This image I've seen before, and now it slots into place. The fractured puzzle of my broken mind coming together.

I am led away, though the reason why I'm not simply shot and thrown into the sea eludes me. Except that as soon as I think it, I hear Tegwin's voice say, 'Bring her. We'll throw her off the cliff. Make it look like an accident. Maybe suicide.' And that voice heralds another cascade of memories, finally tumbling into place.

'How long have you been down here?' I ask Lila, after what feels like hours but is probably only a few seconds.

'I . . . not know. No day, no night. Is long time.'

I gently pull away from her, then struggle to my feet and step over to the door. My eyes have accustomed themselves to the gloom as much as they're going to, but it's still not much illumination as I hold up my hands and inspect the zip ties around my wrist. Time was I'd have got them undone in a few seconds – but now my hands are numb, and I'm badly out of practice.

'I help?' Lila comes to my side. In the weak light, she looks a mess. I hold out my wrists and she squints at the ties, giving me the opportunity to study her more closely. Her face is thinner, although the bruising and split lip have gone. Has she really been down here all this time? Why would they do that?

'I saw you. That night, with the boat and the people?'

'They find me. After I run from the car, from your house. Take me back to Kieran. I try to be nice, way he likes it. But I am too old for him now. He has new girl.' Lila's fingers tremble as she works at the ties, but I can feel them loosening now.

'And the boat?'

'Some of people from Ukraine. I translate for them. Make self useful, or who knows what happen to me?'

The ties come apart and I let out a little sigh of relief, followed by a sharp intake of breath as the pins and needles hit. Flexing my fingers through the pain, I start to massage my wrists back to life.

'Doesn't seem to have worked so well.'

Lila stares at the floor. 'I take passports of people. Refugees. Not all. Just few at a time. I hide them away. Hope maybe find people, give them back. Old man notice them not there. He angry whole time now. Kieran angry too. Is not just passports. They say everything change.' Now she looks up at me, and in the faint light I can see the tears tracking through the grime and dirt on her cheeks. 'They say you bad luck. Blame me for bringing you here.'

My hands are beginning to feel almost normal again, only the points of my fingers still tingling, so I reach out and fold Lila into a hug. I've never been much of a one for hugging, but sometimes it's the best thing in the world. I can feel how thin she is under her clothes, the way her breath catches in sobs as she breathes. She winces as if her ribs pain her, and she smells sour, sick as well as unwashed. Now I'm paying attention, I notice a dull odour of human waste tainting the air too. If she's been here for days or weeks, she must have a bucket to go in somewhere. One with a lid or the air would be unbreathable by now.

'We need to get out of here.' I let Lila go and turn my attention to the door. It's old, made with thick wooden planks, solid and unyielding. I remember the way the lock opened without any obvious effort on Tegwin's part, the well-greased hinges. I run my fingers around the edges of the door, searching for any sign of an internal latch mechanism, but there's nothing.

And then I feel a flat metal disc with a dimple at the top. Unlike the lock it conceals, it's stiff with lack of use, but I manage to slide it around. A beam of pale light falls through from the passage outside in the shape of a keyhole and I imagine it painting my cheek like an unusual tattoo.

'I need something thin. Stiff enough to try and pick this lock.' I straighten up and almost fall over as my head goes faint. Luckily, Lila is so close behind me she can act as a prop until I'm able to gather myself together. Curse this damned tiredness. I thought I was getting better, but now the adrenaline's worn off and I'm overdue a crash.

'You are not well?'

'Being thrown off a cliff will do that to you. Just need to sit down and catch my breath for a while, OK?'

In the near-total darkness I just about make out Lila's head as she nods, and then she's lowering me gently to the ground. I end up with my back to the door, the light from the keyhole and tiny window disappearing into inky blackness. I can't see anything except a circle of floor perhaps two or three metres before it becomes indistinct.

'How big is this place?' I ask, and again I hear my voice echo slightly. This is no small dungeon cell but a much larger space.

'Is big. You stay. I go fetch.'

In a whisper, she's gone. I take the time to feel through my pockets for anything that might make a lockpick. It's futile, of course. They must have searched me while I was still uncon-scious, taken everything but my clothes. I've that to be grateful for, I suppose.

'Can use this?' Lila reappears at my side. She's holding something close to my face. A cheap metal fork, spoon and blunt knife with a round-nosed end. Fine for eating with, no use for attacking your gaoler. Or picking a lock, if I'm being honest. But even in this terrible darkness I can see the gleam of hope in Lila's eyes, so I haul my weary body up onto my knees, shuffle round until I'm facing the lock, and try my best.

I've done a bit of lock picking in my time. My old boss, Pete Copperthwaite, was quite the dab hand with a set of tiny picks, and he showed me how to do it once. This lock is nothing like the modern things with tumblers and barrels and all the other stuff they put in to make them secure. It's ancient, made of iron, and if it hadn't been so well-greased I'd have had no chance at all. As it is, the handle of the fork is just the right size to fit in the keyhole and waggle around until I find something that gives under pressure. It takes a couple of attempts, and there's a heart-stopping moment when I drop the fork and can't see where it's gone. Lila is on it like a flash, handing it back to me and then kneeling close by my side.

'Almost got it, I think.' I angle the fork one last time, wedge the knife into the tines for extra leverage, and gently twist. There's a satisfying clunk as the bolt slides back. I stand, reach for the tiny window, push my finger through the metal bars and pull. The door swings inwards on silent hinges to reveal the empty tunnel beyond.

34

'Where to go now?'

Lila's question brings me up short. The elation I felt from successfully picking the lock with nothing more than an old knife and fork doesn't sustain me long, and by the time we reach the first junction I'm flagging badly. Lila's not in any better shape than me, either. Probably cracked ribs, judging by the way she's holding her side and breathing in short, shallow gasps.

'I don't know.' I really have no idea. There's nothing to indicate which of our two options might be the right one. Both are lit by far-spaced low-wattage bulkhead lights. I can't remember too many sharp turns on my way here, but these two tunnels intersect in a shallow Y. When Tegwin led me this way, I was even more knackered than I am now, and I had the added worry of a gun in my back. Even so, I don't remember noticing another passage this close to our dungeon at all.

'Is maybe this way?' Lila gestures to the right. I let out a low groan of effort as I crouch down to inspect the floor, made of hard packed fine gravel. It doesn't show up any sign of footfall. No clues there.

'It's as good a choice as any,' I say, and we set off along our chosen path. There's a familiarity to the rough-hewn walls. The carved arch of the ceiling makes me feel like I have to stoop constantly. The lights are spaced so far apart that they don't illuminate the whole path, either. Little wells of light in the distance, we have to brave unseen perils in the darkness in between.

And then they all go out at once.

On instinct, I reach out in the blackness, catch Lila's hand. Her grip is fierce with fright, and I can hardly blame her. I've never liked enclosed spaces. This utter dark reminds me all too much of the sarcophagus I was trapped in. The one they put my mother in when she died.

'Stay calm.' I whisper it low, even though I don't feel like following my own instructions. 'We keep walking the way we were going. Slowly.' I reach out with my free hand until I can feel the stone wall. 'Put your hand out. If you feel an opening, we'll stop.'

Lila says nothing, but her grip tightens. We set off even more slowly than before, and it's all I can do to keep down the rising panic as the darkness presses in from all sides. This tunnel must go somewhere, otherwise why have permanent lighting? But then why did they turn it off? Has someone found our cell empty? Are they even now rushing to find us?

'Stop a moment.' I tug Lila's hand gently and get a pained grunt in response. Of course, it's her other side that was bothering her, so holding that arm out to feel the way will only make that worse.

'What is it?' she asks.

'Listen.' I strain my ears for the slightest sound, expecting to hear the crunch of boot on gravel. Or maybe the distant echoing boom of waves on a beach in a cave. But all I can distinguish is the pounding of my heart, the rush of blood in my ears, the rasp of mine and Lila's breaths.

But then, there's something else. A quiet snuffling noise that should be terrifying but is instead oddly comforting. I can feel Lila tense, hear her sharp intake of breath as she senses whatever is approaching too.

'C . . . Con?' She sounds like a little girl.

'It's OK. Here.' I pull her closer to me, and then we crouch in the darkness. I hope I'm right. Know, somehow, that I am right. The memory is there, after all. Dragging myself up a shallow, gritty beach. Arm broken, legs – who knows? Almost ready to give up until . . .

The shuffling stops and then I feel a cold, wet nose press itself against my free hand. I can see nothing, but I hear a gentle wuffle of excitement, the wagging swish of a tail, and then a loud fart that echoes in the narrow tunnel.

'Hey there, Gelert. How'd you find us then?' I scratch the dog behind the ears, feel Lila shrinking away in terror. 'It's Gareth . . . Lord Caernant's dog. Don't be scared.'

I find her hand and guide it to the dog's neck, or at least what I hope is the dog's neck. He gives another excited wuffle noise, not a bark as such. Then he pulls away from us both, shakes his head as if he's just been bathed. Although the smell of him suggests that's not happened in a while.

'How is here?' Lila asks. I shrug, but that's about as helpful as sign language in this utter, pitch black.

'I don't know.' I have a suspicion, but the logic of it doesn't work. Then again, the logic of these tunnels existing largely unknown doesn't work. And neither does the logic of my surviving being thrown off a cliff, of surviving without any physical injuries, of a missing day and fractured memories. None of it makes any sense.

I hear that flap of shaken ears again, a bit further away this time. Gelert has moved off in the direction we were already going. I feel for Lila's hand, and stand up straight again. 'I think we should follow.'

★ ★ ★

In the darkness, everything feels like a dream. Nothing makes sense any more, but that doesn't seem to matter. I can feel Lila's hand in mine, hear her ragged breathing, and yet a part of me wonders if she is actually there. If this is all some fever dream, then maybe she's a part of it too. I can hear Gelert as he leads us ever onwards, but he can't be here either, can he? There's no way the tunnels along the coast can connect with Plas Caernant, miles inland. That's insane.

Or I am.

Still, I am getting stronger with each step. My breathing has settled into a steady walking rhythm, not the laboured gasps of recent weeks. My head is still a little fuzzy, the memories disjointed, but the constant dull pressure that had worn me down has gone.

Time no longer has any meaning, so I don't know when I first notice the light. It's a slow realisation that I can make out shapes in the black, see the faintest glimmer on the damp surface of the rocks. The air is warmer, too. I start to catch scents other than Gelert's old dog ears and Lila's sour, ill taint. There's a mineral edge to the air, like bath salts poured onto hot water. And now I can make out the silhouette of the deerhound ahead of me, the gravel at my feet. I can see the shape of the tunnel, where it has been carefully carved from the rock and where it follows natural clefts and passages.

I notice something else, too. 'There are no lamps here,' I say out loud.

It's as if we've stepped into a different world, the darkness marking the boundary between mundane and myth. I am compelled to follow Gelert along these endless tunnels, a strange limbo between life and death. Until finally he stops, sits down and glances around. His bony tail thumps on the ground in expectation.

I approach him slowly, carefully, because now I can see something of what lies ahead and I am sure I must be dreaming. Lila still clutches my hand. I feel her grip tighten as we step from the tunnel and into the largest cavern I have ever seen. I can only make out the far side because it glitters with sparkling white crystals. There are more of them in the walls closer by, and up so high overhead it cricks my neck to look at them. They seem to glow from within, or is there a light source somewhere that they refract and amplify, like nature's own lasers? I don't know. It's all I can do to stop my mouth falling open in wonder and surprise.

The ground falls away from our tunnel entrance in a gentle slope of broken slate. Was this a mine once? Did human hands dig out this vast hall, or was it some race of giants? At the thought, my mind turns to Aisha and her tales of Celtic myths, even as my eyes focus on the central feature of this place and I wonder how I didn't see it straight away.

A lake.

Its surface spreads like a flawless black mirror, reflecting the crystals high overhead. From where Lila and I stand, it appears to be perfectly circular, perhaps thirty metres in diameter. The chipped and broken slate mounds up from its edges in a gentle beach of darkest grey.

Lila finally lets go of my hand and steps forward to take it all in. She's still favouring her side. Now that there's a bit more light, I can see how awkwardly she's walking, the twist to her hip and the pain in one knee. They've given her a thorough going over before throwing her in that dungeon to rot, and yet not once since we've been traipsing blindly along these tunnels has she complained. Not even a whimper. They make them tough in Ukraine.

'Be careful,' I say as she approaches the pool. The last thing I want is to dive in after her. Gelert wags his tail again, swishing against broken slate. Then he gets up and ambles down to where Lila kneels by the water. There is no time to shout a warning, and no hesitation as the dog butts her in the back with his great shaggy head. She lets out a short squeal of surprise and topples in.

Everything slows.

I watch Lila pitch forwards, breaking the perfect mirror of the water's surface. Ripples circle outwards until they hit the far shore and reflect back in complicated patterns. But by the time they've returned to the point where she fell in, she's gone.

I'm already moving, running towards the lake to Gelert's obvious delight. He gets in the way, tail wagging, tongue lolling, as I try to reach the edge, searching the dark surface for any sign of my friend below.

Nothing.

'Lila?' It's a stupid thing to shout. My voice disappears into the void before echoing back at me. My knees dig into the shale as I crouch down at the edge of the pool, feel the moistness seep into my trousers, surprisingly warm. All the ripples have faded to nothing now, as if the liquid is some viscous oil, not water at all.

I plunge my hand in, deep as I dare, feeling the bottom as it falls steeply towards the centre, loose stones tumbling from my touch and down into darkness. She should be just here, it's been only moments, and yet she's gone.

'Lila?' I ask the question again, more quietly this time, as my reflection comes back into focus in the calming waters. There is something very wrong here, and it takes me too long to understand what it is. High up above me, the cavern roof is made of stone, those sharp, white crystals running through it at strange angles and casting their illumination on the scene. I know this place. I've been here before in my dreams. Or are those memories? And if they are memories, then what does that mean? For Lila? For me? For my sanity?

Gelert slumps beside me, his bony body a surprising weight. His wagging tail sends small chips of slate splashing into the lake, and they shimmer the surface again. When it clears I think I can see something floating a few feet below. Not the reflection of my own gaunt features, but the faintest of flickering lights. Or is it a pale face and blonde hair turning in slow currents? The shock of realisation as the image coalesces in my mind is like a jolt of electricity, spurring me to action.

No thought for my safety, no thought for anything, I stand up, breathe deep and plunge into the pool.

35

I wake up with a start, confused. My mind tells me I should be plunging into warm water, but I'm cold. Lying on hard stone, my hands still awkwardly behind my back, tied together.

What the fuck?

I open my eyes to darkness, although not the complete inky blackness of the unlit tunnels. Neither is it the total nothingness of the pool. Was that really the Cauldron of Life, from Aisha's tales? More like some kind of desperate fever dream.

Rolling onto my back, I manage to lift my legs up, shuffle my hands under my bum and bring them in front of me, like I thought I'd done hours ago. My shoulders are agony, but that's to be expected. What's less expected but far more welcome is how I feel supple and strong again. The bone-crushing weariness is gone. I'm not fighting fit, for sure. But as I shuffle to my knees, and then onto my feet, I don't feel like I'm about to come crashing back down to the floor again. Nor do I want to gather up as much straw as I can, arrange it into a more comfortable bed, and go back to sleep.

Sleep. The thought of it makes me wonder. Is that what I've been doing since I was locked in here? I remember leaning forward, head aching, the cool of the flagstones. Did I slip into unconsciousness then? Was everything that happened afterwards some vivid hallucination as the last of whatever illness has been draining all my energy burned itself out? If I didn't free my hands and pick the lock then . . .

'Lila?'

There is no answer. Not even the scurrying of startled rats.

'Lila?'

Again, nothing, and I have to concede she's not here. My disappointment verges on true grief at the loss, but I push it away. No time for that, Con. Escape first, puzzle out what's happened to your mind afterwards.

Searching the cavern, I find a trough carved from the stone, and discover the hard way that it's full of fresh spring water. Indistinct shapes turn out to be stout wooden boxes, the sort of thing heavy machinery is delivered in. Some are still unopened and unmoveable; others have been crowbarred and emptied of their contents. There isn't enough light to read the stencils on the sides of the boxes, but as I look at them it occurs to me they wouldn't fit through the door easily. There must be another way in. And possibly out.

I find it a little further into the darkness, but any hope I might escape is swiftly dashed. There's a steel door wide enough to drive a car through, and when I press my ear against it, I can just about hear the rhythmic sound of waves. It sparks a memory, being led through another, larger cavern, its sloped concrete floor disappearing under water towards what must be a cave entrance at low tide. At the top of that ramp, there had been a rusty steel door. I remember it now. Somehow, I am certain that I'm currently standing on the other side of that door. As trapped as I was then, unless I can find a way to open it.

I continue my circuit of the room, until I find what feels like a nest. The straw is deep here, pulled from one of the opened boxes where it must have been used to protect whatever had been packed inside. Close by, I almost kick over a bucket, knocking the lid off it. A powerful stink rises up, until I find the lid and clamp it back on. There's a ledge in the stone wall here, and that's where I find what I've been looking for all along. A tin plate scraped clean and a set of cheap metal cutlery.

But no Lila. So, what did I see before? Her ghost?

I shake the idea away, swallow the lump it brings to my throat. The knife isn't sharp, but it makes quick work of the plastic tie holding my hands together. The pain of release is acute, but I work through it as the life eases back into my fingers. I hurry back to the small door where I was thrown in before. My memory of picking the lock the last time has a dream-like quality to it, but when I push the fork handle into the hole it fits exactly as I'd expected it to. The bolt is well oiled, and slides back. Within moments, the door springs open. There's a switch on the wall outside. I flick it on, more bulkhead lamps lighting up my prison. It's little more than a storeroom, only that industrial-scale door on the opposite wall making it look unusual. That, and the nest of packaging materials in the driest corner.

Something about the box they've been dragged from catches my attention enough for me to prop the door open and go take a quick closer look. There are five in total, including the empty one, the size of the tea chests that used to live in the attic at Harston Magna Hall, filled with old paintings and other long-forgotten rubbish. They're made of thin wood, the edges held together with metal strips, and the base of each one has gaps for a pallet truck to move them around. The writing stencilled on the sides is in Cyrillic letters. My Russian is far too rusty to even remember how to read that alphabet, but I don't need a translator to recognise the international symbol for explosives.

I gently push against the top of the nearest unopened box, hoping that it might be empty. It isn't, and judging from the way I can't make it move at all, there's enough explosive in this room to significantly change the coastline of Ceredigion. Why the hell do they need it? Who are they selling it to? And more to the point, what have they done with the contents of the empty crate?

I have a horrible idea that I know. Something Tegwin said when I was up in the steadings at the farm, about clearing everything out. They're not going to stop their operations just because I've shone a light on them, but they'll move away from Penparc Uchaf, collapse the tunnels into the old steadings and start up again somewhere else. And what better way to cover up than an unfortunate accident at their shiny new anaerobic digester? All that gas go boom.

Only, I've sent evidence to my team that will have them all converging on the farm any time now. And they've no idea what they're walking into.

The tunnels are much less sinister as I work my way back in what I hope is the right direction for the farm. There are also considerably fewer junctions than when I wandered them earlier with Lila. Perhaps it's growing familiarity that makes them seem less extensive, but given my recent strange experiences I can't shake the idea there might be more to it than that.

I've only walked a few dozen strides when the tunnel opens up onto another cavern that I'm confident I came through with Tegwin earlier. As confident as I am about anything in my current mental state. Glancing around, I can see the different entrances and exits to this place. There's the one I've come from, and close by it the one that must lead to the other side of the big metal door, the narrow gully and a way up to the cliffs. Outside. I'm tempted to go that way, but the light falling on the entrance to a fourth tunnel shows steps climbing upwards. That night, before they threw me off the cliff, we climbed narrow stone steps that led to the little combe, the jumble of rocks artfully hiding the exit. If I go that way, I can get out onto the clifftop path, make my way above ground to the farm. Maybe even find some way of contacting Karen, warning the team not to come near. My claustrophobia has been growing since I woke up in the cell, and knowing there are explosives that could collapse the tunnels is not helping.

I change course, and head for the stairs.

The lights give out long before I reach the surface. I suppose there's a logic to not having them too close to any entrance where they might be seen at night. It would only take one forgetful smuggler to give away all these long-held secrets. I guide myself up the steps by letting my fingers brush lightly against the wall, feeling with each foot before trusting my weight to it fully. It slows me down, and that only heightens my anxiety, but there's no other way.

The darkness begins to change at around the same time my hand brushes against a thin wire. I can smell a different scent on the air, too. Where before it had been flat, mineral, the un-changing dampness of caves, now I can smell earth and feel the faintest of breezes. I keep going, my fingers using the wire as a guide until they bump up against something hard, smooth, rectangular. About the size of a brick sliced in half lengthways. Instinctively I recoil, knowing it for a block of explosive without needing to see. Some kind of plastic, Semtex or the like. It's been duct-taped to the tunnel wall, another three in an arch to make sure the job is done properly.

I hate explosives almost as much as I hate guns, but I know enough about both to leave well alone. Tempting though it is to remove the detonators from the plastic, I've no idea whether that would trigger them to blow or not. Best leave it to the experts.

How I manage to stop myself from running the last few tens of metres, I've no idea. Perhaps it's the knowledge that my friends are in danger and a sprained ankle down here could be the difference between life and death for all of us. By the time I emerge from the narrow gap in the tumble of rocks and out into the night air, my heart is hammering away in my chest so hard it must be audible for miles. For a moment, all I can do is bend over, hands on my knees, and breathe deeply, all too aware that time is running out.

There's the faintest of dawn tints to the night sky, but the fact that it is still night gives me hope as I scramble out of the combe and head towards the clifftop path. Tegwin wanted everything cleared by dawn. What little evidence there might have been of this part of his smuggling empire will be gone soon, my colleagues and friends with it. Even Billy Latham doesn't deserve that.

I can't linger here. Mustn't linger here. The feelings are too raw, the memories vivid. When I turn away from the cliff, force myself along the path towards Penparc Uchaf, my legs are shaking, my whole body jittery. I may be stronger now than I've felt in weeks, but mentally I'm still a work in progress if not an actual wreck. It takes concentration to push myself forward into danger, not run back all the way to the cottage I no longer have a set of keys for.

Which is probably why I don't notice the men coming towards me until it's too late.

36

'Well, look what we've got here, boyo. If it isn't a little mouse escaped from its cage.'

They loom out of the darkness, so sudden and unexpected I take an involuntary step backwards. Then remember what's behind me, and stand my ground. William Kendall, Slaphead, is keeping his bald head warm under a woolly bonnet, hands shoved into the pockets of a camouflage jacket that almost works in this scant pre-dawn light. Beside him, the man Tegwin called Hefin wears his habitual scowl, and I can feel the weariness boiling off him. He's been awake, sorting things out, shouting at people and generally doing what his boss tells him to do for the whole night. I know with startling clarity that he's been sent to walk the cliffs all the way to Twmp, to make sure there are no night walkers like me to hear the explosions when they bring down all the hidden tunnel entrances along this stretch. Not that he cares if people get hurt, just doesn't want it to be obvious it's not the new digester going up. He's the one who has spoken, but I can tell by the way his hands flex by his side that he doesn't have his gun with him; almost read the frustration in his mind as if he's saying it out loud.

'Come to fetch me have you, boys?' I try to project as much confidence into my voice as I can, even if I don't actually feel any. At least they've stopped walking towards me, the distance between us enough that if they rush I might be able to react before they catch me. Not sure what I'll do, mind you. I might be stronger than I was yesterday, and I don't want to think too hard about how that works, but I'm still not in the shape I was when Slaphead and his last best friend tried to jump me.

'Reckon you're hardly worth the effort.' Hefin takes a step forwards. 'But the boss'll want to know you've got out, I guess.'

He lunges, but I duck and swerve, trip him as he goes past me and then jab my other boot to the back of his knee. He goes down with a squeal of pain, but I'm already moving. Slaphead's reactions are quicker than Hefin's; I guess he's seen me fight before. Even so, I can tell exactly what he's going to do a split second before he does it. The punch would probably have knocked me unconscious if it had connected, but it sails past me through the space where my head had been only moments before. Hefin's struggling to get back up as I pivot around, spinning Slaphead away from me. The two of them collide, and then with a scream of terror that rips to my very core, Slaphead steps backwards into nothing.

There's a moment when the whole world seems to stop. It's like Wile E. Coyote and the Roadrunner, except that there's nothing funny here at all. Slaphead's eyes are so wide I think they're going to pop out, and he windmills his arms so fast he might almost fly. I'm reaching for him, even as I know it's hopeless. He's too far away, too heavy. If I did grab him then I'd be like Greasy Rat. And then one foot goes from under him, kicking up loose gravel across the path. He lets out more of a whimper this time, and he's gone.

'Fuckin' gonna die for that, bitch.'

If he ever had any discipline, Hefin's lost it now. I'm almost caught out by his ferocity, horrified as I am by what's just happened to Slaphead. I dodge Hefin's flailing fists as his anger turns to blind rage, robbing him of any skill he might have had. When it comes, the opening is as clear as if it were full daylight and we'd been practising this choreographed fight scene for days. He springs forward, opens his mouth to roar at me again, and I jab my knuckles hard into his unprotected throat.

I can't pretend it isn't deeply satisfying watching him crumple to the ground, gasping to breathe, face darkening with the effort. For a moment I stand over him, staring down as my heartbeat slows. I can still feel his anger and hatred as if I'm somehow plugged into his mind, which isn't the most pleasant of images. And then I hear a noise behind me, feel an undercurrent of utter terror and panic.

Turning swiftly, I see nothing but the black of night leaching into grey as dawn approaches. A few tufts of wiry grass cling to the top of the cliff, rippling in the morning breeze. Somewhere a seagull cries, and beyond it I hear that noise again. A sobbing wail of hopeless fear.

A quick check confirms Hefin's not going anywhere soon. I move cautiously to the cliff, all too aware that this is the exact spot where I was thrown from, and look down towards the distant sea. Slaphead is about a metre below the edge, desperate hands clinging to the tiniest of ledges. His bonnet's gone, and I can see the shiny dome of his shaved head glow in the faint light.

I can't honestly say I'm not tempted to let him fall, just for a fraction of a second. Only a fraction, mind you. He might have tried to rape me, might have been part of the gang that have brought drugs into the country, trafficked women for illegal sex work. He might be a pitiful excuse for a human being, but he doesn't deserve to die this way. I should know; I've done it myself after all.

'Hold on. I'll get you.' I've no idea how; he's too far to reach even if I lay flat, and it's doubtful I'd have the strength to pull him up on my own. He looks up as he hears my voice, eyes white and wide.

'Please. Help.'

'Just hold on.' I move back from the edge, look around for something, anything, I can use. There's only Hefin, still lying on the ground trying to breathe. Fine. Needs must when the devil drives, and all that. I hurry to his side, check he's still too pre-occupied to put up a fight.

'Going to need this.' I undo his belt, pull it out through the loops. He tries to stop me, but he's got no strength. Nice to be on the other side of that equation for a change. His boots take a little longer to remove, and pulling down his trousers gives me no great thrill. He tries to choke out a 'Why?' as I roll him over and help myself to his coat too, but there's no time to explain.

I tie Hefin's coat and trousers together, then attach them to his belt looped around my middle. It's long enough, barely, so that I can kneel at the cliff edge and use the clothes as a makeshift climbing rope. Slaphead's so wrapped up in his misery and fear, I worry he might let go and fall to his death when I call to him again, but he manages to hold on.

'You'll have to climb up yourself!' I yell over the rising wind. 'I can take the weight, but no way I can pull you up.'

A single nod of understanding, and then I lean back, bracing myself as the knotted coat and trousers go taut. He's not a big man, Slaphead, but he's solid after many narcissistic hours in the gym. I feel the rough gravel and stone of the path dig into my knees, the pull of Hefin's belt as it tightens around my back. And then a hand reaches over the top of the cliff, followed by another. I shuffle back to allow him space, unclip the belt as he flops onto the path and rolls over, gasping.

It takes a moment for both of us to get our breath back. Slaphead is the first to speak.

'Tha . . . Thank you. Thou . . . Thought I was a . . . goner.'

'Yeah, well. Don't get too cocky. You're still under arrest.'

Slaphead doesn't say anything to that, so I guess he's going into shock now. I can see his arms trembling from the strain of holding on for dear life. I don't feel all that bad about rolling him over onto his front, pulling them up tight behind him and tying them together with Hefin's belt. He lies there all the while, accepting it and not saying anything. He doesn't need to; I can read the misery in his thoughts.

I can also hear Hefin's choking sounds growing louder, and when I look to see if he's OK, I find he's trying to laugh. He's up on his hands and knees now, struggling to stand but still having trouble breathing. All I sense from him is hatred, blind and unreasoning. And I can see his face now in my memory, the look of glee as he grabbed my arm and shoved me towards the cliff.

'You're . . . too . . . late . . .' He forces out each word before dragging in a painful breath. 'Gonna . . . blow . . . sky . . . high . . .'

I stride over, grab him by the throat and lift him up so that he has to look me in the eye. The scorn on his face turns to a grimace as I squeeze, which suggests I've done more damage to his windpipe than I'd realised. What a shame.

'The explosives you've rigged all around here. Where's the detonator?'

I know what he's going to say before he says it. 'Fugg . . . you . . .' He even tries to spit at me, but ends up dribbling down his chin. I give his throat another squeeze, then let him go. He drops back onto all fours as I stand up, gasping for more breath until I kick him hard in the head. Then he collapses and stops moving.

'The old man has it.'

I look around, realising that the light is quickly seeping into the day now. Slaphead sits upright, hands behind his back where

I've tied them. He's regained some of his composure, and unlike the waves of utter revulsion I was getting from his friend, all I read from him is regret.

'Tegwin?'

'Yeah. It's a remote switch thing. Linked to his phone, I think. We were supposed to meet him at Islwyn's Cove after we'd checked the coast was clear.'

'Islwyn's Cove?'

Slaphead nods in the direction leading away from the farm. 'Where we found you the last time. Tide's low, so he'll be taking the boat into the cave alongside. Load up the last of the gear and then we'll rendezvous with the *Anwen's Favour* out in the bay. Soon as we're out on the water – boom.' He shrugs his shoulders as the best mimicry of explosion he can manage.

'How long will he wait for you?' I crouch down beside the bundle of Hefin's trousers and coat as I ask the question, start going through his pockets like I should have done before I turned them into a makeshift rope.

'Not long. We should be there already. I'd have said he'd wait a while, but if what you said about Karl is true?'

'It is. Pushed him over the edge himself.' I find Hefin's phone, flip the case open and hope it's not one of these face recognition ones. It isn't, but it needs a thumbprint. When I roll the unconscious man over, I see a trickle of blood from his nose, take a second to check he has a pulse. I wouldn't mourn him if he was dead, but it would mean a lot of awkward questions, and quite probably paperwork.

'Karl was Tegwin's nephew. His sister's only child. What kind of man kills his own nephew?'

I tune Slaphead out as I press Hefin's right thumb to the phone. The home screen appears, a couple of angry texts from his boss showing as notifications. Ignoring them, I start dialling Karen's number, hoping my memory's up to scratch. Silence for a moment, and I pray it doesn't go to voicemail. Then the ringtone, once, twice.

'Hello? Who is this?'

'K, it's me. Con. Where are you right now?'

'Con? Christ, where are you? Whose phone is this? What's—'

'K. Listen to me. I'm fine. Where are you? Because if it's anywhere near Penparc Uchaf Farm you need to get the fuck out of there. It's rigged with enough explosives to give Cardigan a new bay.'

The silence on the line confirms my worst fears. I take the time to rearrange Hefin into the recovery position. In the growing light, I notice a head torch lying a few paces away. He must have lost it in our short fight.

'Stay with him,' I say to Slaphead, then I grab the torch and start walking towards the combe. When Karen comes back on the line I can hear her breathing heavily, sounds of hurried movement in the background.

'Where are you, Con? Your car's here, but the house and yard are empty. Just a big shed full of cows looking like they want to be milked.'

My car. Dammit, if the old Volvo gets blown up by some idiot Welsh drug smuggler I'm going to be more pissed off at that than anything. 'You all clearing out?'

'Fast as we can. Billy found a block of Semtex in one of the old stone buildings. He was going to pull the blast cap out of it, but Diane managed to stop him in time.'

'Yeah. They're all wired to a remote detonator. Looks like Tegwin Johns doesn't take too kindly to having his plans buggered.'

'Seems a bit spiteful, blowing everything up.'

'He threw me off a cliff, K.'

'Yeah, I guess there is that.' For a moment, all I can hear is laboured breathing, and then someone shouting orders in the background that I can't quite make out. 'Where are you, Con? We traced your phone to the farm, but . . .'

I've reached the hidden entrance to the tunnels now. It's not so easy getting in with one hand holding the phone to my ear and the other with the torch. I don't pause, though. If I did that, then I'd probably think hard enough about what I'm about to do to realise it's a bad idea. 'There's no time to explain. I'm not far away, but I'm probably going to lose the signal any moment.'

'Con? What are you up to?'

'Go to the cottage. Where I was staying before all this happened. I'll meet you there.' I don't wait for Karen's response, knowing she's only going to try to talk me out of this. As I tap the phone's screen to end the call I see another text message from Tegwin.

Leaving in five minutes. With or without you.

The timestamp's one minute ago, which gives me four to get down the tunnels to the cave. A day ago, I wouldn't have been able to walk for four minutes without having to stop to catch my breath. Now I feel an angry energy filling me. How dare he destroy this place like it's his own private playground and not the work of millennia? How fucking dare he?

I switch on the torch and play the beam along the ground so I can avoid tripping. Then I start to run.

37

I slow down before I reach the end of the tunnel leading to the last cavern and the sea. Partly because it's always a good idea to approach danger with caution, but mostly because even my new-found energy has its limits. As I walk the last few metres, keeping close to the tunnel wall, I can hear the low echoing burble of an idling outboard motor. Not painfully loud, but enough to block out all other sounds. Hopefully that means they won't hear me coming.

It's just as well the bulkhead lights are lit, as I almost forget to turn off Hefin's head torch before I'm close enough to the tunnel mouth for it to be seen. I shove it in my pocket alongside the phone, then crouch down as low as I can manage before risking a peek into the cavern. It's at once familiar from my last, brief visit, and yet very different. The tide must be almost as low as it ever gets, if the shiny seaweed and barnacles clinging to the rock wall of the far side are any indication. The space is lit by more than the lamps too, and there's a hint of natural light flickering off water, although I can't see the cave mouth from here.

'Where the fuck are they?'

The voice echoes in the cavern, but I get enough of a sense of direction from it to know the speaker is down towards the water.

A stack of boxes gives me some cover, and I crawl up to them, as quiet as a mouse.

'That's five minutes up, now. Come on. We're leaving.'

I recognise Tegwin's voice, and as I peer through a narrow gap between boxes, I can see the old man standing at the wheel of a large semi-rigid inflatable. He's got his phone in one hand, and that gives me an idea. I pull out Hefin's, glad I remembered to disable the lock screen. Tap in a quick reply to the old man's last text. Hope there's a signal down here.

Fairchild escaped. Caught her on clifftops. Bringing with us. Five mins.

I've no idea if it will convince Tegwin, but it'll slow him down long enough. Long enough for what, though? I need to stop them; keep them here. No way they're going to set off any explosives if they're not already far away. The obvious solution would be to disable the boat somehow. Sink it, maybe? But how? There's at least two of them, and I'm not in as good shape as I'd like to be.

'Fucking typical.' Tegwin lifts up his phone and stares at the screen. So the text must have gone through.

'What is it?'

I freeze as I hear the other voice. It's Kieran, that voice is unmistakeable. And he's so close I can almost sense him. No, that's not true. I can sense him. I can feel his frustration, worry, an underlying current of anger that's directed almost entirely at me. Well, it's nice to be noticed, I guess.

'That fucking Fairchild woman's got out.' Tegwin waves his free hand towards the large metal door. 'Go check the receiver. Last thing we need is for her to have tampered with it.'

'Is she . . . ?' Kieran doesn't finish the question, and neither has he moved to carry out his father's command. Just as well, since I've got a clear view of the big door, which means when he goes over there, he'll have a clear view of me.

'They've caught her. Bringing her with them. I'll take great pleasure in tying a couple of creels to her legs and throwing her to the lobsters.' He shoves the phone in his pocket. 'Now, hurry. Check that receiver.'

I make myself as small as possible, huddling in among the boxes as I watch Kieran stride up the slope towards the big metal door. The floor is a concrete ramp that levels off at the top to form an area wide enough to park a boat trailer. There's a grey metal box set into the concrete surround, and when Kieran opens it, I see a heavy lever switch that wouldn't look out of place in a World War Two bunker. Perhaps that's what this is, some long-forgotten defence against a potential German invasion. He reaches in, pulls it down, and with much clanking the door swings open. Of course, that's when he turns around to look at his father in the boat.

I freeze, not even daring to breathe. Not even daring to think, as his gaze slides over the shadowed corner where I'm hiding in plain sight. All I can do is watch, as he pulls out his own phone and then slowly turns and steps into the storeroom that was until recently my prison. Once the big metal door has swung completely open, I can see the far door with its little barred window at the top, half open onto the tunnel beyond. In moments, Kieran has pushed through it, and turned the opposite way to where I went. Presumably that's where the receiver is for whatever remote detonator Tegwin is using. Linked to his phone, didn't Slaphead say? That would explain why the old man's keeping a hold of it.

A plan begins to form in my head. All I need to do is get the phone off Tegwin. Chances are that Kieran will have the number too, though. So, I'll need to get his phone as well. One of them, I might stand a chance, but both?

I scan the cavern, looking for a weapon. Leaning up against the opposite wall, I spot a long pole with a hook on the end. It has a nautical name, but I can't for the life of me think what. You can use it for fishing buoys out of the water, or fending a boat away from the quayside. It looks a little unwieldy, but formidable. All I need to do is cross about fifteen metres of open ground without being seen.

'Well, look what we have here.'

The voice sends a chill deep into my core. It's right behind me and I know exactly who it is without needing to turn and look. I don't dare turn and look anyway, as the other thing chilling me is a horribly familiar cold metal barrel pressed into the back of my head. How the hell did Kieran manage to double back and come down the same tunnel I used?

'Up.'

It's not a command I can easily refuse, so I stand slowly, raising my arms to show I'm not a threat. Kieran steps in close, pats me down. He feels the torch and phone in my pocket, pulls them out.

'In the boat. Quick about it.' The gun jabs me painfully in the back, pushing me off balance so that I have no option but to step forwards. Tegwin's eyes narrow in suspicion when he sees me. He says nothing, though, only watching as Kieran marches me down the narrow jetty. He still has his phone in one hand, the other resting on the wheel.

'Looks like Hefin and Will won't be joining us.' Kieran holds up Hefin's phone. 'Bitch had this in her pocket. Reckon she probably sent you that last text.'

Tegwin grunts something I don't quite catch. Then he hooks a thumb over his shoulder. 'Chuck her in the back and cast off. Time we were getting out of here. *Anwen's Favour* will be waiting for us.'

I'm stepping over the inflatable tube that makes up one half of the hull when Kieran shoves me hard in the back, sending me sprawling into a pile of boxes and other detritus. There are some lobster creels there, and Tegwin's earlier words about a watery grave come back to haunt me. Now would probably be my best chance to wrestle the phone off the old man, but before I can even get my feet underneath me, Kieran's untied the ropes and hopped aboard, pushing the boat away from the jetty. He has better sea legs than me, finding his balance easily as he levels the gun at my face. Tegwin guns the engine, and we glide out of the cave into open water.

38

More light has leached into the day as Tegwin pilots the boat expertly out of the cave and navigates a path through the rocks at the base of the cliffs. I'm mostly searching around for something I can use as a weapon, but I can't help noticing how the coming dawn paints the underside of the low clouds in rippling shades of pink and orange. A storm on its way, perhaps. Certainly, the wind has picked up, whipping the tops of the waves into foam. Not quite white horses yet, but maybe white foals. They bicker and prance, pushing us back the way we have come.

I landed awkwardly when Kieran shoved me to the back of the boat, but I'm reluctant to move too much while he's got his gun trained on me. Lying down feels safer as the waves pitch us this way and that. Further out, things would probably settle down to a rhythmic bobbing, but close to the towering walls of granite, the sea is choppy and unpredictable. Tegwin has both hands occupied controlling the boat, his phone wedged into a cradle taped to the metal frame that holds the wheel and instruments, and which looks like it should be suckered to the windscreen of a car, not out here on the ocean. There's not much in the boat apart from the three of us. A couple of well-stuffed waterproof duffel bags are stowed towards the bows, presumably their luggage. The rigid part of the hull has a slatted wooden deck, but nowhere to sit. Either side of me, at the stern, red plastic fuel tanks are bolted in, pipes leading to the outboard engine. Stacked alongside them, four empty lobster creels look out of place.

I can't see anything that would be of any use in a fight.

'What about this one?' Kieran half turns to his father, nodding his head at me. He sways with the motion of the boat, but the gun stays uncomfortably level.

'Tie her to those creels.' Tegwin lobs a thumb over his shoulder without looking back, his voice raised against the wind, the growl of the outboard motor and the crash of sea against cliff. He takes his hand off the throttle lever for an instant, and the boat tips awkwardly as it catches a wave side on. Is it just my imagination, or are those ponies becoming stallions?

I taste salt spray on my face, hear Tegwin's curses as he struggles with the wheel against a suddenly stiffer breeze. Kieran's balance is good, but he can't stay upright and keep the gun on me. Not without a handrail to hold. He takes a step closer, crouches and grabs the rope that runs the length of the inflatable upper part of the hull.

'You heard,' he shouts over the growing noise. 'Those two creels. Tie them to your ankles.'

The creels have thin ropes neatly attached to them and coiled for stowage. They're not long; maybe only a couple of metres. Enough to tie them to the longer ropes that are lowered to the seabed, presumably.

'No sudden moves. I'll shoot you if I have to.' Kieran waggles the gun as I shift onto my knees.

'You won't get away with it,' I say as I reach for the first creel, take a hold of the rope and slowly unwind it. My eyes are half on Kieran and the gun, half on the choppy waters. I can see a wave coming in from the side again, and while I've no doubt Tegwin has seen it too, if I can keep Kieran distracted for a moment longer, I might just have a chance.

'We've been getting away with it for centuries. This is a minor setback, believe me.'

'No. It really isn't. You may have been fine running rum and tobacco past the excise men, might even have been OK bringing cocaine in for the idle rich in London. But you crossed a line when you started trafficking in slaves, didn't you? Bringing in children for men to pay to rape. I've heard you like them young yourself, eh, Kieran?' I take the free end of the rope in one hand, run the other along its length to where it's attached, test the weight of the creel. Only one chance.

'Shut your fucking mouth and tie that rope.' Kieran motions with the gun again, the flush of anger in his eyes as they stare straight at me. Good, he's not paying attention to the sea.

The wave hits the boat at exactly the same time as the gun stops pointing my way. I've one leg under me, and as the boat tilts I use the momentum to stand. The creel is heavier than I'd estimated, but not so heavy I can't manage to lift it, swing it round with all my might.

It catches his arm, knocks him sideways. The sound of the gun is like a thunderclap, echoing off the cliffs behind us. I've no idea where the bullet goes, but before Kieran can fire again, a second, larger wave catches the boat. Tegwin turns to see what's happening, pulling the wheel with him, and the boat tilts further still. Kieran screams in alarm as he grabs at the creel to try and stop himself going over the side. Two short steps, and I'm right in front of him. One short shove, and he's in the water, rope tangling around his arm and neck as the creel pulls him under.

For a split second, I think he's somehow managed to fire the gun again. A roar like an explosion rises over the din. We're in among jagged rocks, a reef not far off the shore, but the sound is not the sea. Tegwin's bellow of fury is like a thunderclap, and I duck just in time as his fist sails past my ear. The boat pitches like a mad animal, throwing us both off balance. The old man recovers swiftly, more accustomed to the sea than I am.

'You fucking bitch. Should have put a bullet in you the first time.'

He launches himself at me, surprisingly fast and agile. There's not much room in the boat, and the waves have shaken loose the other creels, tumbling them around our feet. I dodge the first blow, but there's nowhere to go; I can't keep away from him forever.

And then I notice that both his hands are clenched into fists. A brief glance at the wheel, and I see his phone still in its holder. Kieran's phone will be useless now, Hefin's too. Only that one left to set off all those explosives.

I feint towards the stern of the boat and the still-burbling outboard motor as Tegwin comes in for another attack. At the last possible moment, I drop and launch myself the other way. He's so enraged, I can tell that he's not thinking strategically anymore. I'm tempted to use that against him. I can't risk it though; there's too much at stake.

Scrambling to my feet, I stagger to the wheel, snatch the phone from its cradle and throw it into the sea. An instant later, the old man crashes into me, eyes mad with fury, face so red he might explode, spittle flecking the corners of his mouth.

Before I know it, his hands are round my throat, squeezing hard as we both fall to the slatted deck. I flail, trying to grab something. My hand hits the throttle lever, knocking it all the way back, and the boat surges forward with a howl from the outboard engine. For a moment, all I can see past mad Tegwin's puce face is the angry slate grey sky. Then the world turns upside down as the boat hits something hard and flips on its end. We're thrown into the air, but the old man is so far gone he doesn't seem to notice. His hands are tight around my throat, choking the life out of me as we fall towards the rocks and the sea, and all I can think is 'Fuck, not this again.'

Tegwin hits first. Our impact with the water forces him to let go of me. The sea swallows us in its briny embrace. I have to fight every instinct to take in a huge breath. Mouth clamped tight shut, I kick away. My boots collide with something that might be a rock, or might be Tegwin Johns. I no longer care. All I want is to breathe.

The water boils and crashes around me, waves throwing me about. I can't tell what way is up and what way down.

If I don't breathe soon, I'll drown.

My sodden clothes are dragging me to the bottom, boots filled with water. The sea is cold, leaching what little strength there was from my muscles. Come on, Con. Get yourself together.

No second chances.

A wave pushes me against something hard, and for a moment I think I'm going to be dashed on the rocks. Then whatever it is gives slightly. I grab, feel a rope and the smooth, tubular surface of the boat's inflatable section. It's upside down, but it's on the surface. I haul myself up, almost screaming with the effort as my head breaks through.

Breathing never felt so good, nor so painful. For a while, all I can do is cling on and gulp down as much air as possible. The sea has become a mad swirl of waves and froth, the wind howling out of nowhere. Waves crash against the cliffs, and I know there are rocks nearby encrusted with shells that will rip my flesh to shreds. I can see no one, but then I can't see far in any direction, my eyes stinging with salt spray, head barely above the surface. Only the looming grey mass of the cliffs gives me any sense of direction, and they're both too close for comfort and too far away to reach.

At least they haven't exploded. I can congratulate myself on that. Well done, Con. You've saved the day. Now all you need to do is save yourself.

A wave picks up the boat unexpectedly, spinning it around with me still clinging on to the rope. My shoulder's almost wrenched out of its socket as I'm lifted from the water, and then my grip gives up. I'm falling again, no fight left in me.

I hit the sea hard, another wave leaping up to greet me before I'm ready. My head bends forward, chin smacking against my chest, knocking me senseless. And as the blackness washes over me, I can't help thinking that at least this time I went out on my own terms.

39

Seagulls scream, their calls piercing my head. I want to tell them to fuck off and stop spoiling my rest, but then it occurs to me I don't remember lying down. Certainly, I don't remember lying down on a stony beach.

Something makes a noise close by. Not the soft wash of waves; this sounds more like somebody rattling a cloth sack filled with wet bones. I know that noise, but I can't quite place it, until I hear the soft crunch of feet on pebbles, and then something warm and slimy starts to lick my face.

I mean to go 'urgh', but instead I vomit up my own body weight in seawater, great heaving gouts of it emptying from my stomach. There's so much, it comes out of my nose, the sting of it bringing tears to my eyes.

'Urgh.' This time I manage a sound, although my throat feels as rough as if I'd been shouting all night. I haul myself up onto all fours. Through blurred vision, I can make out the familiar sight of Twmp Beach, and right beside me Gelert the deerhound. He's soaking wet, salt-water dripping from his beard. He wags his tail when he sees me looking at him, then hawks up almost as much seawater as I did. When he's finished, he shakes himself, then stoops to lick my cheek again.

'Enough, already.' I reach up, wobbly and weak, and part fend him off, part give him a scratch behind the ears. He sits down patiently, and I slowly push myself up onto my knees. I'm close to the end of the beach nearest the village, about five metres or so above the surf. I look up to see a pale blue sky striped with high cirrus cloud.

And then I remember.

Everything.

'Well, fuck me sideways.' I shift around and flop down onto my backside, staring out to sea. On the horizon, I can just about make out a large boat heading north. Nothing to do with Tegwin and Kieran Johns and their smuggling operation. Just an ordinary ship going about its ordinary, legal business. I check my pockets, find them empty. I've no idea what time it is, except that the sun is maybe two thirds into the sky. Mid-morning at this time of year, I'd guess. Who knows what day, though?

I don't really care. I'm soaked through, it's true, but the wind's died down and the sun warms my face. That strange, violent storm blown out as quickly as it appeared. I can sit here for a while without freezing to death. I've got Gelert to keep me warm if needs be.

That's how they find me.

I hear the footsteps crunch slowly across the shingle, then speed up as they get closer. Gelert sounds off, a happy bark not a protective one. He stands up and goes to greet them, but I still can't seem to turn around. All I can do is hug my knees to my chest and stare out to sea.

'Con?' It's Karen.

'Constance?' Amy adds her own voice.

'Con? Are you OK?' This last voice breaks whatever spell has kept me still. My legs are stiff, back sore and I think I may have one or two cracked ribs, so it takes me a while to gaze upon the odd little group who have come to fetch me back from the edge of the world.

Karen looks like she wants to grab me into a fierce hug. Lila has no such reservation, rushing up to me with tears in her eyes. I wince as she wraps her arms around me, but the pain isn't as bad as I'd thought. Maybe just bruises after all.

I can't begin to understand how she is here. I don't know whether she was in the dungeon with me, or I simply dreamed all of that. It doesn't matter. Not now. I know this is real because of the other figure in the group. Diane Shepherd. Her face is stern, no hint of concern for my wellbeing.

'Detective Constable Fairchild. I would like a full report please.'

I don't really start to feel anything like normal until we're back at Plas Caernant and I've changed out of my sopping wet clothes. I'd dearly love to lie in a bath for an hour, but that's not an option right now, so I dress in a hurry before going down to the kitchen. It's an odd collection of people I find sitting around the table. Karen's been here before, of course, as has Lila. Diane Shepherd looks perfectly at home, and I can imagine her getting on just fine with Lord and Lady Caernant. Billy Latham, on the other hand, seems weighed down by the sheer number of chips on his shoulders.

'Sit before you fall down, dear.' Amy pulls out a chair. She brings over a mug of coffee and places it in my hands. I stare at it for far longer than should be necessary before fully understanding what it is and taking a drink. It's not quite as good as Mrs Feltham's, but then I don't think anyone else has that magic recipe.

'Are you OK to talk?' Diane asks once I've put the mug back down. 'Only, there's a bomb squad currently working its way through a set of tunnels nobody knew anything about until today, and a team of engineers venting gas from an anaerobic digester I was assured hadn't been finished yet. There's a body washed up on that beach where we found you, too. We're waiting for confirmation, but it's male and carrying a wallet with cards belonging to one Alwyn Kieran Johns.'

Only one body?

I feel certain the sea has taken Tegwin into its cold embrace. Will it toy with him like it did Karl Peterson? Discard him when there's nothing left for the fish to nibble? I find I can't bring myself to care much about the dead. Only those I left alive.

'What about William Kendall? And a bloke called Hefin?'

Shepherd looks to Billy Latham, who glares at me before speaking. 'Hefin Jenkins is in the hospital with concussion and a bruised windpipe. William Kendall handed himself in to the first policeman he found at Penparc Uchaf Farm. Told us some mad story about you saving his life when he fell off the cliff.'

'Is that so mad, Billy?' I enjoy watching him flinch when I use his first name.

'What happened, Con?' Shepherd asks. 'Last I heard, you left London even though you could barely climb three flights of stairs. Now you're putting grown men in hospital, or worse.'

I take another generous swig of coffee, feel the heat of it slide down my throat. It burns at the rawness that is the result of breathing in too much seawater. Or maybe screaming my rage at the world. Talking's going to hurt, but the sooner I get it over and done with, the sooner I can have that bath.

'There's a lot doesn't make much sense to me, but I'll do my best.'

I tell them everything that's happened since I found the passports hidden in the empty council flat. But, when it comes to the part about finding Lila in the storeroom, our escape and the strangely dreamlike events afterwards, I pause. Gelert the deerhound has sat up from where he was lying in front of the Aga, and now he stares at me with eyes far too knowing. Gareth Caernant is standing too, his hands resting on the back of the chair Amy has sat in. They say nothing, but their expressions give me pause. So, I skip the part about the Cauldron of Life and how it swallowed up a badly injured Lila. She's showing no sign of those cracked ribs, after all. Not thin and haggard. She looks healthier than I think I've ever seen her, and she has that same expression on her face, too.

'I managed to escape the cell they'd put me in. Found my way back up to the surface. That's where I found Kendall and . . . Jenkins, you say?'

Latham's face is a permanent sneer, but he nods in reply to my question.

'It's pretty much like Kendall said. They attacked me, I fought back, and Kendall went over the edge. He managed to grab a ledge not too far down. I didn't pull him up, just helped him climb back. That's when I used Jenkins' phone to call Karen, and then went after the two Johns.'

There are questions, far more than I'd like. I do my best to answer, knowing that this is just the first of many debriefings to come. Eventually, Amy comes to my rescue, insisting with all the authority of a St Bert's girl that I need rest, and that this interview can continue another time. For once, Shepherd agrees. The NCA team leave shortly after. As Amy shows them to the front door, Gareth crouches down beside me, one hand lightly on my shoulder.

'Thank you, Con. You've done us all a great service.'

'I think I should be thanking you.' I nod my head in the direction of Gelert, who has lain back down and is now cleaning his balls with his tongue. 'And him. That's at least twice he's pulled me out of the sea now.'

'What can I say? He likes you.'

As if to emphasise the point, Gelert lets out a loud fart.

'Is it true though, Gareth? What I saw down there. What we saw?' I don't have the energy to point, but I look at Lila as I speak.

'Ah, Con. What is truth? What is myth?'

'The first time. When I was thrown off the cliff. I was badly injured. Broken arm. Couldn't feel my legs, so probably my spine was snapped too. I could hardly breathe when I washed up. And yet two weeks later, I woke in hospital with not a scratch on me. Just that terrible weakness and lethargy. That was the Cauldron, wasn't it? The Pair Dadeni?'

'An old wives' tale.' Gareth grins. 'Like the grail in our underground chapel here. That's most likely a late fourteenth-century mazer bowl that's somehow survived down the years and accumulated a legend of its own. Or possibly it's an eighteenth-century fake made by some foolish romantic wanting to bring more tourists to the area.' He pauses. 'The Cauldron of Life is the same. A story told around winter fires, warped and twisted from the telling long before anyone thought to write it down. The literature's full of tales just like it, and they all likely come from similar roots. Some injured warrior bathes in a lake few people ever visit. He gets better, and everyone says it's because of the lake. Nobody remembers the hundreds of injured warriors who took a bath and still died of their wounds.'

I know he's lying. Not because I can feel the shape of his thoughts, although I can. It's because he's fallen into the trap of all liars, and put far too much detail into the lie. It doesn't matter. Not now. I'm grateful for his hospitality as much as saving my life.

'Well, it might not be a magical lake, but there's a deep bath upstairs that I would very much like to lie in for a while. And if I die from my wounds, at least I'll be warm and clean.'

Gareth gives a great belly laugh, and then he helps me stand up, since I'm altogether too unsteady to do it myself.

'What will do now?'

The halting, accented English reminds me of who else is in the room. I look across at Lila, still sitting at the table. 'First, I'm going to sleep. But I promised I'd take you somewhere safe. I like to keep my promises.'

'We go Scot Land?' She pronounces it as two words and I haven't the heart to correct her. The excitement on her face makes her look like she's twelve. Then it disappears almost as soon as it came. 'But you have work. Answer questions. Make report.'

It's true. I have to answer a lot of questions. But the smuggling operation has been closed down and now it's the turn of the forensic accountants to follow the money; for the international teams to look into all those passports; for the Maritime and Coastguard Agency to track all the boats that have been coerced into helping the Johns with their operation. None of these things require any input from me.

'How about we go tomorrow?'

40

I'd forgotten how long this country is, when you travel from south to north. We left Plas Caernant not long after an early breakfast, and it's still approaching evening before my trusty Volvo rolls into the little Angus village of Friockheim. Not that I've been driving particularly quickly. I seem to have lost my fondness for speed somewhere between almost dying and being brought back to life by a mythical cauldron. Either that, or I'm getting old.

Lila didn't say much for the first couple of hours driving, but after we'd stopped outside Chester for fuel, coffee and a pee, she slowly began to open up. Perhaps it was the dawning realisation that a long and particularly horrific chapter in her life was finally done. She told me very little about her journey from Ukraine to Wales, and the life she'd lived as part of the Johns' drug and modern-day slavery empire. But the stories of her childhood before war tore her world apart make me both desperately sad for her and also strangely keen to visit Kiev and the towns further east. Maybe, when the world has come to terms with this terrible virus, I'll make the journey. For now, a well-hidden mansion in the countryside north of Dundee will suffice.

'This is the place?' Lila's awe is unmistakable as we approach the massive gate house towers that form the main entrance to the Burntwoods estate.

'This is just the beginning. Wait until you see the house.'

She leans forward in her seat, peering through the windscreen as the drive leads us through a mature forest and then out into open parkland. Finally, the drive curves around, trees falling away on each side to reveal the house.

Lila says something under her breath that could be Russian or Ukrainian.

'Impressive, no?' I pull into the car park, noticing that my car is by no means the most battered here. 'Now, remember. You don't have to stay here. We can find you somewhere else to go. Even back to Ukraine if you want. It's your choice.'

Lila clambers out of the car, stretches like a gymnast and stares up at the massive edifice that is the front of Burntwoods mansion. I take a little longer to get out of my seat, joints creaking and muscles reminding me of the punishment I've doled out to my body recently. By the time I've closed my door, a small group of people have appeared, walking swiftly towards us across the gravel. One of them breaks from the group and runs to greet me.

'Con! You should have said you were coming!' Izzy hugs me tight for a moment before releasing me and stepping back, her face taking on a quizzical look. 'Love the hair, but you look thin, big sis. Mrs F not feeding you any more?'

Before I have a chance to answer, the rest of the party has arrived. I don't recognise most of them, but one I do. Tall, as thin as a willow, and with pure white hair that falls straight from either side of a centre parting down well past her waist so that she looks like some wizard from *The Lord of the Rings*. Mirriam Downham, founder of this refuge for abused women and almost certainly a witch to boot, glances only briefly in my direction before turning her full attention to my passenger.

'You must be Lila Ivanova,' she says, before slipping into what I assume is either Russian or Ukrainian. I have no idea what she says, but I can see by Lila's enthusiastic nodding and flustered responses that she's going to be taking up the offer of sanctuary here. Not that I was ever in much doubt.

'There's tea in the front drawing room,' Dr Downham says, and it takes me a moment to realise she's talking to me. 'There's a room made up for you, too.'

Before I can answer, she's turned and walked away, one arm protectively around Lila's shoulders. I watch them go, happy to feel the sun on my face and to not be sitting down after far too many hours behind the wheel.

'You going to stay then, Con?' Izzy asks. She's leaning against the bonnet of the car, looking annoyingly pleased with herself. 'Or are you all too eager to dash down to London and fight crime?'

I gaze up at the house, then do a slow three-sixty degree turn taking in the park, the distant woodland and even further distant mountains to the west. Izzy's still standing right in front of me when I get back to where I started, her face a disconcerting mixture of mine and her mother's. With just a hint of my father in there too.

'No. I'm in no rush to go back right now. Think I might stick around here for a while.'

Acknowledgements

A lot of people have worked very hard to make my strange imaginings into an actual book you can hold and read. I sprung this one on my publishers by surprise, too, so this is as much an apology as thanks. The whole team at Wildfire have been brilliant to work with, and special mention must go to Alex Clarke, Jack Butler, Serena Arthur and Antonia Whitton.

I wouldn't be doing this at all without the tireless support and sage advice of my agent, the indomitable Juliet Mushens, ably assisted by Liza DeBlock and Kiya Evans at Mushens Entertainment. Thank you all.

If you have kept from reading this bit until the end, like a normal person, you'll already have discovered that this book is set mostly in Wales. Look for the village of Llantwmp, though, and you'll be disappointed. Caernant Hall is yet another figment of my imagination, although locals will recognise the inspiration for the place, and anyone with much of an interest in Grail mythology will probably have heard of Nanteos Mansion. Look it up with the internet search engine of your preference if you haven't; it's fascinating stuff.

As is my way, I have also played a little fast and loose with geography, particularly the clifftop paths between Aberystwyth and Aberaeron, but this is a work of fiction, after all. I hope my depiction of Ceredigion life doesn't offend too many people. I lived there for ten happy years, in the difficult-to-pronounce village of Cwmystwyth, a thousand feet up in the Cambrian Mountains. This book is, in many ways, a fond remembrance of that decade and my own strange way of saying thank you. Diolch yn fawr pawb!

And last, but never least, I owe a huge debt of gratitude to my better half, Barbara, who keeps everything together while I'm away with the faeries (and dragons, giants, witches, knights in armour . . .).

Biography

James Oswald is the author of the *Sunday Times* bestselling Inspector McLean series of detective mysteries and the epic fantasy series *The Ballad of Sir Benfro*, as well as the new DC Constance Fairchild series. James's first two books, *Natural Causes* and *The Book of Souls*, were both shortlisted for the prestigious CWA Debut Dagger Award and he was shortlisted for the National Book Awards New Writer of the Year in 2013. *Nowhere to Run* is the third book in the DC Constance Fairchild series.

James lives in North East Fife, where he farms Highland cows by day and writes disturbing fiction by night.